TRUTH FROM THE BATHROOM

WRITTEN BY
BOB WHIRE

Book Cover Design by www.ebooklaunch.com

ISBN: 978-0-9794607-4-6

Truth from the Bathroom

What the crap does she want me to say?

So, Janine takes me out shopping today with her and Sammy because she wants a new pair of slacks. She goes in and puts them on, and she wants me to tell her what I think. What did I think? What was I thinking?

Fine. They're fine.

What does she want me to say?

What am I even doing sitting on a fuzzy pink ottoman in front of the women's dressing room? What guy does that? Why does this have anything to do with me in any way? Okay, I understand, she says she wants my opinion on some really ugly pants. But she doesn't. It doesn't matter what I say. It won't influence her decision at all. So why am I sitting here in this stupid space next to a rack of bras? I'm tired of the dirty looks I'm getting from all the fat ladies waiting to try on girdles.

The truth is that they look like crap. The pants, not the bras and girdles. They look like something that my ninety-six-year-old grandmother would wear. They make her buns look all pinched together, like she's trying to hold a dime in her ass.

That's the kind of truth I should tell her. I'd be doing her a favor! She's a beautiful woman, and she should be wearing clothing that makes her look good. But that's not what she wants from me. What does she want? I don't know.

So I sit there and say, 'They're fine.'

Sammy doesn't even react like a typical teenaged girl. She just shakes her head a little and goes back to whatever she was doing. She never says: 'They're cyuuuat!!!!!'

Is that what she's waiting to hear me say? I'm never going to say it. I'm a guy. She's never going to hear me call her clothes cyuuuat. Especially not these crap-colored gramma pants.

Sammy says, 'I don't know, mom!' and she walks around and around her mother. But Janine ignores Sammy and looks at me.

"You don't like them, I can tell."

But it's not like, 'We've known each other for twenty-five years, and we have a romantic love bond, so I can tell what he's thinking."

It's more like she's Professor Snape, and I'm Harry Potter, and she's accusing me of stealing some secret book of spells. I sit there shaking my head innocently and saying, 'they're fine'.

She grimaces a grimace from hell and sneers at me.

"Good grief!"

She rolls her eyes so hard that her eye lids flutter, and she throws a shoulder into me as she storms past me and back to the changing room.

She bought the damn pants.

So now we're home and she's storming around the house, sighing, grumbling, and complaining that she'll have to go back and return them tomorrow, and she had a million things to do tomorrow, and it looks like she just doesn't deserve to have nice clothes. She says it all glaring at me over her shoulder, as if I've done something wrong.

What the hell does she want from me? I didn't do this! Dammit, I didn't buy the pants, I didn't make the pants, and I didn't scheme and plan and come up with some evil way to make her look bad in those ugly pants. It's ridiculous, and she tries to make it all seem like it's my fault somehow.

Saturday.

I can't believe I'm writing this.

I think I need to explain this a little bit.

I'm coming to you, from the bathroom. That last little tirade was written while actually sitting on the toilet. And I think it's going to happen again. Well, it's absolutely going to happen again, or I'm going to die of an intestinal blockage. Actually, it's happening right now. I'm writing from the bathroom, or the master bath off my bedroom. I'm not actually using the toilet, I just told my wife I needed to use the bathroom so I could have an excuse to come in here and write this. I don't know if that's too much information.

I don't know how much I should actually explain about what I'm doing in here, I just want to make sure it's the truth. Everything I write in here must be the truth. I've already decided that. Yes, I'll make excuses to come in here to write. Yes, I'm hiding. But it's got to happen. What I mean ultimately is that I'm going to write again, on the toilet. Nature gives me the needed excuse to find the privacy to write all this. It's a perfect storm that happens about every day of my life. Nature tells me to head for my designated toilet, and while I'm there I've got a lot to say. I'm going to be a toilet writer, a new pastime that I will explain in a minute.

But who am I explaining this to? Who are you? Are you this notebook I've found? Are you some unknown reader who has found this notebook? Not if I can help it. I don't think I would want anyone to every read the things I'm going to write in here. Not right now anyway. I don't know if I'll ever change my mind about that.

Maybe one day I'll put this notebook in a bottle and throw it in the ocean, and you'll find it and you'll be reading it on some exotic pacific island. Maybe.

For now I can only say that it really felt good to vent the other night when she asked me about those damn pants. Who's going to read about it? No one. Ever. I just need to write this.

I don't even know what would happen if she knew. I shudder to think. But she'll never know. I need to make sure of that.

I can't believe I'm actually writing this in the bathroom. It's pathetic.

Why am I writing about her while sitting on the toilet instead of talking to her face to face? Am I afraid of her? No. Is she mean or violent or cruel to me? Not really. I don't know. It's hard to explain.

Who am I talking about? My wife. I've wanted to tell somebody, anybody, all the infuriating things she says and does to me. She's the steering wheel in my pants. You'd think that we're constantly fighting and arguing. But that's just not me. I don't complain. I don't confront. I don't disobey. I just keep gently trying to maintain the status quo.

Pathetic. I'm reading what I'm writing and it makes me want to puke. I admit that it's satisfying to get this off my chest in this way, but I'm already seeing what an ugly image my life is.

I came in here last week to take a dump, that day my wife bought those damn pants, and found this notebook. It was tucked away on a shelf where the towels use to go. Somebody probably bought it for school and then forgot it. Completely unused. Completely blank. It's mine now. It's perfect. It's just what I've been looking for. I sat there for a while and doodled. I mean, I drew things in the notebook. I had to use a marker that my wife had in the medicine cabinet, but it was fun. I felt like I was hiding something. I drew my wife as a monster with ugly pants.

When I was done, I ran and found a pen. I went back to the bathroom and sat on the toilet. With the lid down. I'm not that crazy, please. I started to write a letter to Janine. I told her to stop asking me about stupid things like ugly pants, and then blaming me that she looks bad. Almost as soon as I started writing, I knew I would never give it to her. Then I started listing all the things that were bugging me about my wife. That's when this notebook became a relief to me. Maybe that was because I was in the bathroom. The toilet, the pepto, the Preparation H, they all subliminally point to relief. That that's what this notebook has become. Relief. But it's kind of like a mirror, too. What I'm seeing in that mirror isn't pretty.

I'm going to keep this notebook hidden here in my bathroom. I think it will be pretty safe in here. This is our master bath, but it's kind of my own private bathroom. Janine just uses the space to store bathroom related stuff. No one else but me comes in here. This will all work out perfectly. I'm going to write exactly what I'm thinking, and I don't want anyone to find this and read it. I'm going to be frank, honest, cruel, chaste, benevolent, and I'm going to do a good turn daily. Or at least a good movement.

This bathroom is a great place for writing and complaining. It's my last holdout. It's my castle. But it's only a half bath, and it desperately needs remodeling. That's why Janine hardly ever comes in here. The water in the sink doesn't work. I'm supposed to fix that, but I keep making excuses, and that keeps Janine from coming in here. And since I've claimed this as my literal throne, I think this bathroom kind of disgusts her. And that's great! It all ensures that I'll have some privacy in here. It's the only place in this entire damned world where I can feel private and alone.

Not even the shower provides this kind of luxury. I can't read in the shower, and Janine doesn't let me lock the bathroom door when I shower. So when I'm feeling some pressure, when I've got a load on my mind, when I need some alone time, when things really stink in my life, I come here. This is my bathroom.

A little side note here. I was watching "Dances With Wolves" last night. There is a scene where Kevin Costner is being driven out west by this crude little guy with a wagon and a team of horses. Kevin is writing in his journal, writing and writing. They stop for the night, make a fire and prepare dinner. Suddenly the crude little guy stands up, pokes his butt out and farts. It's a loud, long, juicy fart, and the crude little guy laughs really hard.

"Put that in your book!" He says with a taunt to Costner. That's me now. That's what I'm putting in this book.

Bathroom humor. I knew it would work its way into all this. This notebook is where the shit is really going to hit the fan.

You know, I usually read in the bathroom. I've always got a couple of my favorite books in here. My wife thinks that's funny. My books are disappearing all the time because she takes them out of here. She says that books don't belong in the bathroom. That's not true. Lots of people read in the bathroom. Books are sold that are intended to be read in the bathroom. It's even in their titles. I need to read in the bathroom for some reason. I take more time in the bathroom than most people do. I need time to myself away from my wife. Did you see that? I'm already sharing embarrassing, truthful things in this notebook. That's my choice.

So, some people read in the bathroom, I write. I warned you not to read this notebook if you don't want to be offended. But why should it offend you? First of all, it's the truth, and if the truth offends you, hey, that's your problem. And second, it's all about my wife, so she's the only one who should be offended, and if she ever finds this notebook, well. Well what? I'm guessing I'll never take a peaceful crap again in my life.

ENTRY # 1

I can just tell that I'm going to be writing in here regularly, and that's what I want, regularity. It's the hallmark of a good bathroom experience. I'm a bathroom writer now, and I'm going to fill this notebook up to the brim.

Let's continue to analyze this all a little bit.

WHY THE BATHROOM?

Well I'm hiding, of course. I don't want anyone to know what I'm doing. And by anyone, I obviously mean my wife. So meet Janine. Janine is my wife, and the subject of this notebook. We'll be talking about her here in this notebook, bagging on her, ripping on her, complaining about her, and trying to figure her out. And I'm Scott, the scared mouse of a husband, by the way.

This hasn't been an easy decision, but I've decided I'm going to write down the things about my wife and marriage that have been bugging me for years. Wait a minute, on second thought this IS an easy decision. To tell the truth I started bitching about my wife on these pages as soon as I sat down. And I'm going to keep on doing it. I'm going to do it because it's petty and mean and because she can't stop me.

By making the decision to write this down in this notebook, instead of going to my wife to argue my points and try to seek a resolution to my problems with her, I acknowledge that we have one of those marriages where the wife wears the pants.

There. I said it.

My wife wears the pants in this marriage.

She tells me what to do, tells me what I can't do, yells at me when I step out of line. And what do I do about it? I sit in here and complain on the pages of this notebook.

You're probably asking yourself what I tell her and how I explain the time I spend in the bathroom. I know that's what I'm asking myself.

I told her I have IBS. She didn't care. My health is my problem. My responsibility is to manage my health, so it doesn't get in the way of the family. I think I actually did have IBS for a while. I was always uncomfortable, and I always felt sick. The doctor said it was stress. Stress at work, stress at home, stress everywhere. Hell, I probably still do have IBS or some other kind of digestive problem. I just spend more time than most people do in the bathroom. It takes me longer than it takes other people, and it's never pretty. I should see a doctor again or something. Whether or not it's IBS, she complains bitterly about the stink when I'm in the bathroom. I always apologize and remind her about my IBS. She doesn't want to know anything about it, so she leaves me alone when I come in here.

The IBS story has an aside. I know a lot about public restrooms. That has nothing to do with this book, but I can tell you where the best public restrooms are within a one-hundred-mile radius. When I'm not home, and I have to make a mad dash for the can, I don't want to use the dirty restroom at the gas station.

So I know all the best office buildings and stores that have clean, isolated restrooms where I can get in and out without causing a scene. Never go to the first floor. People who are thinking like me and are just looking for a restroom will go to the one on the first floor. So take the elevator up a floor or two. If an office building has a restroom in the hallway, it will be rarely used because the offices will have their own restroom inside. That's always comforting. In a store, find the restrooms in the lady's section. They're always cleaner where the ladies are, and there aren't many men there looking for restrooms. Better yet, stop at a store that caters to women. They will still usually have a men's restroom. You might get a few disapproving looks as you make your way through the night gowns on your way to see a man about a horse, but what do you care? When you've got to go, you've got to go.

Yes, I can see how my passion for just the right toilet has had something to do with this new project. I'm very particular about my bathroom habits. I think a lot when I'm in the bathroom.

It's not like I'm going to spend hours and hours in here writing. I'm not obsessed. I'm not going off the deep end. I'm just going to grab this notebook when I'm in here and put down my thoughts. It's one quick entry, flush, and then I'm finished.

It will never mean anything, and I'll never show it to anyone. It will just make me feel a whole lot better. Just like everything else that happens in here.

ENTRY # 2

WHY AM I DOING THIS?

I feel like I'm crazy. I have all these thoughts and feelings, and no one on earth would ever believe me, or even want to hear about it. Men don't have feelings. Men aren't supposed to complain about stuff like this. Men go to work and do the yard work. Men fix things around the house and lay around on the couch watching sports. Men have hobbies and buddies. I don't know this firsthand, but I've seen guys like this.

I fix things around the house, and I go to work, and I do the yard work, but I don't do anything in my life because I choose to. That's the difference between me and other men. I am told what to do. From the minute I wake up in the morning until I lay down at night to go to sleep, and even sometimes after that. And I'm not asked nicely to do the things I do, and once I've done them, I'm not told that I've done a good job, and no one says thank you.

I know it sounds like I'm whining and complaining and probably exaggerating, but I'm not. This is my life. This is the way things have played out over the last, oh, ten years. Maybe it was Janine's cruel design, or maybe it all just happened without anyone noticing, but that's the way it is for me, as of this writing. There's no one I can tell, no one who can fix this for me.

So I come into the bathroom, pretend like I've got IBS, and write down this crap.

Why don't I just write in the living room, or at the kitchen table, or on the couch?

I'd have to explain to her what I'm writing, and why, and then she would have something to say about it. This isn't exactly complimentary stuff. I'm going to vent here. It's going to get ugly. If she knew about this she might yell. She would almost certainly insult me. She would complain and say that I was writing cruel things about her. And that's exactly what

I'm doing, so you see why it's important for her to never find out about it. She's the stinking steering wheel in my pants.

I really like this notebook, though. It's a spiral bound, so I can open it to the page where I'm writing and the former pages and the cover fold right around to the back and then it can sit flat on my bare lap. That's great. I actually found this notebook accidentally. I was looking for a user manual for the weed wacker. We keep the manuals for everything we've ever bought on the top shelf of the linen closet in here. While I was looking, I found this notebook. It must have belonged to one of my kids and they probably needed it for school. I'm sure they bought another one. But here I was, with this empty notebook, and I just started to write down a bullet list of the things about my wife that bug me.

Her snarl.

Her temper.

Her sigh.

Her tensed up buns.

Her stare.

Her arrogant swagger.

The way she swings her shoulders when she marches.

The fact that she marches instead of walking.

Her stomping march.

Her eye roll.

Her smirk.

Her fake laugh.

Her snap judgments.

Her demeaning tone.

Her sarcastic smile.

The list just came flowing out of me. I could have come up with a thousand things about my wife that are problematic. It was exciting. It was fun. It was relieving. I couldn't believe how fast I was writing. I never knew I had so much to say about this subject. Looking back on what I just wrote, I find it funny that this experience is relieving, in the bathroom.

This reminds me of a game I used to play in church when I was a child. It was different than this toilet writing game I'm playing right now. We weren't offended, we were just bored. My sister and I would have fun during the sermon in church by writing "in the bathroom" behind the titles of the hymns in the hymn book. Pretty hilarious. We had to be sneaky and try to keep anyone from seeing what we were doing. We always used a pencil so someone else could erase what we had done later.

Some samples:

"Each Day I'll Do a Golden Deed" in the bathroom

"ABIDE WITH ME" in the bathroom

"AGAIN THE MORN OF GLADNESS" in the bathroom

"GET RIGHT WITH GOD" in the bathroom

"THE NAME WHICH I WHISPER" in the bathroom

"NEVER GIVE UP" in the bathroom

"I NEED THEE EVERY HOUR" in the bathroom

"NOW LET US REJOICE" in the bathroom

"GUIDE ME TO THEE" in the bathroom

How about that? I'm just playing a new version of that old game. Writing in secret, trying not to get caught. I never would have thought that a silly little game that I played as a child in Church would become a reality of my life when I was married.

So what is this? A journal? Just a collection of notes? Evidence that my wife is an abusive bully? Maybe this is just a whiney assed collection of whiney ass complaints. I don't know. I just know that I feel better when I can hide in here for a few minutes and write this all down.

Does this mean I hate my wife? Absolutely not. I loved her when we got married, and I still love her today. She's just being a jerk lately. Lately for the past ten years. She's just the steering wheel in my pants. Well, she's been being a jerk for about ten years, I guess. It hasn't always been this way. I guess she's always been bossy, but over the years it got worse and worse.

I guess this is pretty funny, isn't it? I just hope it's not pathetic. I'm not going to confront her about my feelings, because I think that would make this all seem pathetic. It would be like begging the bully to leave you alone. Bullies love that. You tell them that they are making you feel bad, and they do it more!

Yes, this is funny. I'm feeling hurt, persecuted, smothered, and pushed around, but she doesn't know it because I'm not telling her. It's funny because I'm afraid of her and hiding from her on the toilet. I get it. But maybe by writing all this down, one day I'll figure out what to do or say so that I can help her realize that she's kind of running me over.

I keep saying that she's the steering wheel in my pants. I got that from a joke I once heard.

A pirate goes in to a bar and there's a steering wheel sticking out of his pants.

The guy next to him at the bar notices and says to him:

"Hey, buddy, are you aware that there's a steering wheel sticking out of your pants?"

And the pirate, he says: "Arggggh! It's driving me nuts!"

That's why Janine is the steering wheel in my pants. I sometimes feel that her main purpose in life is to drive me nuts. Silly. I'm being silly, right?

She's a rational adult, isn't she? Now there's something to think about!

What if she's treating me this way on purpose? What if all this mean and abusive behavior is thought out and planned? Why would she do that? Is she trying to teach me to defend myself? Is she waiting for me to stand up to her? Does she really think I'm lazy and stupid and she's hoping that by pushing me I'll find my true potential?

If only all that were true. If only I could discover a reason for all this and then formulate a plan to resolve it.

My gut instinct is that Janine is just mean and spiteful. Was she always that way? I think to some degree she was. I can picture her as a pushy ten-year-old, bullying the nerdy kids. I can picture her as a conniving teenager, manipulating her friends. And now she's married and the focus of her behavior is her husband. Me. It's become more and more intense over the last ten years. She's learned that I'll put up with her bullying. She's lucky to have me. I'm like a punching bag. Whenever she needs a good work out and needs someone to punch and push around, there I am.

I'm writing this and I'm picturing what questions you might be asking me. Why don't I just go to her and tell her all these things that I'm feeling? And as I've said, it's not because I'm afraid of her.

Okay, I'm afraid of her. There, I said it.

But really the reason is because she should know about it without having to be told. I shouldn't have to tell her all the things I'm writing in this notebook. She should be sensitive to the way I feel, and to the things I need. She should see the things I'm going through. You might say that's a piss poor excuse, but I don't think so. I'm sensitive to her. I try to anticipate her needs. I try to understand the things she wants and the things she's going through. Marriage should be like that. Marriage should be a two-way street. Our marriage is not like that.

Who else knows about my situation? I'm not sure. Maybe no one. I think my kids have a sense of the way things are. They've lived with their parents, surely they see what goes on. And I know that people have seemed to sympathize over the years, though it's always with looks and whispers and little comments about how I'm a great guy and how my wife is really special, but no one has ever really talked to me about my family life.

Why do I put up with it? Why am I happy to wear a target? I don't know. There are lots of reasons. I want to keep my family together. I want peace in my home. I'm a coward. And worst of all, I'm just used to it. It's a bad habit.

And here's me pretending to be a psychiatrist: I think Janine is frustrated and unhappy with her own life. She's getting older. Her siblings avoid her. She doesn't have true, faithful friends. Her friends are really just people who are polite to her. She doesn't have the fancy career she longed for. So she bullies me to make herself feel better.

I wonder what this notebook would be like if Janine was writing. Yes, I realize that there are two sides to every story. I'll bet there are things about me that legitimately annoy her.

I've done some things wrong, and I know it. Sometimes I've deserved it when she's been angry with me. Like the time when I took my shoes off at her parent's house. They had just had some new carpet installed, and they didn't want any dirty shoes walking around on their new carpet. So everybody kicked their shoes off right there in the doorway. I went ahead and took my shoes off, just like I was told to, and there was a big hole in my sock, and my big toe was sticking out of it. I didn't know there was a hole in my sock! Janine's the one who buys my socks for me. And it wasn't me who made the rule that everyone who enters her parents' house must take off their shoes because of the new carpet.

Boy was I in trouble! To have my toe sticking out of my sock in her parents' house! What could be worse?

And I even remember the very first time I pissed her off. It was the day we got married. Oh, we had disagreements before that. Janine had been cross with me before that, but it was different on our wedding day. I never thought Janine would even look. I never thought at the time that it even mattered. I was young. I didn't understand how the world worked.

What was the horrible thing I did? I wore sweat socks with my tuxedo. We had been standing under the little arch where the people were greeting us, and I remember she kept looking at my feet. I couldn't understand why. Then she asked, "Are those sweat socks?" I told her I wanted to be comfortable. She looked horrified. I assured her they were grey. But she threw her bouquet on the ground and stormed out of the room. Everyone was shocked. She cried to her mom and threatened to leave the reception. Some people laughed at me, some chastised me. Lots of people didn't care.

What did I do about it back then? My uncle changed socks with me. That didn't help things. I learned on my wedding day just how angry Janine could get.

But I have no problem being aware of my mistakes and faults. That's not what this is all about. We learn from our mistakes, and sometimes we can't see our mistakes unless someone else points them out.

Frankly, I'd like to know. Knowing about my own defects would help me become a better person. That's easy to say when no one is complaining about me to my face. Do I think that Janine would like to know about all this? Would it make Janine do some self-inspection and maybe change a few things in her life? Actually, I think it would make her head explode.

Janine is a proud person. She's proud of everything about her life. Mostly she's proud of seeing herself as a leader, as a very successful person in many ways, and as an alpha dog.

Did I just call my wife a dog? What can I say? She acts like an alpha dog, she needs to be prepared to hear someone call her a dog. But she'd never want to hear or admit that she's wrong about anything. And she'd do some serious damage to anyone who would dare to propose that she's wrong about anything.

Entry # 3

I DON'T REALLY HAVE TO GO, BUT I WANTED TO WRITE SOMETHING.

I actually came in here, dropped my pants, and sat down because I wanted to write. Here's the thing. I did have something specific that I wanted to complain about.

Whatever I say or think, I'm wrong. Whatever my opinion is, it's wrong. Whatever I like, it's bad. If I think something is funny, it's stupid. Not just sometimes, not just when she disagrees with me. It's all the time. It's every time. My wrongness is like a barometer in our house. What is right is anything that is the exact opposite of what I say or think.

Literally. She literally uses her contempt of my opinions to make her own decisions. When she asks me for input on anything, and I mean everything, she always goes for the opposite of what I say. She asks me about clothing she's shopping for, new ways to arrange the furniture, what to have for dinner, and whatever I say, she goes for the opposite. If I say I like the skirt she's looking at, she puts it back. She asks if I would like chicken for dinner. I say yes, and she makes a roast.

I'm baffled by the fact that she constantly asks for my opinion anyway. She is always asking me about something. Especially if I'm already engrossed in something else. She wants to know what I think about the latest thing the neighbors did. She wants to know what I think about a shelf she wants to hang in the kitchen. She wants to know what I think about some plants she wants to buy. She wants to know what I think about painting the kitchen. She wants to know what I think about what's going on at the high school. And she mostly wants to know these things when I'm watching tv, or talking on the telephone, or eating, or reading.

And this is classic: Just when I get started doing something she's told me to do, she tells me to do something else, and then scolds me when the two different things don't get done at the same time. For example, I was told to wash the dishes. In fact, I was growled at because the dishes from the night before had never been done. So off I went. I don't mind washing dishes. It's one of my favorite chores. But just as I get right in the middle of washing the dishes, I'm all wet and soapy, she's suddenly storms through the kitchen and tells me she needs me to take the trash out. One minute later the dishes weren't finished and the trash wasn't out, and I was in trouble.

There's a teenaged girl in our house. Our daughter Sammy. I always wonder why my wife doesn't call upon Sammy to take on some of these chores that she has me do. But she doesn't. Sammy sits comfortably watching tv while Janine complains because I'm not doing everything at once, and doing it more quickly.

Even more aggravating is how she blames me for the things in her life that aren't my fault. Just this morning as I was getting ready for work, she body checked me as we passed in the hallway and growled at me that Sammie was going to be late for school. It was the tone of her voice. It sounded like she meant that it was all my fault.

I thought about that incident all day. When I got home from work, I asked Janine if Sammie had been late for school. She shrugged as if she had no idea what I was talking about and said that she didn't think so. So I told her that I had gotten the impression that Sammie was going to be late, and that it was because of something that I had done. Janine stared at me in amazement for a long moment and asked me why I thought it was my fault. I told her how she had pushed past me and growled at me.

Then she laughed. Bullies always laugh. She told me I was being paranoid. She laughed harder. She denied making any implications about Sammy or her school day at all. She said that she was just in a hurry, and nothing else. She said that I should really get a better grip on my emotions.

The amazing thing is that I pointed it out to her. I've never done that before. She didn't say much about it other than to tell me I was ridiculous and annoying. But she didn't deny it either.

That's fine. So she didn't mean anything by growling at me. It still sounded like she was telling me that it was my fault. I mention it here because it happens all the time. We run out of milk. Something gets lost. Something gets broken. Janine forgets an appointment. Anything. I get growled at. She implies that it's my fault.

And would you like to know what's always my fault? Anything I have to do, anything I've planned to do, anything I want to do. It's all wrong. Whatever it is, if it's something I'm doing, or need to do, or want to do, it has ruined her fricking life! It's destroyed her day, it's threatened our family, it's breaking down the very foundations of our society.

Anything that happens around me is my fault. Earlier this summer we went to a picnic with some aunts and uncles and cousins on Janine's side of the family. We were up near a beautiful lake in the mountains.

I was sitting at a picnic bench, eating a sandwich. That's all I was doing. A cute little three-year-old girl started climbing onto the bench on the side where I was sitting. Not next to me. Just on the same side. Well, the little girl lost her balance and fell over backwards onto the ground.

I gasped when I saw her fall out of the corner of my eye, but she wasn't close enough for me to grab. And there wasn't time. It happened so fast. I heard a few other gasps, and then I heard a horrible sound.

I heard Janine scream, "Scott!" But it wasn't like, "Scott! Help that little girl!" It was more like, "Scott! You evil bastard! What have you done?"

Then the little girl started to scream in pain and I jumped up and ran to her. Others, including her mother, had reached her first, and I was standing there helplessly. And then I heard it again.

"Scott!" It sounded like an accusation. It was a moment of judge, jury, and executioner. I looked up innocently at my wife, and she let out a growl from the pits of hell.

"What did you do?"

I shrugged and started to stutter defensively. Someone on their knees by the crying little girl looked up at me and weakly said, "I don't think Scott did anything, I think she just fell."

But it was too late. It was my fault. Everyone was giving me "that" look. I had done something. That seemed certain. The little girl's mother tried to smile.

"She's fine! No harm done! I don't think it was Scott's fault at all. It's just one of those things that happens."

Everyone tried to focus on cheering the little girl, but I was left standing there like a teenaged boy caught with a girlie magazine. I didn't know what to say or what to do. Janine was glaring at me and shaking her head. I walked over to her. I started to whisper anxiously.

"I didn't see her until she had already fallen. I didn't know she was going to fall. I don't think I could have reached her in time."

Janine didn't care. It was my fault. Like everything else in the entire world. And the attitude rubbed off on the rest of our group. For the rest of the day, people tried to avoid eye contact with me while staring at me at the same time. I was a child molester. I was a criminal. I was that horrible guy who had pushed a three-year-old girl off a bench. And that's an example of the way things are always my fault.

It's daily stuff too. It doesn't matter if it's something benign and point-less. It doesn't matter if it's something necessary and helpful. If I do it, she's inconvenienced, and it's my fault.

I need to run to the store to get a part for the lawn mower.

I need to go to the post office to mail a bill.

I need a tool from the garage.

I need the broom in the kitchen.

When I tell her I have something to do, the look on her face is absolutely one of horror. I am the worst person in the world for even suggesting that I might have something to do that she hasn't pre-approved.

Even more amazing is how things are my fault before they've even hap-pened. I was fixing the cabinet doors, hard at work, and she stopped to check my progress.

"You're finishing this job tonight! Don't even tell me you're finishing it tomorrow!"

"I never said I was going to finish it tomorrow."

Even though I said it, it's not good enough. I'm in trouble for trying to finish the project tomorrow, even though I've assured her that I'm going to finish tonight.

"You always drag these things out. I'm not having that!

Then she makes the ugliest face she can as she screws her mouth up in a pout and mocks my voice: "Oh! I lost the screws! I need to buy new screws! Then they don't fit and they don't match and you've got a hundred reasons to put this job off till tomorrow. You're not going to lose those screws! You're going to finish this tonight."

So there I stand, diligently working on the doors, being yelled at for losing the screws and putting off the job till the next day, and none of it has even happened yet!

Two weeks ago, a business contact invited me to have lunch on a Saturday. Janine was horrified. She was outraged. She was offended. Who plans a business lunch on a Saturday? Doesn't this guy know I have a wife and family? Why does it have to be lunch? Why can't he just meet with you in your office on Monday? He must be some single playboy, probably a pervert! Call him, call him right now! Tell him to forget it!

There's no reasoning with her in a moment like that. There's no way to explain to her that I would be really embarrassed to call this client and tell him I had to cancel because my wife told me to. She doesn't listen, and she doesn't seem to understand. She would never see the damage it would cause to my career. She's way out of line, and she doesn't care, or doesn't see it.

Did I go to lunch with the client? Of course I did. I have to provide for my family, even if Janine is too stupid to see what I'm doing. But I pay a heavy price for it. The tension in our house was horrible for days after that. It's just ridiculous. I deserve more consideration than that.

There are lots of reasons like this for her to be kind and considerate of me. I work hard for our family. The things I need to do, the things I want to do, many of them affect our family income.

But it's more than that. Being nice and considerate to other people is important. It says a lot about what kind of person you are. Can't she see that?

Entry # 4

I'm back

So here I am, back in the bathroom with my notebook on my bare lap again. Good thing I've got some paper. Thought I'd give an example of a typical day around here.

This afternoon, as my workday was winding down, I was thinking about relaxing on the couch in front of the television for a while with a cool drink.

That didn't happen.

Janine had projects for me. She's always believed in separation of men's and women's roles. Women are always naturally doing what women should do. In fact, anything women do is what a woman's role is. They're always doing what women should do. So, men should do what men should do. But a man's role is much more specific. He doesn't have choices. And it's up to women to define a man's role. That means that when I get home from work, I've got things to do.

The towel rack in the bathroom is coming loose. The vacuum is making a funny sound. The dog needs a bath. The shelves in the laundry room have to be rearranged.

Then I had to leave the house with her. And by that I mean that she walked to the door, looked at me over her shoulder, and said, "Let's go." I didn't know why or where. My job is to follow. It turns out that our neighborhood is planning a block party, and Janine expected me to go with her to the meeting. It didn't surprise me. Janine always has me go with her wherever she goes. We got to a neighbor's house and I was the only husband there. I just sat there in silence, but Janine felt that it was important that we went as a couple.

I wasn't the only one at that meeting who felt Janine's contempt. She shot down every idea. She made it clear that she felt she should have the last word on the menu and things like that. So I sat there silently for an hour and then we walked home.

Finally, just before the news came on, I told Janine I needed to head upstairs to the bathroom. She sighed at me and told me that she needed me to help her with the dishes. I whined. I told her that I was old enough to know when I needed to use the bathroom. Did she want me dancing around and hyperventilating in the kitchen? She scowled and waved me off. Now, here I am. Alone at last. Sitting on the toilet and writing about all this.

I'll finish up at my own leisure, brush my teeth, and get in bed. I'll turn on the tv to watch a late-night talk show for a minute, and she'll grab the remote from me and turn it off.

Yes this has been a typical day, but sometimes we have what I call, 'little struggles'. I'm not the milk-toast guy you're thinking I am.

I like to keep a good quality fingernail clipper here in my bathroom. There is a little ceramic dish where I like to keep my clippers. Sometimes I buy a fingernail clipper, and it's a bad one. Do you know the kind? They mash and tear instead of making a clean clip. So I toss a bad one in the garbage when that happens, and I buy a new one. What is it? A buck fifty purchase? I don't mind. I want a good one that makes a clean, crisp clip.

But sometimes my good clippers disappear mysteriously. I have always suspected that someone in my family finds my good clipper and steals it. That's okay. Sometimes we need clippers and we search the bathrooms until we find one, and we keep it. I can buy another one. The thing is, though, that my clippers seem to disappear at an alarming rate.

One day, I don't remember how long ago, Janine did her caveman scream when she stepped into this bathroom for some reason. She started bellowing my name. I came running to see what was wrong. She was holding up my clipper as if it were some kind of horrible drug paraphernalia.

"What is this?"

What is that? Doesn't she recognize a fingernail clipper? I told her what it was.

"Did you just buy this?"

Yes. Yes I did.

"We've got a MILLION of these!"

I remained calm and sarcastic.

"Well, I didn't have one here on my ceramic dish, so I bought one when I was at the store, and let me tell you, it's a great one! Nice, clean, crisp clips."

Janine was contorted with anger. She rolled her eyes and clucked her tongue and took exaggerated gasps of frustration.

"There's a reason why there wasn't a clipper in this ceramic dish. They don't belong here!"

Janine started her army march through the bedroom. She was throwing her shoulders and elbows like a drill sergeant.

"Follow me!"

I followed her somewhere. I honestly don't remember. But suddenly she had a yellow makeup back in her hand. She held it up menacingly in my face and pulled on the zipper. What do you know? The bag was full of fingernail clippers.

"Every time I find a clipper in that ceramic dish, I put it in here! Finger-nail clippers don't belong in the ceramic dish! They belong in this bag!"

I was baffled.

"Well, that's just dumb. I need a good clipper where I can reach it when I need it. The best time for clipping is, you know, when I'm in there. The ceramic dish is the best place for my personal, quality fingernail clipper."

Janine was trembling.

"When you need to clip your fingernails, you will come and find this bag, and get a clipper. You'll use it, and return it to this bag. Under-stand?"

I didn't answer, and she didn't wait for a response.

Not long after that, I was at the grocery store buying milk when I also bought a new fingernail clipper. It was perfect. It made a nice, clean cut. It sat on that ceramic dish for weeks. Maybe months. I don't remember. Then, just last week, I heard Janine scream,

"God Dammit!"

I ran to the bedroom expecting to see blood. Janine had my clippers in one hand, and her yellow makeup bag in the other.

"I told you! The clippers are in this bag! Did you buy this? Did you put this clipper in that ceramic dish? Why? I told you where they were! Why didn't you use one of these?"

Honestly? I had forgotten all about it. I don't think about Janine's makeup. I don't think about bags and kits and makeup holders. I just think about having what I need where I can easily get to it.

"I didn't remember where your yellow bag was."

Big, big eye roll. Followed by trembling and gnashing of teeth, and fists to heaven. She turned and entered the hallway bathroom. The one all decorated in frilly yellow. She slammed open a drawer. Violently.

"Right here, God dammit! The yellow makeup bag with the nail clippers in it is always right here in the bottom left hand drawer under the counter top!"

She ran downstairs grumbling furiously under her breath. "I cannot freaking believe it."

I felt so small. But I was angry too. I wasn't asking for much. I just wanted my own clippers in my own bathroom where I could easily reach them. But I've said that enough already. So, I ripped a sheet of paper from the back of this very notebook, and I sloppily scrawled on it:

THE NAIL CLIPPERS ARE IN THE YELLOW MAKEUP BAG IN THE BOTTOM LEFT HAND DRAWER UNDER THE COUNTERTOP IN THE BATHROOM IN THE HALL.

I taped that message on the wall of our bedroom near the door to my bathroom. When I left for work it was still there, and when I got home from work it was still there. When I went into my bedroom to get ready for bed that night, the sign was gone, and a little chip of paint was gone where the sign had been violently ripped off the wall.

Scotch tape will do that if you're not careful about how you remove it.

Good night everybody.

ENTRY # 5

As I'm trying to write about a typical day here in my life, I'm trying to think of a reference that will help you understand.

Have you ever seen the English comedy: Keeping Up Appearances? Hyacinth and Richard are a couple who are approaching retirement age. They are alone in the house. Hyacinth makes Richard's life hell, and she doesn't listen to him or take his feelings or opinions into account. I laugh like hell at that show.

Well, life in my house is a lot like that show. But Hyacinth isn't nearly as mean as Janine is. And we aren't alone in the house and we aren't approaching retirement age. Other than that, picture Hyacinth screaming constantly at Richard, and then completely ignoring anything he has to say. And picture Richard's zombie like obedience to his wife because it is just futile to resist. That's us. Janine is Hyacinth, and I'm Richard. Laugh it up.

Even funnier than the show is the fact that Janine loves it and thinks it's hilarious. She likes to point out how people in the show are like people in my family. My family? How the hell is that show like my family? What a stupid thing to say, especially when many of the episodes seem to follow Janine and my marriage so closely, it makes me wonder if the house is bugged.

Now, we're not going to even talk about Everybody Loves Raymond. Is my life like that? Obviously there are similarities. People have pointed it out to me a million times. Janine insults and yells at me, and people, neighbors, family, somebody points out that they saw Debra treat Ray the same way on an episode of that show. But it's different. Debra hates her life, hates Ray's family, and she's just frustrated.

Janine isn't frustrated. She's mean and controlling.

And really, neither show is really like my life, because I'm not wallowing like Richard, and I'm not bumbling and selfish like Raymond. So, I see the humorous reflection in each show, but they are just tv programs. My life with Janine is something that has taken years to put together. And it's hard to explain. I could never do it in a half hour tv show.

One of the similarities between our life and television is public embarrassment.

Janine is always spoiling for a fight. She has no filter. She'll say anything to anyone. I think I've made that abundantly clear. The situations and encounters are unbelievable, but very common.

In early June we were at a barbeque that had been put on by a local church group. It was a charity fund raiser. Janine loves that kind of thing, so we were there.

Two guys with beards were sitting on the porch near us, when they started discussing their facial hair. It seems that one guy was frustrated because his beard was crinkly and unruly. Janine was eavesdropping. I knew she would be. She was talking with a lady who had asked her about our daughter and how she liked the high school, but her heart was in the discussion about beards. One guy commented to the other that he used beard oil to make his beard more manageable. That was the last straw for Janine.

"Beards are so disgusting."

That surprised the bearded conversationalists.

"Excuse me?"

Janine dropped her chatting partner as if she didn't even exist and turned to face her new opponent head on.

"Beards are disgusting. I would never let my husband grow a beard."

"Okay. You don't like beards. We do. Thanks for sharing."

Janine wasn't going to be shut down.

"And what were you saying about oil? You put 'product' in your beard? Do you want me to lend you a tampon too?"

Janine didn't know it, but she had head butted someone who wasn't afraid of her.

"Look, lady. If you don't like my beard, then you don't have to give me a blow job."

He turned away from Janine, clearly finished with her. Janine spun around to look at me, to see if I would jump to her defense. I pretended that I hadn't been listening and strolled over to the desert table. I was careful to stay within earshot.

"No one would ever give a blow job to someone with a disgusting beard! You guys grow those nasty things because you're insecure about your manhood!"

Janine's opponent looked annoyed. He clearly had hoped a sharp insult would drive her away. He heaved a heavy sigh and turned back around to face Janine.

"We're insecure? Let me ask you a question. Is that your natural hair color?"

Janine bristled like a startled Pit Bull.

"Don't give me that! I'm a woman. Women have been coloring their hair for centuries. Women are expected to use product in their hair, and try on different cuts and styles. That's not the same as men letting disgusting hair grow on their faces, and then acting like women and putting all kinds of mouse and product in the mess."

The beard guy laughed confidently.

"Do you know what? If you could grow a beard, to go with that moustache you've got going, you'd grow a beard. In fact, if women could grow beards, beard styling and coloring and beard products would be a billion-dollar business. You don't like my beard because you can't grow one."

Janine was knocked off balance a little bit by the last insult, but she was loving this. She was totally in her element.

"That's bullcrap! The only reason you grow a beard is because you're compensating. You're afraid you're not manly enough, and you think that crap on your face makes the difference."

"I'm compensating? What about you? What woman wears a blouse like that? Going to a cattle drive after dinner?"

Janine had not expected an insult about her clothing. Janine considers herself a top-fashion dresser.

"What's wrong with this blouse? Now you're just taking random shots."

Then bearded guy tapped his finger on the side of his head as he squinted at Janine.

"The only way that blouse would look feminine is if you went bra-less and undid a couple more buttons. That would look classy without looking slutty. Now, for slutty, you'd go without pants and underwear. That blouse would pull off that look perfectly!"

Janine's mouth dropped open and she looked dizzy. She was finished. I could tell.

"Filthy!"

That was all she said, and she stood up and marched in my direction.

"We're leaving."

The ride home wasn't fun. She railed at me for not defending her. She started throwing insults at me for not being man enough to do the gallant thing. I was definitely back pedaling.

"I heard you talking about hair products. I wondered why you were getting all worked up about hair, but I didn't want to get involved, because I don't know anything about hair products."

It was a lie. I heard everything that went on in Janine's crazy fight. She was twitching angrily, and I could tell she was very wound up. I wondered if we were going to have a huge fight when we got home.

"You should have heard the awful things that guy was saying to me."

She was chewing her thumb nail now and staring out the window. When we got home, Janine marched straight to our room. She shut herself in my bathroom, and I heard rustling around. I stood and watched the door nervously. This notebook, you know?

When Janine came out of the bathroom she walked straight over to our stand mirror. She looked good. I watched her carefully. She wasn't wearing a bra and there were two buttons undone on her blouse. She put her hands on her hips and swiveled from side to side, staring at herself in the mirror.

"Does this look alright to you?"

I was surprised to hear her voice so calm. I walked over closer and looked in the mirror with her.

"That looks really nice. Very good."

"Not slutty?"

"Surprisingly, no. You look very elegant."

"I'm not wearing a bra, you know."

"Yes, I noticed that right away. I am a man after all."

"But it doesn't look slutty?"

"Classy. That's what I'd say. Very classy."

Janine turned and looked into my eyes. She caressed my chin with the back of her fingers.

"You've never worn any kind of facial hair, have you? Never a moustache, or anything?"

I looked back at her and shook my head.

"Never. I've never done anything but shave every morning."

She smiled and caressed my cheek with her palm.

"You've never felt less of a man because of it, have you?"

I didn't answer. I wanted to say, "Not because of facial hair." But I didn't. Janine dropped an unexpected compliment.

"You're a good man. You know what it means to be a man. You don't have to compensate with any stupid posturing."

Janine spun away from me just as suddenly and marched back into the bathroom. There was more rustling. Again I stood and watched the door. When Janine finally exited the bathroom, she wasn't wearing pants. The blouse was the same, but no pants. She was biting her lower lip, and grinning like crazy. She did a little twirl. There were no panties, either.

"Does this look sexy?"

My heart started to race.

"I'll say it does! What brought this on?"

I couldn't believe it. Janine's fight had made her horny! That night I got the blow job that her bearded foe had told her he didn't want. It was kind of like an erotic continuation of that fight about facial hair, that lasted until 2:30 am.

Give'em hell, Janine.

Entry # 6

Who leads?

I'm still thinking about what a stranger might ask me about my marriage. When we dance, who leads?

Or better yet, who drives the car when we go someplace?

That's a great question!

We have the kind of marriage where Janine says, 'What's mine is mine and what's your's is ours.'

We each have our "own" car. How do we decide that? We don't. Janine decides which car is hers, and which is mine. Her decision might change as her moods and needs modulate. But this is definitely an area where she lays down the law. Driving in a car is a very serious matter to Janine.

Once when the kids were little, we were driving in Janine's car. We were going to visit her cousin's family. It was about a two hour trip. She was driving, I was reading a magazine. Suddenly there was a commotion in the back seat. The kids were fighting. Sammy suddenly grabbed Daniel's Walkman and threw it out the window. An impulsive act from a child fighting with a sibling. The wrong thing to do. Daniel was horrified. He was screaming mad. I get that. It was his freaking Walkman! Sammy was very frightened. It wasn't something she had thought about doing, it was just something she did.

Janine started to scream at Sammy. She started to scream at me. She wanted me to discipline Sammy. Sammy was frightened. She was hugging her doll. I couldn't say anything. I should have told her to calm down. She should have pulled the car over so we could handle the situation. But she didn't. Janine was screaming, and trying to turn around to reach Sammy. The car was accelerating. We were going faster because Janine was tensing up. Sammy was crying harder and harder. Daniel was frozen in fear.

Janine was screaming at Sammy to throw her doll out of the car window. That was the price. She had to make it even. The doll for the Walkman. She was serious! She wanted Sammy's doll thrown out of the window as justice for Sammy throwing Daniel's Walkman out the window.

Sammy was crying and trying to hug and protect her doll. Janine was swerving the car all over the place, paying more attention to the fight in the car than her own driving. Daniel and I were staring at the situation with our mouths open. Janine was getting more and more hysterical, because she couldn't control the situation and drive the car at the same time.

Suddenly Janine whipped her head around at me with a scary, vicious snarl on her face.

"Get the doll!"

Get the doll? What am I? A mob enforcer? I stared at Janine in disbelief and she could see that I wasn't going to cooperate. Janine pounded the brakes with both feet, the car skidded to a stop, and we all braced ourselves the best we could.

"Why don't you listen to me?"

It's moments like that when I should have brought calm to the situation and asserted my position of father in the family. But I could only just shake my head and shrug my shoulders.

I think my kids noticed my weakness that day, and it caused permanent hurt in my family.

ENTRY # 7

WHO'S A FOOL?

I came back in here because something's bothering me.

Janine treats me as if I were the biggest fool in the world. I have to just sit there and accept it as if I agree that I'm a fool. I have to admit that it's kind of always been that way for me. I was a class clown in school, I was a poor student,

But who's the real fool?

Janine likes to sing, and she secretly thinks she's an unusually good singer. So she's not afraid to belt out a song without any notice.

No one ever says, "Hey, you're a great singer!" And she's not. She's really not. She's a horrible singer. She sounds like a dog whining when she sings. There's that dog reference again.

And besides that, she always gets the lyrics wrong.

She likes to sing "Jeramiah was a Bullfrog".

Simple song, but she gets the lyrics wrong every time.

She sings: "Joy to the people in the deep blue sea, joy to you and me".

I told her once: "there are no people in the deep blue sea."

She sneered at me and said: "What??? What in the world are you talking about?"

And she sings, "So buy me some American pie ...."

And on an unrelated note, when she's determined to do something, she says, "come hell or ice water."

So, I'm saying she gets things wrong. Especially song lyrics.

But she keeps on belting out those songs, with lots of theatrical enthusiasm. She sings along with the instrumental music in stores and elevators.

And Janine gets jokes wrong. She tells them all wrong and always ruins the punch line. People give her charity laughs because they feel sorry for her, or because they are afraid of her. Janine doesn't understand that people are faking their laughs, so she thinks her jokes are great. I sometimes think Janine doesn't understand jokes at all.

Janine likes slapstick comedy. She likes to see people fall down. She likes when someone pulls a funny face become someone else slapped them.

Sometimes when we go to the movies and see an action movie, Janine laughs like it's the funniest thing in the world. She laughs at the fights and she laughs when the cars crash. She's always the only one in the theater who's laughing, but she doesn't care. It embarrasses me.

I can just keep going and going.

You haven't lived until you've heard Janine try to tell about a movie she's seen. She just can't do it. She can't make any sense out of what she's seen. She stumbles and stutters and gets the plot and story all wrong. And she gets angry and offended if anyone tries to help or correct her. I used to help her tell about movies we saw, years ago. But she would really let me have it when we were alone after, so I stopped doing it. I just let her get herself all tangled up until the person who is trying to listen to her finally changes the subject in awkward desperation.

Then a funny thing happens. The person who couldn't make sense of what Janine had been trying to tell her, this person, maybe a friend, a neighbor or someone in her family, this person will casually ask me what I thought of the movie, and then ask me to tell them about it.

Janine absolutely hates that. I always catch hell for that later.

Did you see that?

I catch hell no matter what I do. When I used to help and correct her, it made her angry. Now I ignore her, and talk about the movie when she's done making an idiot of herself, and I STILL get in trouble. That's what I'm trying to tell you here.

No sense of humor. None.

And yet I'm always trying to use humor to make her see what's going on.

We were out shopping early Saturday morning. As we were driving home, I realized that I really had to use the bathroom. Number one. Not a crisis, but still urgent. I got out the car quickly when we pulled into the driveway of our house.

"Why do you hurry so much?" She asked it with a snarl in her voice. Who cares how fast I get out of the car? What difference does it make? She's just always looking for a reason to pick.

"I need to use the bathroom."

I said it without slowing or looking at her.

"Can't even open the door for your wife?"

Holy crap. I never open the door for her. She just gets out of the car. Every errand isn't a date. I'm not a pig, I just don't think of things like that after shopping. But I sighed and turned and walked back to the car. She was out before I could get there. So I turned again toward the car.

Inside, I was briskly walking toward the bathroom when she snarled again.

"Can you wait just a second? I have something to ask you! JEEZ!"

I paused impatiently and turned halfway around.

"When are we going to take care of the problem with the head light on my car?"

"We can go later today. Or right now if you want. Just let me use the bathroom."

She kept going. I was sure she was purposely torturing me.

"I need it fixed, because it's all cloudy. It looks terrible and it's dim at night. They'll be busy today. We might not get in today. What if we have to wait till Monday?"

Stupid questions, stupid conversation, all designed to keep me out of the bathroom. So I decided to be funny. I turned fully around and started to unzip my pants and reach into the fly. Her lips and nose curled in horror, and she stepped backwards as if some snake was going to jump out and bit her.

"What in the hell are you doing?"

I gave her a knowing look.

"I really really need to use the bathroom, and I want to be totally ready when you're finished talking. So I'm going to get my penis out and be ready to dash in there and just start going as soon as I'm able."

I got her. She was speechless. Her body was contorted, but she was motionless and silent.

"Finished? Am I good to go?"

She didn't answer, and I ran to the bathroom. When I got out, she was still standing in the same spot. She wouldn't look at me. But she was steaming mad. I made a wide half circle around her, and at the moment when I was exactly behind her, she spoke. It was like the devil's voice, hissing from hell.

"What's wrong with you? Who does something like that? Seriously. You're really screwed up, buddy."

I chuckled and stepped outside to get the stuff we got from the store.

Entry # 8

Oh crap.

Here I am again, sitting here in the bathroom, and I realize that I've got nothing to say. My wife bosses me around, I feel picked on. The end. You already know that. I'm just saying it over and over again. Maybe that's all I'm going to get out of this. But it's more than that. This little writing project has made me take a hard look at my marriage. Things aren't right. They haven't been right for a long time. I'm thinking about it on a daily basis.

Nothing bad has happened today. Yet I still feel the need to complain. Why is that? If I were talking to someone face to face, I'd sound like such a whiner. Maybe I still sound that way in this notebook.

But here's the thing. It's the way she talks to me. I guess that's the best I can do today. It's not exactly like she's talking to a child, or talking to an employee. It's not even really that she talks down to me. And she's not generally insulting. Don't get me wrong, there are moments, too many moments, when she is all of those things. Demeaning, insulting, insinuating, talking to me like I was a child or an idiot. I know that it's not generally the way things are between us. I know I'm exaggerating my feelings a little bit. But the way she talks to me is still aggravating.

She talks to me as if she already knows what I'm going to say. Or it's more that I'm supposed to respond a certain way. It's always a given that I agree with her. When I've done something wrong, or had neglected to do something she wanted me to do, she scolds me. But she doesn't scold me exactly like an adult would scold a child, she scolds me as if it really bothers her that for a moment we're not totally synchronized.

That hurts. Why would she assume that my thoughts are just an echo of her thoughts? For years I've wondered if she thinks that I don't have thoughts of my own, or something important running around in my head that I'm concerned about. What if I'm not in tune with what she wants me to think or do because I'm worried about something important?

Either she doesn't know, or doesn't care. I'm sure that she thinks that there is nothing more important in this whole world than what she thinks and wants. Even my kids complain about that. Everything is always her way, and she always has the last word on everything. Even when the kids have friends over, Janine tells them what to do, and how they should do everything. And Janine's always up for a good fight. I'm embarrassed to admit that I'm the only one who rarely faces off with her. I've learned that it's just easier to let her win.

Janine has fought with all the neighbors, all the parents of other kids from school, all the parents of the kids who are friends with our kids, and all the teachers at the schools where our kids have attended. She's fought with our pastor. She's fought with waiters, cashiers and salespeople. And it's always something really stupid. It's never something worth fighting over.

Our kid didn't get a good part in the school play.

The fries are cold.

Your dog pooped in our yard.

Your mail got delivered to our mailbox.

A neighbor looked at her wrong at the grocery store.

Someone invited us to do something we've never tried before.

She's sure someone's kind comment was really sarcastic and meant as a burn.

And as you've seen already, if a guy has a beard.

Do these people fight back? Rarely. The guy with the beard was a very unusual case. I've been trying to figure that out. Some people see Janine, and patronize her. They let her blow off steam, stomp around, and intimidate. They ignore the attitude and move on. Some of them ignore what she is saying, and some respond as if they are pretending that she has been polite and understanding. Other people are indeed afraid of her, and just try to stay out of her way. I am the first one to admit that her moods can be scary. And yes, a few people face off with her and try to put her in her place. That usually results in a very long interchange of loud voices. I always try to tune out when that happens. It's embarrassing, and it's awkward.

Janine is never offended though. She might come away from an aggressive encounter with strong feelings about why her opponent is wrong, and she might have feelings about why her opponent is weak or stupid, but she's never offended. She doesn't sit and pout. She's too proud for that. She moves on to the next fight. Don't feel bad if she's tangled with you. Believe me, I get the brunt of her attitude. Most things are my fault.

Even more aggravating is how she assumes that I'm always physically close to her. She talks to me without looking to see if I'm there. Sometimes I'm nearby, but sometimes I'm in a completely different room. And if I don't answer, if she has to look for me, I'm in trouble. If we're shopping together, and I wander off to look at something that caught my eye, she'll eventually say something to me over her shoulder as if I'm following her like an obedient child, or a lady in waiting. Then when she finds me, she yells. I embarrassed her. I left her talking to herself. People thought she was crazy. I'm always tempted to mumble, "You are crazy!"

She does it at home, too. If she's in the kitchen, she just starts talking to me without looking to see if I'm in there with her. So by the time I hear her shouting at me from the other room, she's already angry.

I guess that's what today's entry will be. You can just about bet that when I leave the bathroom and go back downstairs, she's going to growl at me and say, "Where were you?" And I'll shrug and act all innocent and say, "I was in the bathroom." And she'll roll her eyes. Then she'll tell me that she was trying to talk to me and how she was asking me if I bought new line for the trimmer or something like that and she'll start complaining that the yard is starting to look really bad.

One day I'll snap. One day I'll tell her that I don't give a crap how the yard looks, and that I don't want to waste more money on trimmer line when I could be spending it on porn. Then I'll tell her that I've been considering dousing the yard in gasoline and setting it on fire. I know. It's brave talk for a guy with his pants down around his ankles.

The worst thing of all, the absolute worst of all the horrible little things she does to me, is her disgusting eye roll. I hate the way she rolls her eyes more than I hate anything else she does. I'm going to write about that every time she does it, so I'm going to write about it over and over again.

Here's how it works. She calls my name. That's how it starts. It doesn't matter the reason or what she wants. She always starts by calling my name. It might be when we're with our family, or just the two of us alone. It might be with friends or extended family. It might be in a very public place surrounded by strangers. But she'll call my name. It always sounds like she's calling my name because I've done something wrong, or because I'm stupid, like maybe I'm not paying attention. When I turn to respond to her, she'll roll her eyes. Not subtly. She rolls her eyes with a big, exaggerated flourish.

What did I do? Seriously. What the hell did I do? Why do I deserve to have her roll her eyes at me?

Here's another one. I make a suggestion that we go for a drive on a Saturday. It's a nice day and I'm offering to take my wife and family for a nice drive and maybe a stop somewhere nice for lunch. But watch how she reacts. You'd think that I had said we should go smoke crack in an alley while soliciting prostitutes.

She stares at me for a moment with an exaggerated, stupid expression on her face, as if mocking how stupid my suggestion is. Then she rolls her eyes and her whole head with a big wave. Then she starts listing all the things we still have to do on that Saturday, and she does it like I'm five years old.

One more. We're having dinner with her family. I tell her parents about a movie I recently enjoyed seeing. As I'm talking, out of the corner of my eye, I'm aware that my wife is reacting. I look at her. She's rolling her eyes. She's having an entire conversation with her sister or with our daughter, all through the use of eye rolls.

I say, "What?" She answers, "What?" Innocence. Total innocence. After a minute she sarcastically asks her mother. "So, does anybody want to run out and see Scott's movie? Nobody? Okay, let's change the subject then." I feel embarrassed and betrayed. She's not being honest with herself or anyone else. She saw the movie too, and I thought she liked it.

Here's the thing. It's all the time. She rolls her eyes at me constantly.

Now, think about it. What does an eye roll mean? Nothing? No words? I'm telling you she nags a thousand words with her eye rolls. Here's what it says to me: "Good Lord he's so damn stupid!" But if I say, "Stop doing that!" she's sure to respond as if I'm crazy. "Stop doing what? You're imagining things!"

In fact, when I've casually brought up how much eye rolls annoy me in general, she'll agree with me and bring up someone who once rolled their eyes at her and got on her nerves. It's as if she has no idea that she does it to me. Could it be true? Is she really unaware of the things she does that make me feel emotionally cornered?

Another great eye trick that Janine does is the "ole one eye". I've called this trick the "Mr. Spock" from time to time, but mostly it's the "ole one eye". I got that one yesterday.

I had the day off, and I was going to relax in front of the tv. Janine came in and told me that the yard looked like crap. If you've been paying attention at all, you know by now that this is something she tells me more than once a week.

Anyway, I looked up at her and told her that I had just been out looking things over, and that there was nothing really to do out there. The grass wouldn't need mowing till Saturday, the edges were so edged that they looked like the edge of a knife. There wasn't a weed in sight. Everything looked perfect.

When I finished talking, Janine turned her head so that she was looking at me mostly with her right eye, which was getting wider by the second, and her right eyebrow was arching higher and higher, like Mr. Spock does with his eyebrow. That's the "ole one eye". It means that I need to do whatever she has told me to do immediately without any further argument.

I know this all makes me sound like a meek little beaten mouse, but I have my little moments of victory sometimes. That's what happened yesterday. I went outside, in the sun and heat, and started looking around for something to do. The walks didn't even need sweeping. I swear that woman is obsessive compulsive.

Then I noticed through the window that Janine was talking on the phone to someone, probably her sister, and that she was working through the tv channels with the remote. She gets to relax on the couch with the phone and the tv while I work in the yard? There had to be something I could do about that. There was.

I got the yard hose all unwound, and I started watering the plants near the window. Janine didn't even look up to see what I was doing. Very casually I pretended to notice something out of place above the window, and I put my thumb over the end of the hose and started spraying the window with the high pressure.

I know how loud that sounds inside the house. Janine jumped and looked up at me with a start. She narrowed her eyebrows at me and waved me away. I pointed at a high space on the window and pretended to talk to her, pointing out an imaginary problem spot that needed to be cleaned. Janine shook her head at me angrily and went back to her phone conversation.

I waited about a minute and then pretended to see something on the window again. I thumbed the hose again and sprayed the window again, and Janine jumped again. She looked very annoyed that time. She waved me away vigorously with her arm AND her head. I pointed at the imaginary spot again and pretended to explain. I was moving my mouth but not really saying anything or even making sound. It felt really good. I could tell by the look on Janine's face that she was complaining about my watering to the person on the phone. Probably her sister.

She waved me off very vigorously and with great annoyance.

I shrugged and went back to watering the plants.

I waited another minute and sprayed the window again.

I could see Janine starting to tense up and get flustered. She jerked her head at me to yell, but realized I couldn't hear her. She stood up and started to pace. She made fists at heaven. That's another one we'll talk about later. Fists at heaven. That one always amuses me. Then Janine marched over to the window. I was still just standing there like a dufus, spraying the window as if I were doing what I had been told to do.

Janine looked right at me and I could see her ask the person on the phone to wait a minute. Then she gave me the ole one eye and pointed toward the sidewalk. I looked up and across the street and over the tops of the houses. I shaded my eyes with my hand and pretended to search for something she was trying to point out to me. I left the hose spraying on the window. Then turned back to Janine and shrugged my shoulders and shook my head like a confused child.

What did she do? You already know. She rolled her eyes. It was a big roll this time. Her eye roll turned her whole body around and she stormed out of the family room.

Now, I've already said that I hate her eye roll more than anything else, and that's true. But there is a higher level of pressure that I'm subjected to.

This higher level of spousal disgust has a few different parts.

First, it only happens when we're with people she wants to impress. A rich neighbor at a party for example, or someone she went to school with.

Second, it only happens if I have something to say. Even if I'm responding to something someone has asked me directly, I get the treatment. To be honest, I haven't really noticed if the treatment includes eye rolling. I try not to make eye contact with Janine when I get the treatment. I try to pretend that I'm not getting the treatment.

I should probably mention that the treatment doesn't happen all that often, because I don't push the envelope with Janine that much when we're with other people. I don't really talk too much when we're in social situations, but when I do, it quickly becomes clear that I should be seen and not heard. Let me diagram the treatment for you.

Here's how it goes:

I start to talk. Maybe it's because I have something to say, or maybe it's because I'm answering a question. Janine comes dancing over. She hovers, then she sits by me. Sound terrible? It is. Just wait.

Next, Janine looks away from me, I mean in the complete opposite direction, and quietly says, "honey". I'm supposed to stop talking at this point, no matter where I am in my sentence. If I don't, the treatment continues.

What does she think people see when she's patting me on the leg and repeating "honey" over and over? It makes us look stupid. It reveals a lot about our relationship.

So let's say I pretend not to hear her say, "honey", and I keep talking. This happens sometimes, if I'm feeling especially assertive or if I'm talking with someone about something I know or care about. It doesn't happen a lot, mind you. Most of the time when she says "honey", I let the subject drop and just look out the window. But there are definitely times when I pretend that I haven't noticed her hand on my knee, and I just keep talking.

When this happens, Janine looks down, slumps her shoulders, and sighs. Not a gentle, feminine sigh like Scarlet does in Gone With The Wind. Janine's sigh sounds like someone letting the air out of a car tire. But not by pushing on the little plunger in the valve. It sounds like air escaping from a tire because it's been stabbed by a dagger that was stolen from the very bowels of hell.

But we're not done yet. If I still won't shut up, the treatment gets taken to its highest level. Janine looks up to heaven this time, and puts her hand on my leg. Then she pats or rubs my knee. She bites her bottom lip, or sometimes purses her lips, and says, "sweetheart". It's like she wants to say, "sweet heart, can you get me a drink of punch?" but only the "sweetheart" part comes out.

Now, if I don't shut up at this point, it's clear that there's going to be trouble when we get home. She lets me know just with the look on her face. I always wonder if other people in the room can read that look on her face. To me it couldn't be more obvious if she was wearing war paint and dancing around in a circle, beating a tom tom. Anyone can see just by looking at her that she's mad and she's looking for a fight. But she clearly doesn't think they can tell. And I don't think it's just a matter of her not caring if they can read her or not. She's right, and she thinks our little conflict is private. She doesn't think other people see the way she's reacting to me. She doesn't even believe there's a problem with the way she reacts to me.

Now what, you may ask, was I saying in the first place to bring on the treatment? It doesn't matter. It really doesn't matter. I get the treatment if I open my mouth in public at all. If I say anything at all when we're with somebody important, I'll get the treatment. We could be talking about pets or politics, yard work or religion. We could be in our own home, or at some other house. It happens just the same way.

It happens because she doesn't respect anything I might say. I'm forever on the verge of embarrassing her with my opinions.

I've often wondered if other people noticed. I'm pretty sure that at least a few of them have. Once in a while, after enduring the treatment, the person I was talking to will riddle me with questions in an obvious effort to keep me talking. It almost seems like they are provoking a fight with Janine, to prove that I should be able to chat with them without her interfering. Janine will stare them down, and she'll say "honey" and "sweetheart" more enthusiastically. She'll try to interrupt me and change the subject, all in an effort to get me to shut up and sit there like an obedient Labrador. Several times I've been tempted to start to pant.

But I figure that if someone wants to hear what I have to say, I have a right to say it. It might sound funny, but as long as I can't see her rolling her eyes, I don't care. If I don't care about the conversation, I do shut up. But if I'm having an interesting conversation, or I like the person I'm talking with, I let them push the point, even though it will result in a tirade when we get home.

Why were you ignoring me tonight?

You were so stupid tonight.

I can't believe what you were saying.

You really embarrassed me.

Why can't you just sit there and politely listen to the conversation?

I don't care. I put up with crap like that every damn day of my life. Day after day after day.

By the way, it just occurred to me that in all our family portraits, she's sitting by me with her hand on my knee.

Entry # 9

Is Janine ever wrong?

That's the next question you would ask me if you could.

Years ago, Janine would sometimes see, like any other person, that she was wrong about something. It's annoying to be wrong. We all understand that. But as time has gone by, Janine has grown tired of being wrong. She has learned to justify almost any position she takes. She has given up being wrong altogether.

She would never admit now that she was wrong about anything. Telling her she's wrong just makes her angry. And even if you've got overwhelming evidence that she's wrong, she just starts to act crazy. She walks away from the conversation. She starts singing nonsense lyrics to a made up song. She throws herself into a task. She avoids further conversation about the subject.

Certainly she will never want to talk about her wrongness calmly. She's a bluffer. After a wild exhibition of crazy, busy behavior, she gets quiet. She avoids everybody. After an appropriate amount of time, she acts like nothing ever happened.

Part of the problem is that Janine lives in her own world, and it's tough to prove to anyone who lives in their own world that they are wrong about anything.

Much of my jousting with Janine occurs on Saturdays when I'm doing yardwork. Janine putters around in the yard doing "gardening", but really she's watching over me like a prison warden.

Recently I mowed the grass. Nothing special about that, I mow the grass every Saturday. But on this particular Saturday, after finishing the entire yard, I went into the house to get a drink of water. I hadn't put the mower away, because I intended to rearrange the yard tools in the garage a little after I had finished my water.

Suddenly I heard the mower start up again. At least I thought I heard the mower start again. I thought for a minute that it could have been the neighbor's mower. But soon enough, I recognized the sound of my own mower. I ran to the window to see what was happening. Janine was mowing the lawn that I had just finished mowing. I opened the window and yelled.

"What are you doing? I just mowed that!"

Janine looked up, startled. She put her hand to her ear to signal that she couldn't hear me. I stepped to the door and went outside. Janine scowled at me as she turned off the mower. I pointed at the yard. Before I could speak she started chastising me.

"You left, so I'm finishing the mowing. It has to be finished today. I don't know why you walked away, but I guess it's up to me to get it done now."

I was dumbfounded.

"I just finished mowing the whole yard! Look at it! It's perfectly mowed. Can't you see that?"

Janine was caught off guard, just a little. She looked around the yard with a tiny bit of embarrassment.

"It looks like you just left the mower here because you didn't want to finish."

I was really starting to feel frustrated.

"No! I left the mower here because I went in to get a drink of water before I put all the tools away in the garage. I wanted to do a little cleaning in there."

Janine's eye started twitching and she leaned in toward me, looking at me with one, big, wide opened eye.

"You should put stuff away BEFORE you get a drink!"

I shook my head slowly.

"Why?"

She didn't have an answer. Bottom line: she was mowing a just-mowed lawn. She curled her lip as she looked around her.

"It doesn't look like you did a very good job. It's all uneven here, and there, and over there. I guess I'll have to finish it."

And with that, she fired up the mower and continued mowing a just-mowed lawn.

No, Janine is never wrong.

ENTRY # 10

IT WAS SCARY TONIGHT.

Janine screamed and insulted me like a crazy person. I feel so stupid. I'm literally hiding in here tonight. Here's what happened.

Janine sent me to the garage earlier to get some chicken from the freezer. So I did. I found the bag of frozen chicken, and I ripped it open and I took some out. Then I folded the bag around itself and put it back where I found it.

Later Janine was in the garage and she started screaming. It sounded like the world had ended. It was as if she had found her parents mutilated and hanging from the garage door opener. It was a scream from the bottom of her guts. Like in a horror movie. It was crazy. She had found the chicken I opened.

Okay, I didn't notice that the bag of frozen chicken had one of those re-sealable openings. I didn't have to rip the bag open. I could have just opened the zip thingy and then resealed it when I got the chicken out.

So that was earlier, and just now, when Janine went to the garage and started screaming, she had opened the freezer to get something she needed, and she saw the bag of frozen chicken that I had opened. Apparently it made her so mad that she started screaming. So I rushed to the garage to see what the matter was.

"It has a re-sealable opening! You don't have to tear it open!"

I didn't know what to say. She was so upset! I was trying to understand why this was the end of the world. Janine was getting more and more upset, mostly because I didn't seem as devastated by this as she was, so suddenly she just threw the bag of chicken across the garage and the bag burst open when it hit the wall. There was frozen chicken all over the garage floor. Janine screamed at me one more time before shoving past me back into the house.

"You are so unaware!"

ENTRY # 11

SHE'S QUIRKY.

Now this time I feel really bad about doing this. Everybody has their little quirky habits, and no one wants to be mocked or criticized for the quirky things they do. But Janine's very quirky. She doesn't deserve to have me rip her apart like this. I can hear her right now on the other side of this bathroom door, shuffling around the bedroom, arranging this and that. She's not bothering me at all, and she's knows I'm in here. Totally innocent this time.

But since I'm writing this stuff down, I'll go ahead and write this very petty and childish entry.

Okay, here goes:

Janine has weird habits.

She turns down the television and stereo like some weird compulsion. Even if she's not watching the television, she'll grab the remote every time she walks through the room and turn the sound a little bit. It's especially annoying when we're all gathered in the family room watching tv. Janine acts like she's the only one who is concerned about the television. She makes several passes through the room, turning down the tv each time. After a while we can't hear the tv at all. When we complain to her she tells us that loud electronic sound can damage our hearing.

She's obsessed with being in control of the television. She'll randomly change the channel, even when someone is watching something. She'll just say, "This is stupid." And then she'll just change the channel. It doesn't matter who protests or how earnestly they beg her to change the channel back. If you tell her that you were watching a show you especially had been waiting to see, she'll snarl and tell you that it looked stupid to her. She especially hates comedy shows. I think it's because she doesn't understand the humor. She doesn't get the jokes. So she just angrily changes the channel.

And she grumbles and mumbles when she complains. When she's cooking, or cleaning, or doing any of her regular chores, she grumbles to herself about how it's all somehow unfair to her. What exactly is unfair? Who knows? Lots of people have families and prepare dinners or do other things in the kitchen.

Now, it seems to me that we all have chores and responsibilities. But Janine will grumble at a steady, low pace about how no one cares about her, and how we would all live like pigs if she died, and how she shouldn't have to do everything when she's only one person.

The truth is that she doesn't do everything. I do.

Now that's really funny. Now it looks like we're two spoiled children arguing over who does more work around the house. I guess this book is my own version of grumbling and mumbling.

But read that again. I'm serious. I do everything. Janine tells me to do it, and then I do. I guess in her mind, because she's giving the orders, everything gets done because of her. But I'm the one that actually does the work.

So she talks to herself. She grumbles and complains like there's a ghost following her around agreeing with her. And she's quirky when she talks to me. Whenever I say anything to her, anything at all, she answers with "what?". It's almost as if she's deaf, or as if she's suddenly totally lost and confused. I could be standing right in front of her, looking her right in the eye, and she'll still answer with "what?" I guess really it's like I'm not worth her full attention, or as if what I'm saying is beneath her contempt. I must say that this habit is very aggravating. To be answered by "What?" every time I say anything to her. It's like fingernails on a chalkboard.

What else? Okay, now I'm going to get petty and childish. Janine grunts when she works. Whenever she does anything that requires any physical effort, she grunts like a caveman. It's disgusting. I'm talking about real, caveman grunts from the bottom of her groin. Repeating, rhythmic grunts. Breath, breath, grunt. Breath, breath, grunt. It's like she's working up a might dump.

It happens when she's mixing ingredients for a cake, or turning a screw with a screw driver, or working the push sweeper thing. It sounds like she's having a horrendous movement.

And this is going to make me look like a real insensitive jerk. But Janine blows her nose a lot. I mean, Janine blows her nose, a lot. I think that she tries to blow her nose for no reason, like when there's nothing there. Why would she do that? I think it's a nervous habit. Like cracking your knuckles. But when she blows her nose, it irritates her sinuses, and they swell up and her nose starts to run. Then suddenly she really is stuffed up and she needs a tissue and it all escalates.

So her nose issues are all in her head. No, I'm not a doctor. But it's all just very, very clear. All she needs to do to solve it, is to just relax and leave her nose alone. It's all in her imagination. Her nose is never really stuffed up.

Do you know what would happen if I posed that theory to her? You try it. I've learned by experience to just keep my mouth shut and listen to her honk her nose like the horn on a semi-truck.

I did, however, point out once that she hadn't sounded congested before she blew her nose. When I do something like that, she locks on to me with eye contact. She asked me over and over again what I was trying to say. I just kept pointing out that she didn't sound congested, and I asked innocently if she thought she was getting sick. She sat there and concentrated on her eye contact with me like some cheap county fair fortune teller and said that she wasn't sick, she was just blowing her nose.

I mumbled quietly that I couldn't understand why she was blowing her nose if she wasn't sick. She ordered me to repeat what I had said more loudly so that she could hear me, and I acted like I was really concerned and asked if her ear canals were stuffed up too. I launched into this routine of concern and told her I was worried that she might be getting sick, and she finally told me to just drop it.

The rest of the evening she slammed everything. That's another one of her quirks. When she's in a bad mood, she slams. She slams the bowl onto the table. She slams the cupboard doors. She slams the milk container back into the fridge. She slams the books back into the book case. She was a slamming mammy that night.

And yes, it occurs to me that writing petty little complains in a notebook while using the bathroom is a little quirky too.

Not to beat a dead horse, but one of Janine's quirks, is her temper. Janine just plain likes to be angry. She's at her best when she's angry. Like an athlete taking the field, or a gladiator facing a ferocious Christian. Anything can set her off. It's like she's looking for something to be angry about, because anger makes her feel good.

The doorbell rings, and she starts to guess who it is at the door, and what they need. And whatever it really is doesn't matter, Janine thinks it's something that should make her angry. A salesman with a high-pressure presentation, or a neighbor wanting to borrow something. She knows without checking. By the time she stands up and marches to the door, she's really angry. It's always fun to see visitors react to that built up anger.

A sound comes from the kitchen. No one knows what it was. In an instant, Janine is sure that something important fell. It's expensive and it's broken, and it has broken something else that is important and expensive and no one will ever be able to make it right again. She's fired up and angry before she even gets to the kitchen. If she goes in the kitchen and doesn't find something worth her anger, then she looks around for something worth griping about. Any mess at all, or anything out of place will now be the thing that makes her angry.

And that's not sane. I don't know if that's necessarily insane, but it's quirky.

And last but not least, she's a nail biter. It's just when she's nervous, but it's aggravating to watch. It's not just a little nibbling, its aggressive gnawing. There nothing like having a conversation, turning to look at her, and she's giving oral sex to her thumb. If it were me sucking my thumb, she'd tell me to stop it. And she'd say it angrily. There have been times when she's had her thumb in her mouth in public and it's made me self-conscious, and I've wanted to tell her to get her damn thumb out of her mouth.

So why haven't I? Is it because I'm just a good person, and I don't want to stick my nose in her business? Or am I afraid of her? I can't answer those questions. I just don't know.

One more thing before I drop the subject.

I was thinking about Janine's quirks today because I was writing about it earlier. While we were grocery shopping this evening, I noticed another quirk that I've noticed many times before, but I've always just left it alone.

Janine sighs a lot. It's a deep, heaving sigh, as if she were really depressed about something. If I ask her what is wrong, she either says, "nothing", as if that were the truth, or she growls at me to leave her alone.

So I do.

In fact, I've left her alone about it for years. But sighing sometimes leads to something else. Tonight her sighing led to something else.

As we were driving home, she was leaning her chin on her hand, staring out the window. She started mumbling a long, scattered list of things she was worried about and bothered by. It didn't really seem like a coherent list, and it didn't even seem like she was talking to me or that she expected me to respond in anyway. Then she started to say, "I just... I just.... I just....."

So for the first time in our marriage I interrupted her, and I asked her: "You just what?"

She jumped. It was as if she had been shocked by a live wire.

"What are you talking about?" She sounded angry and defensive.

"Well, you're sitting there saying 'I just, I just, I just', and I asked you what you mean. You just what?"

Janine was staring at me with wide, frightened eyes. It was as if she didn't know me. She growled that she didn't know what I was talking about, and told me to pay attention to my driving and leave her alone.

Now, is that quirky, or am I starting to see some serious problems in Janine's life?

Here's something I'm sure of: Janine would say that I'm quirky too. She would never use the word quirky, but the message is the same in the way she talks to me almost every day.

She told me the other day that I drink way too much water, and it's driving her crazy. There are too many water glasses in the sink and in the dishwasher. And she said it was bad for me. Too much water makes people nervous and sluggish. Now where in the hell did she get that?

I try to defend myself and tell her about how doctors say we should drink plenty of water each day. But, how dare those doctors imply that they know more about health than Janine does?

I wring my hands when I'm nervous or upset. It's a nervous habit. Janine thinks I should seek professional help for that. And she always mocks me when I do it, a lot like a school yard bully would do. She pulls a face like she's having a seizure and shakes her hands like a wild monkey. It's always embarrassing.

Oh, and she says I fart too much, but I can't really argue with that. We won't get into all that again right now. Or maybe we will.

Entry # 12

Were there ever other girls? Before Janine?

Good question!

No, not really. Janine was my first real love.

But I guess I did date a few interesting girls before I met Janine. But was I ever in love before? Probably not.

I remember dating Heather. I met her in college. We had a lot of classes together. I guess Heather was my girlfriend. We flirted and went out a little for three months, and then we dated exclusively for about five weeks. I never kissed Heather, so I don't know if she counts as a girl-friend. Heather was a very interesting girl. She was a model. Not just an ordinary model. Heather modeled woman's underwear in catalogs. But that's not the most interesting thing about Heather.

Heather was about six foot two. She was a stunning sight to see. She had huge eyes that seemed to look right into your soul. How's that for a cliché? But it was true. And her gorgeous cheek bones and mouth made her face look like she was always about to burst into a naughty smile. She was beautiful.

Her height made her beauty all the more impressive if you were just looking at her. It was like seeing a famous movie star. And Heather wanted to be with me! She wanted to date me. She wanted to be my girlfriend. How did that all work out?

I invited Heather to go with me to dinner and a Christmas concert. It was like an evening out of a movie. Heather looked elegant and beautiful. Because of her career, she understood fashion and hair and makeup, I knew everyone was looking at her. She had a very confident, feminine walk. I've never been more proud to be with a beautiful woman in my life. It was like being in a dream.

The dinner was perfect, the concert was perfect, the date was perfect. As we left the concert hall, almost finished with our evening, Heather was walking closer to me than she had before the show. I felt her reach out and take my hand. I guess I've always been a little shy and awkward around beautiful women, so she saw that she would need to take the initiative.

So now we're holding hands, right? What's the problem with that?

Heather was almost four inches taller than me. Her hands were also bigger than mine. It was like holding hands with another man. I just couldn't get past it. I didn't like it. It was a deal breaker for me. I never called Heather again. That's the kind of boyfriend I was.

Maybe I would be a better husband if I understood love a little better. I never had the chance to understand dating and relationships in a meaningful way, but I'm learning about love and family right now.

I asked to use the bathroom at Janine's folk's house last week. Janine gave me a menacing glare. But I really had to go.

I absolutely hate using other people's bathrooms. People are insane with their fluffy lid covers and their delicately embroidered towels. I'm always afraid I'm going to have a disaster and break something. Bathrooms in people's houses seem so personal and intimate. I hate that. Bathrooms are not for art appreciation. Bathrooms are for taking care of some very primal needs. Dirty, disgusting, messy, smelly needs. It just feels wrong to take a crap with colorfully croqueted doilies and dollies and flowers all around you. Who are people trying to kid? I think it's because some people just can't bear to think about their own animalistic functions. But I'm getting away from my story.

So I'm in there and I suddenly realize that mostly what I have to contribute to this world in that moment is lots of very loud methane. I flushed the toilet and ran the water in the sink to hide the horrible rumbling sound, but I was still sweating with the thought that everyone out in the other room could hear me. I didn't mean to be sick at my in-law's house, but I knew I hadn't had a choice. Lots of gas, but lots of sickness. It took a while to clean it all up.

But the smell. The smell from hell. There was nothing I could do about it. I had the vent running, and I sprayed the air freshener, and it didn't help. It smelled like Hilter was trying to get out of hell, right through that very bathroom. I knew I couldn't just stay in there, but I also knew that when I left, someone was going to go in there, and be horrified by that smell.

I felt totally defeated when I walked out of the bathroom. I felt like everyone was staring at me. But as bad as I felt, things suddenly got much worse. Janine's mom stood up and started walking toward me. I felt the blood rush from my head. She was going to try to go in there! She had no idea of the horrors I had left behind, but soon she would think that I was the devil. This seemed at the moment like the worst thing that could ever happen. I seriously considered tackling her and rendering her unconscious by hitting in the head repeatedly with the toaster.

Then something amazing happened. My little Sammy was there for me. Grandma said she was next in the bathroom, but Sammy suddenly said that she couldn't wait and she rushed in there.

Can you believe that? My little girl threw herself onto a stinking grenade for me. And she knows better than that. She knows what a bathroom is like after I've been in there. But by the time Sammy had spent five minutes in there, the smell had dissipated, Sammy had sprayed some room freshener, and any leftover smell was hard to identify as mine or Sammy's.

What a hero! Sammy looked a little light headed and hazy eyed when she came out, but she was still breathing. Grandma entered the bathroom more than a little annoyed.

I walked over to Sammy and squeezed her arm. I told her I couldn't believe she had done that for me. She smiled and told me she didn't mind. She said she's immune after so many years of living with me. She shook her head and said that there was no way she was going to let her grandmother humiliate me again. But she poked me in the forehead and told me that I owed her, big. She'll be surprised when I find the opportunity to repay her.

Entry # 13

JANINE THE ALLY

Wow. Tonight is a huge swing in the opposite direction. Mean, angry Janine has become fun, strong Janine. I admit that with all my heart. Everything feels really weird tonight.

But it shouldn't, not really. Janine defends her family more than anything else in her life.

Today we found out that a girl at the high school did some really cruel things to Sammy. Last year Sammy missed a lot of school because of a serious stomach infection. Apparently rumors flew about Sammy involving suicide attempts and drug use. This girl has been telling other kids stories about Sammy that aren't true, and Sammy was really hurt by some of them.

The name calling has gone on for even longer. This neighbor girl has been referring to Sammy as "sicky". Wow. Not a good rhyme at all. I could have come up with something way better.

Name calling is something that has existed since the beginning of time. When I was growing up there was a neighbor who had an adult son named Lester. Lester worked for a body shop in town. He was heavy set and had a beard. I don't know why he wasn't married, or why he lived with his parents. That's just the way it was. But people gossiped.

Then one day someone caught Lester pleasuring himself to a nudie magazine behind the shed in his yard. It didn't take long for someone to tag him with the nick name: Lester the molester.

Fair? I don't know. But people are always on the lookout for funny monikers to pin on other people.

So as Sammy has come to us about this girl and her teasing and bullying, Janine has started to call them the "Bax-TURDS". Clever? Does Baxter really sound like turd? I don't know. I shouldn't judge. This whole thing has got my blood boiling too.

Sammy came home in tears the other day. The bullying and rumors have really gotten out of hand. It was clear that something needed to be done. That's when Janine is at her best. That's when we are proud to have her in our family.

So following Janine's lead, we confronted the girl's parents. We marched right over to their house like invading French Foreign Legion troops. When we got there, the wind was taken from our sails a little. The girl's parents were polite and welcoming. But Janine didn't let up, and put the situation right out there. She gave a detailed explanation of exactly what had happened. She was stoic. She declared that no more of this behavior would be tolerated by us (her).

Now the parents bristled. They were not going to hear negative things said about their precious daughter. Especially on their own front porch.

It was on.

Right from the beginning it was a no-holds-barred fight. Janine was taking no prisoners. Janine laid out very clearly the reasons for our grievance. They countered with denials. We were being paranoid. We were out to get their precious daughter. Maybe Sammy was the instigator. Maybe Sammy was a liar.

The girl's father is especially repulsive. Squirrely little guy. Prognathic jaw, sanctimonious attitude, retro personality. He crossed his legs and played with the hair on the back of his head as he spoke to us as if we were mentally disabled children. He started to speculate about Sammy's upbringing. He implied that Janine and I were deviants. Janine let him have it.

"We're perverts? What do you even know about sexuality? Just looking at you, I can tell your wife is one of those women who doesn't even know what an orgasm is!"

The guy got very red in the face and started to protest Janine's vulgarity when she nudged me with her elbow and leaned in even closer to her victim.

"Actually, she's a moaner and a screamer, you're just never around when she has one!"

For a moment there I thought the Bax-turds had the upper hand. But Janine hadn't just offended them, she had frightened them. They begged us to leave, promising that no one in their family would ever bother Sammy again.

We were cruel and inappropriate, but when it was over, we all felt like celebrating. I kept looking at Janine. For the rest of the evening, I was looking at the beautiful, vivacious, courageous, forward, and smart girl that I had fallen in love with.

ENTRY # 14

IT'S BEEN A WHILE.

I figured that this bathroom diary would be a passing fad with me. I don't know yet if that if really the case, but I admit that it's been a couple of weeks since I've written in here.

But I had to share this experience with you.

It's Saturday afternoon, and all my chores are done. I've been thinking more and more about how Janine pushes me around. It bugs me more now that I'm talking about it, or writing about it, I guess. I've been clenching my teeth a lot lately, and I keep daydreaming about opportunities to stand up for myself. But there wasn't anything really happening today, so after giving it some real thought, I decided to do something that I've always wanted to do.

I went down to the family room and turned on the tv. Nobody was around. I decided that I was going to watch a tv show that I've always wanted to see, but I knew that Janine would never approve.

I decided I didn't care anymore.

So I got a tall, cold drink, settled down on the couch, and turned on "Sons of Anarchy". I had found a half full bag of Cheetos in the cabinet, and even though it's forbidden to eat on the couch, I had them at my side. I turned the television set up loud so that I could get the whole effect. It was great! I felt free.

I was surprised how long it took her to notice that I wasn't standing at attention, waiting for her to bark her next order. She came looking for me. It might sound crazy to you, but I could hear the impatience in her footsteps on the stairs. She froze when she saw me.

"What are you doing?"

I answered with my mouth full and didn't look at her.

"I'm watching tv."

There was a pause as she was clearly deciding to start over. She had her eyes closed as if she was thinking of all the objections she was going to throw at me. I pointed at the tv just in case she really didn't understand. I think she did understand that I was watching the tv, because she expanded her original question.

"What are you doing? I thought I made it clear how I feel about that show?"

I winked at her and shushed her.

"I love this show. Don't interrupt."

I admit I ducked a little when I said that. She marched over to the tv set and put her hands on her hips. She bent over at the waist as if to inspect the show. Then she stood in front of the tv and started pointing at me, waving her arms, and yelling.

"I'm not going to have this filth in our home!"

What I did next was demeaning, and I'm not sure if it was a step in the right direction or not. I started begging like a little boy.

"Oh come on! We've seen worse than this! I really want to watch this show! Can't you just leave me alone for an hour? I mean, seriously! You've made me watch 'Titanic' a million times, and you say it's a timeless romantic movie. Right? Well, I've never complained about having that one chick's jugs in our home. Remember? That scene where the guy paints the chick's jugs? And we even see her bush for a few seconds each time. I've never complained about that!"

Her jaw dropped open. I thought I was going to hear a scream, but I only heard a sound like a wind tunnel. She started sighing and shaking her head, and she marched angrily from the room, muttering to herself.

"You've really got some problems buddy! Filthy!"

Filthy? Why? Because of Sons of Anarchy. I could accept that; it would even be cool. But what about Titanic? I'm filthy because I noticed that there's a scene where a guy draws a girl in the nude? That's insane.

So, did I win? I can't tell.

But I enjoyed an hour watching 'Sons of Anarchy'. It was the one where Jax beats up a porno actress and calls her a stupid bitch repeatedly.

Cool.

ENTRY # 15

THIS HAS BEEN A TERRIBLE DAY.

It started at work. We had a business presentation from a valued supplier. Part of their big presentation was a hearty, catered lunch. There were all kinds of tempting, exotic foods. There were stuffed mushrooms and Swedish meatballs. What's the problem with that? If you're asking that, you've forgotten about my IBS.

I didn't forget, but I thought, "What could it hurt?"

For a couple hours after lunch, it almost seemed like everything was going to be okay. The head of our department asked me to out to the industrial park with him to inspect some hardware.

Halfway through the tour, I was in agony. I was sweating bullets. I felt dizzy. I asked to use the restroom.

If you could have seen that toilet, you'd understand. It was disgusting. I don't think that toilet had been cleaned for a year. I just couldn't do it. But I didn't think I could hold it either.

One of my greatest goals in life has always been to never crap my pants. Now, with IBS, I've come very close a few times. Today was one of those times. When I get like that, I feel confused and paranoid.

Down the street from the warehouse, on the corner, was a gas station. The toilet there wasn't much better. Who leaves all that mess? Someone with a terrible disease? It's horrifying. Add to that the fact that it was hard to convince the people I was with that I needed to run down the street.

I no longer had a choice. I was going to crap my pants in seconds. I grabbed a bunch of paper towels, soaked them in the sink, and started cleaning the toilet seat. It made me gag, and then throw up. I wasn't sure if I had cleaned the seat very well, but I had to sit down. It was too late. My shorts were stained. It wasn't lumpy, but it was a mess.

I limped back to the plant, and told everyone I was sick and needed to go home.

When I got home, I told my wife what had happened. Janine was very disgusted and impatient.

"What were you thinking? Why don't you just stop eating things that make you sick?"

That's Janine's medical solution. She's as good as a doctor. She thinks the simple way to fix my digestive problems is to just stop eating the things that make me sick. I told you Janine doesn't think I have IBS. She doesn't even think IBS is a real medical condition. She tells everyone I have a "delicate stomach". That sounds so manly.

When I first had IBS symptoms, Janine thought I had cancer. Scared the hell out of me. She knew someone who's brother was a doctor, and she spent a couple of days on the phone with strangers talking about my poop.

Finally, she made an appointment for me to have two series of barium x-rays.

Fun.

The first round was interesting. They wanted me to drink seven barium milkshakes. Milkshakes sound tasty, right? Picture sticks of school room chalk ground up with water. And they expected me to drink seven of them. After two I was angry. I told the S&M nurse that if I took one more swallow, the stuff would come out my ears and nose. A doctor heard our argument and laughed at us. He said he was sure I was ready.

They laid me down on this huge white pedestal in a white room with a big bullet-proof window on one wall. After removing themselves to radiation-free safety, a big canon looking thing was lowered from the ceiling, and everything started to buzz, and the pedestal started moving and slowing spinning. I was being x-rayed.

Round two happened the next week. I went over, checked in, and changed into one of those sexy hospital gowns. I was equipped with the knowledge that I was an empty human being, because the whole procedure had started the night before when I had consumed the tornado

Kool-Aid that doctor had prescribed for my big day. After drinking a few glasses of that stuff, I could shit through a keyhole at forty paces.

Back to the hospital and my thread bare gown. A crack team of technicians and doctors took me to the x-ray room. No one offered me anything to drink this time. They sat me on the pedestal, and we had a talk. One of them put his hand on my shoulder.

"It's going to be tough."

"We'll get you through this."

"Hang in there."

"Be strong, it will all be over in a few minutes."

Then they had me lay down on my stomach. At this point, someone brought in a long, white garden hose. I swear to God; it was a garden hose! With no further ceremony, the white garden hose was shoved up my ass.

"Do you feel okay, there, Scott?"

How should I have felt? I was laying on a big white pedestal with a white hose coming out of my bare ass like a perverted turkey tail. The x-ray device descended, and the pedestal started to rotate. I could feel pressure building. I was being inflated like a birthday balloon. It was the most horrible feeling I had ever experienced. I started to sweat and shake. From the safety of the control room the technicians and doctors were shouting encouragement with a microphone.

"Almost there!"

"You're doing great!"

"You're getting through this like a pro!"

Are there people who stick hoses up their asses professionally? I wondered. I don't know how much time passed, because I was started to see stars. But finally, the pedestal stopped moving and the pressure started to diminish. I was exhausted. The doctors and technicians came back to cheer for me as if I had just won the big state championship. Then one doctor told me I would have my results later that week and everybody excused themselves.

I laid there laughing to myself. Nothing else could go wrong. There was no way I could feel any lower than I felt in that moment. I gently moved my hips and felt that white hose waggling in the air. I was so wrong. Things got worse.

"Okay Scott, can I call you Scott? Let's get you cleaned up and dressed."

It was the sweetest voice you ever heard. Couldn't have come from anyone over twenty-five. I glanced with one eye over my shoulder. I saw a drop-dead gorgeous blond. Once again, in less than five minutes, I was sure that nothing could ever make me feel lower. I was wrong again. I felt one, delicate, beautiful hand on my right buttock. Another beautiful young hand grabbed that white garden hose, and suddenly the silence of the room was filled with the sound of a champagne bottle being uncorked. That had to be the lowest moment.

"Okay, let's get you to the toilet."

The world was spinning as Miss America helped me into a sitting position. She held my elbow as I hobbled like a ninety-year-old man to a small restroom just outside the door. Then my beautiful helper stood in front of me with her hands on my shoulders as I sat on that toilet and let the barium flow out of me. Five minutes, and a descending staircase of "lowest moments".

On Friday Janine answered the phone when the doctor called to tell us that the x-rays had shown nothing wrong with my G.I. tract. I was fine. Nothing to worry about.

Why did I tell this delightful story? It doesn't matter how bad things get with my IBS symptoms, Janine will always roll her eyes and grow at me: "You're fine!" Then she'll yell at me for my poor eating habits.

It's not that simple. Yes, stuffed mushrooms were probably a bad choice for me. I've tried and tried to explain to Janine that my IBS just happens. I don't know why. Sometimes it's provoked by something I eat and sometimes it's provoked by some stressful event. But my IBS can just happen for no reason at all. That's why I keep on eating the foods I love. Why should I be punished and not allowed to eat good food, just because my body sometimes freaks out? That's the way I see it.

Of course, that means I'm an idiot. Even though it's happening to me, Janine knows better.

That's the way it's been whenever I've had a problem, medical or other. If I tell Janine about it, she immediately starts to diagnose, and she starts telling me what to do about it. And she mixes in a heavy dose of criticism.

I can never just have a friend to listen to me. So, as you might have guessed, this has resulted in me not talking to her.

But I don't think she notices. I don't think her mind works that way. You know?

Entry # 16

How did I wind up with a girl like her?

Yes, I know. If she's so terrible, why did I marry her in the first place? And if she's that bad now, why don't I just leave her and get a divorce? I figured that people reading this, if anyone ever read this notebook, might ask me questions like this.

She was very sexy when we met. Outspoken, head strong, and she knew what she wanted and where she was going.

Naturally Janine made the first moves when we met. It was at a party that a friend we had in common was having in his apartment. Janine went to school with this guy, and I knew him from my neighborhood. This friend built me up to his guests like I was someone really cool, and Janine was there, very interested in everything being said about me.

It was all bullshit. My friend was just trying to make me look good, to help set me up with one of the girls there. And it worked. Janine talked to me all night, asking me questions and hanging on my every word. Looking back now, it seemed suspiciously like a job interview. But we were friends by the end of the party, and we stayed in touch. I called her a few times to take her on a date or something, and it snowballed from there.

I didn't know what I wanted back then. I had no experience. It was fun to be with her. She always had a plan. I felt like I had a purpose in life because of her.

We forged a life together, had two beautiful children. Sammy is fourteen years old. Sammy is my joy in life. We've had our issues, and I know I've complained about her, but I love Sammy with all my heart. Sammy is the person in my family that I need to have on my side. But Sammy loves her mother, too. That's natural, I know. I'll admit right here that sometimes I'm tempted to draw lines and make people choose sides. But I never have. It's important to me that my children respect both of their parents.

Sammy's pretty levelheaded. But it wasn't always that way. By the time she was twelve, she had become her mother's little lieutenant. She seemed to feel it was her job to police me and show me that she shared her mother's feelings that everything I did was wrong.

Sammy would be gone shopping with her mother and when they would get back, they might find me watching tv, for example. Janine would immediately ask me if the dog had been walked, and when I didn't answer right away, Sammy would snap at me: "Oh my gosh! Get off your butt and walk the dog! I mean, grow up! How hard is it to walk the dog?"

And this was all the time for a couple of years.

I never said anything to Sammy about it, but the distance between us grew. After those years passed, Sammy went through a time when I seemed to be invisible to her. She wouldn't insult me, but she didn't even acknowledge me at all. She would walk through the house, right past me, as if I wasn't there.

Then, about a year ago, all of the sudden, she started saying little nice things to me, sometimes just saying "hi!" or patting me on the head. She started telling me about things going on in her life and asking me about my day. And even more interesting is the fact that she's smarting off to her mother when Janine bullies me. Janine has ignored it, but it feels like Sammy seems to want to repair her relationship with me. And she'd be very welcome, too.

Daniel is a different story. He's six years older than Sammy. He's named for his aunt, and we'll talk about that later. But Daniel has always been a strange kid. He has always been distant and withdrawn. As a small child he was quiet and shy. He was polite and happy, but he didn't have much to say and didn't like trying new things. As a teenager Daniel was absolutely withdrawn. Didn't like to even come out of his room. I don't remember him ever getting together with friends when he was in high school. I always wanted to connect with Daniel, but I always failed. I didn't know how.

When Daniel was tiny, I always called him, "little guy". That was my name for him. He was my errand buddy. He liked to hold my hand. I would walk through a store, and look down at him, and I'd say, "little guy!" He loved that until he was about in the third grade. He was small for his age, but that didn't worry me. I should have understood, however, that being smaller than the other kids was hard for Daniel. One evening at the grocery store, I was going to ask Daniel about breakfast cereal, and I addressed him as "little guy". He stared at me for a moment, and I saw his eyes well up with tears.

"Please don't call me that."

It was like a lightning bolt. I never called him "little guy" again. But he will forever be my little guy.

Adolescence came and teenage years, and Daniel withdrew, and I lost him. He was just someone living in my house. We didn't talk much, and we didn't do anything together.

Daniel never dated. I mean, take a girl to the dance, go to the movies, go for a burger, etc. He went through an awkward phase in his youth. He struggled with acne, but I don't think that was it. He never made any effort to ask a girl to a school dance even. Then Daniel went away to college, and it feels to me like he's exited my life. Daniel is my one great regret in life. I feel like I've really failed him. He doesn't talk to me, and as far as I know, he doesn't talk much to anyone.

I used to watch Daniel when he was a little kid. I understood him. He was content just to sit quietly by himself and read, or play video games. I wanted him to be happy. I really did. I wanted people to see him for what he was, for him to feel good about it. I'm rambling. What I'm try- ing to say is that I really love Daniel, and I've always known that he's a frustrated person. Even as a little child. I understand that.

Daniel had a girlfriend his last year of high school. I hated her. I think I took out my frustrations about my wife on her. I was always rude to her. I didn't like the way she dominated his time. I didn't like the way she made him push his family and friends away. She wanted to have him all to herself, and she constantly demanded that he assure her that no one but her mattered in his life. Daniel was fiercely in her corner for about a year. There was a lot of tension in our home.

And it's a funny thing, in a way. Daniel and I are more alike than he knows. Maybe that would insult Daniel. I hope not. There's always been a distance between Daniel and me. I'm taller than he is, and I know that has bothered him since he was in high school. But I've always tried to be Daniel's friend. I see myself in him. I really do. I've always wanted him to be able to see how much we're alike. When I can get Daniel talking, we share the same ideas, thoughts and opinions about many things. And when I can get him laughing, we laugh about a lot of the same things.

Daniel is in college right now. He's an engineering student. He's very smart, and very accomplished. I'm proud of him. I just wish I was closer to him.

So that's the story of my children. I don't think I've set a very good example for them. What have I really done for them? Well I guess I've worked hard and tried to provide a home and a future for them. And I've told them to go to school. Education has been very important in our family.

Janine inspired me to go to college. I admit that. I was working as a butcher in a local grocery store when we met. It wasn't bad money. I had a place of my own and a car I liked. I wasn't for or against college when I met Janine. Janine was very enthusiastic about college and convinced me that I could do well in school and that she would do everything she could to help me. Now I'm a successful engineer. But not even that is my own. She tells everybody that I would have worked bagging groceries my whole life if she hadn't encouraged me to go to college.

But that's not true. I've always wanted to tell her that I would have turned out fine no matter who I would have married.

When I met Janine, I didn't have much to compare her with. I didn't date much in my life before I met Janine, I didn't really have girlfriends before her. When I was in high school my parents would tell me that I wasn't much of a catch. What the hell did that mean? I would ask them to explain it to me and they would say really cruel things. I wasn't very sharp. I wasn't very aggressive. Sometimes they were kidding me, but there were a lot of times when they were seriously telling me why girls didn't want to date me.

I've always been a little uncomfortable around women. When I met Janine she made it very easy for me. She was the first to show some interest. She was the one to approach me, before I could summon the courage to approach her. She asked all the questions and made all the moves. She was setting the pace, she was taking the lead. I was open to anything and she was so assertive, it just felt comfortable.

As far as the divorce thing: I don't want to break up my marriage and family. I know, lots of people use that excuse. But I love my wife and I love my children. I have a family, and that's all I've ever wanted. I don't want to be hurt, but I don't want to hurt anyone either. That's not the point of all this. I'm not planning to hurt anybody. But is it too much to ask that I be treated better? That's all I'm trying to figure out. I want to improve my marriage and get my wife to start seeing me differently.

But differently how? How does she really see me now? I don't really know.

Before I leave this entry, I want to be sure I make one point. I'm painting an ugly picture of Janine, but physically it's not that way. Janine is beautiful. She was beautiful when I married her, and she's still very beautiful. I imagine sometimes that people think I put up with her crap because I married out of my league. It's not true. Janine is beautiful, and that's a separate issue.

ENTRY # 17

I ESCAPED.

I escape pretty often now that I think about it.

We watched a video tonight. After it was over, Janine had gone off to bed, and I told her I was going to return the video and that I'd be right back. I love those times when everyone has gone to bed and I'm alone in the family room. I'm free in those moments to do what I want. What was really happening is that I got to feeling that I needed a ride in the car, and I needed a coke. So it occurred to me, as it often does, that if I take the video and return it, we won't get charged for a second day. That's a good thing, right? She should see the logic in that?

Sometimes she does. Kind of. She'll usually growl at me and ask me why I took so long coming to bed. Then when I tell her I took the video back, she'll sit up and yell. "You left the house?" Then I'll try to point out the benefit of getting the video back early. She'll sigh in disgust and lie back down. Then she'll mumble something about how inconsiderate it is for me to not let her sleep.

I don't care.

Jumping in the car at midnight for a ride and a coke is one of the true pleasures that I treasure in my life. It's just a matter of finding the right excuse.

For a while when we would watch a video at home, I would return the video back to wherever we had rented it, and then I would go to the "Hop 'n go" convenience store and gas station, because the girl who worked the night shift would flirt with me. She wasn't very pretty, but she's one of the only girls who has ever flirted with me in my entire life. She calls me her cutie. So I'd grab a coke and she'd make a comment about my late visit, about my haircut, or about how I looked so hand-some, and she'd poke fun at my coke habit. She'd wag her finger at me and tell me that having a coke late at night isn't good for me. I'd tell her

I didn't come for the coke. I'd tell her it was because I had missed her, and she'd grin from ear to ear. As I would leave, she'd tell me not to stay away so long.

One of the best nights of my life was the night Janine and I were coming home from a dinner with friends, and she pointed out that we needed gas. She spotted the "Hop 'n go" station and told me to go there. I could feel the adrenaline surge in me. After pumping the gas, I told Janine I was going in to pay and I asked her if she wanted anything from the store. Janine growled at me for not paying at the pump.

The girl at the counter wouldn't stop commenting on my improved appearance. She really laid it on thick. I was wearing a sport coat and I was all spiffed up. Usually I'm pretty grubby when I go out for my midnight escape, so that night was different. I wondered if the convenience store girl had seen that I was with my wife that night. Maybe that's why she was flirting more. Sometimes girls are that way.

My little girlfriend at the counter started giving me cat calls. Gosh she seemed so sincere! She came out from behind the counter and took a walk all around me and looked me over really good. She said some very complimentary things. She even mentioned my rear end. I'm embarrassed to tell about it here even. So, the "Hop 'n go" girl and I flirted it up good, and then I went back to the car with my coke. Janine complained that I didn't need a coke that late at night.

I think I could have kissed that girl and Janine wouldn't have noticed. Hell, I could have grabbed her, pulled her onto the counter, and ravished her right there in front of the window, and Janine would have complained about my choice of potato chips.

ENTRY # 18

ON THE ROAD.

Today I want to talk about

Wait

Hang on.

Today I'm sitting here at Café Rio, having a wonderful lunch. You should try this place, it's fantastic. The story of how I wound up here is a good one.

So, I've liked writing about this so much, that I bought a little pocket notebook that I can carry around with me so that when I think of something to say, I can write it down. Then later I can copy things over to my real bathroom notebook, like I'm doing right now.

Earlier I was writing on my throne, and I discovered I had a problem. I was distracted. I've told you about my IBS. That means that, well. Look it up. My problem this morning was that I needed to go, and couldn't. Frustrating. Never happens to me. Ever. It really distracted me. I didn't like that feeling. I looked in the medicine cabinet for some milk of magnesia, or some other laxative, but couldn't find anything.

Out to the kitchen I went, where Janine was watching her little tv. I asked her about where I could find a laxative, and she wrinkled her nose at me angrily.

"How should I know? Go look in the bathroom and in the medicine cabinet."

I looked. I looked everywhere that medicine might be. Nothing. So I went back to Janine. She acted all put out and bothered. She shouldered past me and marched to the kitchen cabinet where she keeps the spices. She produced a bottle of laxatives from that cabinet.

What the hell? Who keeps laxatives in the kitchen with the spices? I took the prescribed dosage and went back to my throne. Nothing. So I grabbed my wallet and headed for the door. Janine called after me.

"Where are you going?

"To get Mexican food."

Now she was running after me.

"Don't you dare eat Mexican food! It could kill you!"

I paused and turned to face her.

"Why not? You love Mexican food. Everybody loves Mexican food. I love Mexican food. I'm going out for Mexican food."

And that's why I'm sitting here today eating at Café Rio. Holy crap, it's working. Time to rush to the nearest clean restroom.

Today I'm sitting here in the Siegfried Law office tower downtown, using their lovely restrooms. I don't have any business here, but I know that their restrooms are perfect, and hardly ever used. These are the ones in the hallway. All the attorneys use a private restroom in their office.

It's nice here. It's quiet. There isn't any muzac.

I sound like a French horn in here today. Has to be more than just Mexican food. Must have been the lasagna we had last night. And the echo in here is fantastic. It sounds like four big German guys are breaking wind against each wall. Too bad no one's here to enjoy it. I usually don't like company when I'm using a public restroom, but it would be funny to hear those dress shoes saunter in, only to scamper out when I sound off. That's something that happens a lot when I use a public restroom. I love that.

So I thought I'd tell you about the best restrooms in town. After giving it some thought, I think I definitely have IBS. I have a nervous tick about restrooms. I won't use dirty or crowded public restrooms.

A couple of months ago I was at the airport. Naturally I visited the mensroom. An airport restroom is an amazing place. I've done a lot of traveling because of my job, and I've noticed that airports in general are designed to keep you calm. The cool florescent lighting, the quiet and the calm. They want to keep everyone settled down in a potentially stressful situation. Most of the time when we find ourselves in an airport, we're going somewhere or coming from somewhere, and we don't have much choice about how it all goes. People can get agitated when they feel powerless.

Restrooms in airports are calm places. They are clean and comfortable and quiet and have very little color or variety. Lots of white tile and stainless steel. And they pump in music that is very soothing over the public address system. The stalls feel very private.

So you find one day that you're sitting there in the airport restroom, completely calm, focused on the tasks of your day, and you're comfortable. That's the way it should be. Public toliets should be clean and safe. What you're doing in there is private and important.

There are certain things I look for in a quality public restroom. Of course, cleanliness is very important. Toilets should be so clean that it looks like you could eat scrambled eggs off the seat. And when I desperately need a public toilet that's just exactly what someone's going to think I did.

A really good restroom is all but abandoned. No matter how big the restroom is, it's better if no one walks in while I'm in there. Believe me, no one wants to be aware of what's happening in there with any of their senses.

The restrooms in the ladies' section of major department stores are always clean and safe. Try not to look like a sex offender as you saunter through the lingerie toward the men's room. You'll be thrilled to see how clean and isolated the men's room in the ladies' section of the department store is. It's likely that no one else has used this bathroom all day long.

Comfort. That's what I'm really looking for. That's why I wet paper towels and wipe down toilet seats. I want peace of mind. I like talking about all this here in this notebook. Janine knows about my tendency to be picky and choosy about bathrooms, and it drives her crazy. But she has no idea how deep it goes.

All I ask is a clean toilet for a healthy dump, and some good reading material to pass the time.

Such a modest request.

ENTRY # 19

I CAN'T STOP THINKING ABOUT THIS.

Ever since my first entry, I've been thinking about this. It's turning out to be very good therapy for me. I've got no one that I can really whine and complain to, so I'm writing it all down in here. So here's some more stuff.

I never know when she's going to be in a bad mood. I know, that doesn't sound fair. There's no reason she should have to alter her moods to please me. But sometimes she gives me a pretty smile, and says "hi!", like a pretty teenaged girl who's been waiting for me to walk by. It doesn't happen a lot, but I admit it does happen. Then there are lots of time she just ignores me like I'm invisible. I guess that's probably about half the time. But sometimes, too many times, she pounces on me like a lion and screams at me. And it's not for big things. Sometimes it's for the most stupid things in the world.

I pulled the car too far into the garage. I left a cup on the kitchen counter. I left my shoes by the door. I trimmed the grass too close to the flowers. I left the bathroom a mess. I wrinkled the fabric on the couch cushion. I made her forget the milk at the grocery store.

Now keep in mind, these are all high crimes. They're not just little annoying things that I do, they're evidence that I'm sub human, and probably a demonstration of criminal tendencies. At the very least I deserve to be berated and punished and humiliated for all of them.

I think it's worse when we're in public. I can just tune her out at home. But when she barks my name at the cash register of some little store or fast-food place, I really tense up. Other people notice. She barks my name like a guard who has caught a prisoner escaping. The sound always startles people and they look up at us. My name is already prone to sounding like a bark. It's good for yelling with an angry voice. "Scott! Scott!" There I go again with the barking dog reference. But that's what she sounds like in those very public moments. There is anger and disgust on her face. People wonder what I've done.

What have I done?

It's like having someone hit you over and over and over again with a whiffle bat. It's annoying for a while, then it starts to hurt, and after a while, it feels like it's going to kill you. Even though this notebook makes Janine sound like a monster, she's not. She doesn't stalk me or chase me around the house with a knife. Most of the time she's just doing her own thing. I just happen to be writing about the times when she's mean and insulting. It's not even half the time, but it's at least daily.

ENTRY # 20

IF YOU STAND AT THE BANK OF THE RIVER LONG ENOUGH.

I know what my problem is. At least part of it.

I contemplate stuff too much.

Hence the bathroom book.

Thinking is different from waiting. That's the saying I mentioned when I started this entry. Sun Tzu said, (you all know him, right?) "If you stand at the bank of the river long enough, you will see the bodies of your enemies float by."

Is Janine my enemy? Do I want to see her body float by in the river?

Get real. Yes, I'm frustrated. But what I'm trying to do is outlast her. I'm waiting for her temper tantrum to end. But like I said, waiting is different from thinking. I tend to over-think things.

My mom used to refer to doing a number two as "thinking".

"Where's dad?"

"He's thinking."

Or

"Excuse me for a minute, I need to think."

That's what everybody in my family always said when they needed to make a number two. And that's what I've always done in the bathroom.

Friends I had in school used to say that I took way too much time in the bathroom. And they were right. I didn't just do my duty and then leave, I sat there thinking about stuff.

That's my problem.

A lot of men wouldn't have contemplated their problems with a wife like Janine. They would have just argued, negotiated, and then made whatever adjustments that were necessary for peace. Space, cooperation, divorce, whatever it took. But they wouldn't have analyzed things as much as I do.

I figured this all out today when I stopped to use the bathroom in the office building behind the Sizzler downtown. I've used that bathroom for twenty something years. Maybe more. It's clean and private and nobody ever goes in there. The restrooms are right behind the elevators. All the offices on the first floor have their own restrooms, so they don't need to use the one in the hallway.

I was sitting there in that restroom today and thinking about how it has never changed. It's exactly the same as it was when I was in high school, but it still seems fresh and clean and new.

The office building is close to downtown with all its shopping and businesses, so it's always been convenient for me. No one else seems to care about it, but this restroom has saved my life many, many times.

In school I had a friend named Ted. His parents hated my guts. I wasn't a bad kid, I was just kind of aimless, and I was kind of susceptible to peer pressure. Ted's parents wanted better friends for their son.

Ted wasn't better than me. He didn't know what he wanted out of life any more than I did. Ted liked art. He was amazing at any form of art he tried. He loved to paint and draw and sculpt. He was incredibly creative. But his parents hated his artistic abilities. They always told him that nothing would ever come from all the time he spent drawing and sculpting and stuff like that. You should have seen his room. There were drawings and paintings and sculpted figures of all sizes everywhere you looked. It was like a wonderland of expression. It looked like a museum. It was pretty amazing, and it was clear that Ted has an extraordinary talent.

But Ted always worried about what his parents told him, so he studied education in college, and got his degree and took a job teaching Junior High School.

Ted hated being a teacher, but he worked hard because he met a girl and got married.

Ted got a call out of the blue from the brother of a former girlfriend. He asked Ted if he could still draw cool things. Does that talent ever suddenly disappear? Anyway, he said he still loved to do art things, and so this guy gave Ted the name of his employer. He worked for a video game company, and they needed someone to create art for their games.

Ted didn't get his hopes up. He had never even tried computers, and wasn't really interested. But he went to investigate the possibility. Long story short, soon he was working for a video game company, making more money with his art he had as a teacher.

But the story isn't over yet.

One day Ted was working a graphic arts trade show. Ted was manning his company's booth. A local businessman passed by and was looking at the video sample of the video games they produced.

"Who does your graphics?" he asked.

"I do." Answered Ted. The man raised an eyebrow.

"How would you like to come work for me?"

Ted thanked the man but explained that he was very happy working for his present company and wanted to be loyal to them.

"I'll triple whatever they are paying you."

And that's how Ted became wealthy. His career has been a shining success. He used to fly to Colorado to see all the Avalanche hockey games. He and his wife would fly to Denver, have dinner, see the game, and fly home. That's what his art did for him.

What does this have to do with me, and Janine, and the bathroom in the office complex behind the Sizzler?

Well, Ted's mom used to work in that office building. Her office was right by the elevators, and her blinds were always open. Many times when I would go there to use the restroom, we would see each other as I passed her office. I could always tell how much she hated me, even though she would usually give me a sickly smile and a weak little wave.

One time when I went in there, she was standing in the lobby, talking with some people. As I passed, she excused herself, and called to me.

"Scott! Scott! Just a moment."

I turned to see what she wanted.

"You know, Scott, the restrooms in this building are not public restrooms. They're for the people who work in this building and their clients."

She tipped her head at me as if she had won some kind of a battle. It was such a strange and aggressive moment. I left. That day. But I didn't stop using that restroom when I needed to. It irked me at the time to think that she blamed me for all the exciting twists and turned in Ted's life. Ted was fine. He never made any mistakes. He just learned as he lived. But it wasn't a path that pleased his parents, and they blamed me, at least in part.

About a year ago I saw Ted's mom downtown. She was coming out of a store. She was walking with a cane, very bent over, hobbling slowly along. It was funny to me that it no longer mattered that she didn't approve of me as Ted's friend. Then, just recently, I saw her obituary in the paper.

And there I was today, still using the restroom in that building because I was downtown shopping when I was suddenly hit with the urgent need to do some thinking. Nothing had changed. I'm the same, the restroom is the same, but Ted's mother is no longer part of the equation.

If you wait by the river long enough,

Or,

Out last them. That's what I always say.

ENTRY # 21

FINALLY A PERFECT EXAMPLE.

I should be fighting this out with Janine instead of whining about this in the bathroom, but today was a perfect example of how things are in this house. So here I am sitting on the toilet with my notebook on my lap.

Daniel showed up unexpectedly today. He said he wanted to talk to me. That was wonderful to hear. It was certainly okay with me. But I could see that Janine bristled when she realized that Daniel was asking to talk to me alone and she wasn't invited.

Daniel and I used to do things together without his mom, before he grew up and moved out. When Daniel was younger, we both really liked to go get a Big Mac at McDonalds. It was kind of our thing. When we were working in the yard, or running errands together, I might say to him, "How about Big Mac?" He would always say, "Now you're talking!" We would both act like having a Big Mac was the greatest thing ever. We were both being sarcastic, but we would go and eat a big mac. Daniel and I never talked. We just sat together and enjoyed the day and ate our big macs.

So when Daniel showed up and actually said he wanted to talk to me, I knew it wasn't going to be easy. I had no idea what he wanted, but I knew it was going to be something hard. That's when I thought about our McDonald's thing so many years ago.

So I asked Daniel if he'd like to run to McDonald's with me.

Janine heard me. She had a freak attack.

"We're NOT going to McDonald's!"

We're not going? Who is this 'we' she's talking about? Who invited Janine? Was I missing something? How does anyone just assume that they're taking over something like that? I swear it just blows my mind.

But suddenly there it was. My innocent suggestion that Daniel and I run over to get a Big Mac turned into Janine planning a family dinner out.

"I have to call Aunt Danny and tell her we're going out as a family. And I have to call Grandma and Grandpa."

Then she starts in on her routine. She's talking to me without looking at me or waiting for my input. She's picking the restaurant.

"We need to go to Olive Garden. That's the place we all love. We don't go there often enough."

So all of the sudden I went from having a chance to grab a Big Mac with my son, like we used to do when Daniel was younger, listening to him tell me whatever he wanted to talk to me about, to sitting in the Olive Garden, eating food I didn't want and didn't order. Daniel was sitting so far from me we can't even really say that we had dinner together. Daniel didn't talk to anyone. His mom and his aunt dominated the conversation of the evening. After dinner Daniel went quickly to his car and drove back to his apartment.

I wanted to punch my wife and her slutty sister. When my mother in law asked me how I've been, I gave her a mean glare and didn't answer.

I felt like I couldn't breathe.

But there I sat all evening, staring at my plate, and silently eating lasagna.

ENTRY # 22

ARE YOU LIKE ME?

This pocket notebook gives me the freedom to travel and investigate. I picked it up at the drugstore the other day. It's such a great idea! Now I can write down my thoughts and take notes on my observations no matter where I'm crapping. And I've found this little notebook at just the right time. I've been watching people. Do you ever just watch people when you're in public? Or am I a voyeur?

Watching men hasn't told me anything at all. Men wander the city, and they all seem to be about their business. I can't tell if they're happy or frustrated or if some woman somewhere is making their life hell. They shuffle, they look at nothing.

Women are different. Women are very transparent. You can tell when they're having a bad day, or when they're happy. I've discovered that I'm angry with women. Keep that in mind while you read the following. I'll get over it. Tomorrow I'll probably see that I have no reason to be angry at all women. I'm not blaming all women for the way my wife treats me. I'm sure they aren't all like Janine. I'm sure that there are many of them who are friendly, cooperative, easy going, supportive, fun, productive, understanding, caring people. But I see traits in all women around me that remind me of the bad attitudes that my wife has.

You hear women talk like this all the time. You'll hear them say: "All men are pigs." Or maybe it's dogs. Anyway, they say that because they've had bad experiences. Well, I'm having some bad experiences of my own, and it makes me notice things about women.

Every woman thinks she is a princess. They all seem to prance. Skinny, fat, short, tall, beauties and homely ones. They all seem to think that every man they pass is checking them out. We're not checking them out. That's a common misconception. My mother-in-law frequently states that ANY man would go after ANY woman who gave him the slightest hint that she was interested. Her little motto is:

84

"Men would make a pass at a broom wearing a skirt."

It's not true.

First of all, my sense of faithfulness to my wife would keep me from acting on any opportunity to chase another woman, and second, not all women are attractive to me. Some are out of my age range, too old or too young, some don't fit my taste in women, weight, hair, complexion, personality, etc. I'm not raving over every woman I see. But my mother-in-law says I'm lying. She says that ALL women are at risk of rape at ALL times from ALL men. That's just vain. And it says a lot about how some women see themselves.

Some seem to think that the right sense of fashion, or a big sense of 'attitude' makes up for ugly and fat.

I know men have the same, or at least similar issues, I'm not going to even suggest that men are better than women. But I seem to be noticing the women more right now. So I'm talking about my problems with women in general.

I remember a news program I saw years ago. A reporter was interviewing people, asking them to tell him who was the most attractive or good-looking person in the world.

He did the women first. Women of all ages were approached. The only condition the interview had was that the woman be married. Remember the question? Who's the best looking man on earth? Each woman would pause and think. She would start to rank movie stars and singers. She would come up with a top ten list. The interviewer was fine with that. He gave each lady plenty of time and urged her to finish off her list with some man who was the best looking man in the world. Most of the time it was one of the currant popular movie stars.

Then the reporter moved onto the men. Again, married men of all ages were approached. Each man was asked to tell the reporter who was the most beautiful woman in the world. Each man, without hesitation, proclaimed that his wife was the most beautiful woman in the world. Each man was reminded of movie stars and singers, but each waved away the suggestion. Each man's wife was the most beautiful woman in the world.

The show cut back to the women who had been interviewed. The women were asked about their husbands. Where did they rank on their lists? Almost all the women laughed. Their husbands certainly weren't in the top ten, probably not even in the top one hundred.

That show has always stuck with me.

I can't help but wonder if the people I see out here are going through similar things in their own marriages. How common is this? Are other people deliriously happy? Well, we kind of know the answer to that question. The divorce rate is about fifty percent.

Entry # 23

She takes credit for my success.

I was a failure when she met me, according to her. We started talking about this earlier, right? She straightened me up, made a man of me, and got me into college. I'm not the one who did all that. She did.

I've never contradicted her. I've always just let her write our history as she saw it. I thought for a long time that it was important to support her positions. I appreciate how my life changed when we met. I love the life we've forged together. But we've done it together. I feel like she has gotten as much from this marriage as I have. And I wasn't exactly a screw up when we met.

Our family has been very comfortable. But according to Janine it's not because I've had a good career, it's because she's so good at managing money. Janine is very thrifty. She's always looking for a good deal. She's the one who knows how to plan our financial future. She's said that over and over again for years. And it's true. She's always managed the check book, and she's always had the final say on any money we've ever spent.

That includes my "walking around" money. She gives me an allowance. Can you believe that? If I need more, or ask for more, or want to buy something, we have to talk, and she's guaranteed to get annoyed at me. Most of the time I won't get permission.

Janine thinks she's good with money, but she does a lot of stupid things with money. She spoils the kids. If they ask her for cash for anything, they get it. There was always a "third car" in the driveway when they were in high school. It wasn't officially Daniel's, but it was the car only he drove, and it was way nicer than it should have been. Sammy's going to have the same thing available to her, and that's the way Janine wants things to go. The kids would get money for errands, like putting gas in the car, and they're supposed to bring back change, but they never do. Shopping trips happen multiple times every month. She buys things we don't need. She's constantly decorating and "beautifying" the house. She goes to all the yard sales and thrift shops. She's always bragging about the great deal she got on this and that. She thinks that if she got a good deal, then somehow she's increased our bottom line.

I have to mention here that I have pushed the point with Janine when it comes to money. We've fought about that and I've stood my ground. I've fought back. There have been times when I've needed something, and I've insisted. My camera broke a couple of years ago, and she told me that I'd just have to go without a camera. I told her that she was being ridiculous, and she backed down, a little. She told me I could get a much cheaper camera. I yelled at her. I told her that I work hard, and that I make good money and take good care of my camera. Buying a nice camera to replace the broken one was not too much to ask.

She backed down. I bought the camera. She didn't speak to me for two months, so the camera actually paid for itself. But guess who uses the camera all the time now? That's right. Janine's the family photographer now.

It's hard to reason with an attitude like that. There are differences that Janine and I have. They are things that I didn't see when we were dating. They are things that I didn't see the first few years of our marriage. But they were always there, becoming a very deeply embedded part of our life together.

Care to know what I like? New things. New restaurants to try. New places to visit on vacation. New experiences.

Want to know what Janine hates? New things. If she's in the mood to eat out, I hover nervously. Any suggestion I make will anger her, and if I leave it up to her, she'll be annoyed. So I make a suggestion, and I tell her about a restaurant that I heard someone tell about. They said it was really good.

"We're NOT going to that restaurant. We don't know what the food is like."

It works the same no matter what the new thing is. I mentioned that we'd never been to Florida on vacation before.

"Why in the world would we want to go THERE on vacation? We've never been there before!"

It didn't matter that Disney World and Epcot Center and Universal Studios are there. It's new to her, and therefore we're not going.

She doesn't want new things in her life. That's just that. She wins. I back down and forget it.

The real question is when did I become such a loser? Let me tell you it happens so gradually, that you don't notice at first.

I think I'm a heck of a gentleman. I have always been proud of myself for respecting women. I don't raise my voice, I try not to be contentious, I try to understand what my wife is trying to achieve in her life and in our family. My own mother was so timid, and delicate. My mom and dad have a relationship that is the exact opposite of the relationship I have with Janine.

My dad calls all the shots, makes all the decisions. And he's impatient with my mom. She just goes along with everything he says. I don't know. Are all relationships this way?

Now that I think of it, my dad is a lot like Janine. He still talks to me as if I were a teenager. He acts like I should do what he says without question. I remember, years ago, a neighbor gave us a mattress set that he bought but didn't need. The set was going to be for his daughter's bed, but she didn't like it. I thought it was a pretty good deal. We let Sammy have the mattress set for her bed. So the next time my dad visited, I told him about it. Without skipping beat, he told me that I didn't need a new mattress set, and Sammy didn't need such a big bed, and that he would stop by the next day for it so that he could give it his sister and her husband who really did need a new bed.

I just sat there staring at him, when Janine spoke up and told him that we were giving the mattress set to Sammy, and that was the end of the discussion. It was a great moment, standing there between two unreasonable people. My wife thinks my dad is the devil, and my dad thinks I married a real bitch.

So did I marry my dad? That's a grisly thought.

But I'm a patient, understanding guy, with lots of endurance.

And I'm supportive. That's what I call it. I tell her what she wants to hear. I let her do what she wants, and I try to understand why things are important to her. I make sure she's where she wants to be. I make sure things happen just the way she tells me to make them happen.

So right here I have to make a confession. Janine has mocked me from time to time for not being more assertive. She's pointed out to me that I let myself get pushed around too easily. Isn't that the way it always goes?

My family, the neighbors, my coworkers, she says they all push me around. She's right. That's been my story all my life. People push me around. Sometimes it's in a teasing way, they prod me and make jokes. I put up with it all. Other people warn me that I'm headed for disaster. They know more about me and my destiny than I do.

My own dad said it years ago when I was a teenager. My dad was quite abusive. He believed in corporal punishment, so he would beat the crap out of us when he thought we deserved it. Once when he was going off on me because the dishes hadn't been done, he stopped and seemed aware of what he was doing. It wasn't my night to do the dishes. My brother should have been in there washing dishes, but he had ignored mom when she yelled that the dishes hadn't been washed. I didn't want the evening to turn ugly, so I ran into the kitchen to wash the dishes. But it was too late. Mom was angry because she had been ignored, and Dad was out to punish the offender. Where did he look? Did he look to see who was watching tv? No he ran huffing and puffing to the kitchen, taking off his belt as he went.

I hated to see my dad get that angry, I so ran to the kitchen and started washing dishes. That made me look guilty, and so I was in trouble. Dad was mad at me for something my brother did, or hadn't done. My brother denied knowing it was his turn, he denied hearing my mother yelling about the unwashed dishes. He said I was lying about it not being my night, and that I was just trying to avoid getting in trouble. Dad knew my brother was lying and blaming me for what happened, but he was yelling at me any way. I never fought back when my dad got mean, kind of like I do with Janine. Anyway, this one time when my dad had taken pause and was staring at me, he told me he had some advice for me.

"Never get married. You're too willing to take the fall. A woman will smell that on you, and she'll make your life hell."

What the hell kind of advice is that?

So maybe some of this is my own fault. What I'm confessing is that I'm thinking that maybe I've trained her wrong, without even knowing it.

Entry # 24

She's never had a job.

I thought I should explain that. Janine has never worked. Not a day in her life.

Now, before you get all mad and tell me that raising children and managing a home is work, let me tell you that I know all that, and that I actually admire Janine for the way she's managed our family and life.

But I'm talking about filling out an application, the interview and the offer and then and going everyday somewhere where a boss tells you what to do and where you have deadlines and expectations and parameters, and you can't leave and go home to your family until the clock says five o'clock. Janine has never experienced that. She's never experienced it, but she loves to lecture about it.

You should drop that client.

You should look for a better job.

Why can't you just explain to your boss that you need to leave early today?

Why can't you just explain that you need a raise?

There are just some things in the world of work a day employment that Janine just doesn't understand.

Janine has done lots of community volunteering. She was a Girl Scout leader when Sammy was a girl scout. But obviously that was so that she could manage and control Sammy's experience. And the whole thing was filled with experiences that could only come with Janine's personality.

Scouting was kind of our family thing for a while. Yes, it was all Janine's idea, but it turned out to be something pretty special. I was a Boy Scout leader when Daniel was that age, and I continued to be a scout leader for years after Daniel was finished. I've stayed in contact with many of my scouts, and more than a few have become great friends.

There are so many memories on this scouting road that involve Janine and her unique way of doing things that I don't even know where to start.

Janine was the Girl Scout leader for many years too.

I remember when they had their "camp out". It was really a sleep over at another girl's house. Janine planned the whole thing. They left on a Friday afternoon, and I thought I was going to be able to sleep in on Saturday morning. But it was not to be.

About seven thirty in the morning Janine came exploding through the front door, dragging Sammy by her coat.

"We've got lice!"

She was screaming and losing control. I was calm because I knew how things like this usually went.

I started trying to calm Janine down. I asked her to explain what had happened, but she kept yelling about the lice as she took Sammy to the bathroom and started inspecting her scalp. I kept asking what had happened.

Finally Sammy started to talk. She was pretty scared, but she got the story out between fits of hair pulling from her mother.

It turns out that one of the girls had gotten up early, and Janine had noticed. She also noticed that the girl had been scratching her head a lot the night before. Janine inspected the girl and decided that she had lice, and then all hell broke loose. Janine grabbed Sammy and ran for home, where the scene I just described took place.

Shortly after the scene in the bathroom, the phone started to ring. Mothers wanted know what was going on. Nobody knew. Nobody knew what to do about it all. In the end, nothing came of it. We took Sammy to the doctor, but she didn't have lice.

But let's get back to Janine and her professional lifestyle.

Now, Janine does a really good job managing our money. That part of what she says is true. She manages the bills and keeps track of any credit accounts that we might have. It's just that since I'm the one bringing in the paycheck, I feel like I should have more say about what happens to the money. At least I should have the right to decide how much money is in my wallet at any given time.

She does have a college degree, though. Psychology. Janine and her sister, Danny went away to school together. The Bobbsey twins. Maybe you could say they were the Boobsey twins from some of the stories I've heard about college. Lord knows what went on while they were at school. The subject of their wild college days still comes up a lot, but neither of them actually says anything about it. Lots of winks and nods and giggles. All these years later, they still break up laughing when the subject of college comes up.

After graduation Uncle Leon took them both to Europe as a graduation present. I've almost heard that story a million times. I say almost because every time a story about the trip to Europe comes up, Janine and her sister and her uncle would share a secret smile and then start to giggle uncontrollably. They all seemed to want the rest of us to think that they had experienced a trip that was so great that it was beyond comprehension for the rest of us. And they want us all to think that they did dangerous, bad, and wild things and that Leon made it all possible. I actually used to get along with Leon. He was a decent guy.

Leon was gay. It doesn't matter to me that he was gay. I'm only mentioning that because Janine acts like having a gay uncle really makes her hip and cultured and intellectual. I have an uncle who works for the post office, and that's enough for her to say that my family is weird.

Leon died about three years ago. Now at family dinners and parties and holidays, I have no one to talk to.

But Janine's family is a new subject. I didn't intend to sit here and bag on her family. I don't want to make her family part of this issue, but I guess it's all a part of the story. Her family doesn't make things easier.

Here's the question you're asking right now: What's Janine's mother like?

She's smug. That's the best word I can think of. She thinks she's untouchable. She takes shots at everybody and is never afraid that she's hurt someone's feelings. She isn't mean to me, but that's because she is overly polite in general. Her politeness is condescending. It feels like she saying, "Hi there, are you comfortable? Can I get you anything? How are you? I think you're a piece of dog shit." Have you ever met someone like that? I think you have.

Janine's mom seems to need to be liked. Everyone talks about her like she's some kind of saint. She likes that. She has a reputation to uphold. She's the benevolent saint of the family, and she loves all people. That's the image she wants you to see. But she's so smug, and she looks down her nose at everyone.

How can she be polite and rude at the same time? It's a big show she puts on. I'm sure it took a lifetime of practice.

I don't really dislike Janine's family, but I've never really bonded with them either. All I am to them is "Janine's husband". And it's funny that things have worked out like that. We live relatively close to them, and we've spent a lot of time with them. We've vacationed with them. They've always been friendly and polite to me. They always want to make sure that I'm comfortable and accommodated when I'm with them. But they have always directed the conversation at Janine. I guess that's normal in families.

I keep telling myself that it's all fine. Janine's parents are nice people, I don't have a problem with them. I just don't think they give me too much thought at all. The one member of her family that really drives me crazy is Janine's sister.

Danny. That's why we call my daughter Sammy. Calling Samantha Sammy is like calling Daniela Danny. They're lifelong twinners. Except that Danny is the only one who thinks the connection is special. My daughter can't stand her aunt. At least that's the impression she gives me. She avoids her at family get togethers and she answers her aunt with one or two words when Danny tries to engage her in conversation. Yeah for Sammy. I can't stand Aunt Danny either. She's smug and rude and mean. She makes Janine look like Mother Teresa.

And don't let's even get started on the fact that Daniel is named after his aunt. You can only imagine the influence my wife's sister had over her when our children were born. I just have to call my children's names to be reminded of the two-bit slut that they are related to.

What's so bad about Danny? Yahoo! Another reason to gripe in this notebook! Where do I even begin? Danny's a class-1, grade-a bitch. Danny dresses like a hooker, and she thinks she hides her drinking problem. She would rather die than wear a top or dress with sleeves, and she almost never wears a bra. Her favor conversation topic is expensive liquor. Danny thinks she's a cultured intellectual, but she's so rude and ignorant, I'm frequently embarrassed for her.

Danny hates me, and she makes no secret of it. She loves to prod Janine to heckle me and tell stories about all the stupid things I do. She has the most fun with this when the whole family is together. It's as if she's emphasizing that she warned Janine not to marry me and told the family that she didn't think I was a good choice for Janine. Danny likes to bring up past boyfriends Janine had, and past adventures. These stories always end with the point that Janine's biggest mistake was marrying me.

Janine doesn't know the truth about Danny. No one does. It happened so long ago that it would be pointless and immature to ever bring it up again.

Danny made a huge pass at me before Janine and I got married. At the time Danny was in a relationship with a boyfriend she had since college. That situation wasn't going anywhere. Janine went to California on a school debate trip. Danny's boyfriend had gone home to see his family, and Danny was angry about that. So out of the blue Danny called me and asked if I'd like to grab some lunch with her. Danny was really fun and upbeat when she picked me up. She asked me a lot of questions about how I felt about Janine and she would giggle like crazy at my answers.

Then, little by little, Danny got darker. She started telling me how she didn't think things were working out with her boyfriend. She asked me if I really thought things would work out with Janine. She said that she doubted that Janine and I were going anywhere, and she made a lot of speculations about how she thought Janine wasn't as committed to our relationship as I thought she was. Danny finally took her prodding to the next level by suggesting that since her own relationship was ending, and mine was probably a lie, that she and I make a run for it. We were obviously the best two candidates for a real relationship. She never said anything about being attracted to me or having feelings for me, she just said that we should hook up. I flatly refused her, and she threatened me with my life not to ever tell Janine about the whole incident.

Was it a plot? Was it a test? Or was it just a pyscho slut having a mental fart? I didn't know then, and I don't know now. And honestly, I have never really cared. I just shuttered that night and felt the heebie jeebies at the very thought of hooking up with Dannie, and then I tried very hard to forget it.

Since that day Danny has made it her obsession to bully me, belittle me, and try to make me look bad to Janine.

Danny's on her second marriage, third guy. This latest guy is in real estate and he's really annoying. The best thing about him is that he's never around. He's loud and superficial when he is a part of the family group. But like I said, we hardly ever see this guy. I think his name is Steve. I'm just kidding. Of course his name is Steve. Steve calls me "Sport". He looks like a Steve. "Where's Steve?" That's what everybody always asks Danny whenever she's around. Steve is always in Portland or Dallas or with a client. Or at a game with his posse. It's never even been suggested that I be a part of his posse, so I've never socialized with Steve except the very few times he's been at family events. It's funny to me how Janine always points out to her family that Steve is very successful, but I know that it grates on her nerves that her sister lets a husband have that much free leash to move around. But that's Danny and her current man. Who knows how long it will last?

There were numerous flings before and between and during the marriages and boyfriends. She never married the first real boyfriend. We all had to treat the first guy like part of the family until one day he just disappeared without an explanation. And those are just the relationships she told everyone about. I believe she was the queen of the one-night stand. Probably still is. Am I implying something about Danny? I feel like I have a good reason.

Danny influences the way Janine sees men in general. Together they conclude that if the men Danny has met and dealt with in her life are a bunch of conniving, evil monkeys, then certainly all men are that way.

I've noticed that Janine is especially suspicious and demanding of me after she spends time with her sister.

I haven't pointed out to my wife yet that her sister's experience with men comes right from the bottom of the barrel. She's met every man in her life, at least the one's that I've met or heard about, in bars. Now, I have nothing against bars or the people who frequent them, but if you want to meet people who will form your opinion of the opposite sex, you'll have a different experience in a bar than you would have in a church, or in a physics class at the university, or at an amusement park, or at a ballet. And it's all Danny's experience, when you think about it. Janine was pretty young when we got married, and all her other experience came from dating high school boys.

What I'm trying to say is that Janine and Danny sit around discussing the nature of men in general, and Danny leads the way by using her own experience with the assholes she's met at her favorite clubs as absolute proof that she's right, and men are exactly as she says they are.

Why do I care? Because then my wife comes and stands me up against that measurement and warns me that she's watching me.

Janine loves her sister. She loves Danny more than anything else in this world. Our house is evidence of this, because there are pictures of the two of them together all over the place.

Janine is the oldest child in her family, and she's kind of a big shot. Whatever Janine tells them is the indisputable truth. So if she complains about me to them, she gets sympathy, empathy, and I get smirks or glares or snide remarks. From time to time I get outright accusations.

Come to think of it, over the years that's been the one moment in my life when I feel I get a little revenge. I am completely unmoved when Janine's family is unhappy with me. I couldn't give a rat's ass what Janine's family thinks of me, and they can tell.

If their opinion of me doesn't bother me, something else does.

I've basically turned my back on my own immediate family because of Janine's family. I'm close to individual members of my family, but we aren't close to them as a family. We spend vacations and holidays with Janine's family. There's no discussion. We just do it. I know that's always been painful for my family. It's gone way past the point where I could explain it to my own family.

My folks used to seem hopeful when they would ask if we might be available for Christmas. Now they almost never ask about holidays and birthdays and vacation time.

My family is an example of another problem in my marriage. A visit with my family requires a lot of negotiation, there just never seems to be a convenient time to have them in our home, or to go to them. And when a visit is successful engaged, I have to endure insults about my family from Janine. Whenever I want to see someone in my family, I have to lie to my wife to get around her. The same is true whenever I want to do anything on my own or away from Janine. Whether I've been invited to lunch with a friend, or, as happened a couple of weeks ago, my father asked me to play golf with him. I had to lie to Janine and tell her that I was busy at a power plant reviewing engineering issues.

I even had to sneak my golf clubs out of the house so I could play. It's the lying that really bothers me. I shouldn't have to crawl around like an escaped criminal just because I want to play golf with my dad, or have lunch with a friend. If I tell Janine about it, and believe me it's happened many times, she heaves a sigh, like demons farting from hell, and she starts to rant and rave about how inconsiderate people are to interrupt important things that are going on at our house that require my undivided attention. Then she starts to accuse me of preferring the company of other people to my own family. In the end she wins, if I haven't lied about things, and my family slides farther and farther away from me.

I'm still close to my sister, Kay. We like to exchange emails while we work. Kay is an attorney. We can talk together about anything. Kay really has a great sense of humor, and we really keep each other laughing. But I never have really talked to her about Janine or my marriage.

My brother, Gary, has become a stranger. His kids are nice. My niece Lauren is always sweet to me when I see her. But I don't really know her or any of Gary's kids, and I feel bad about that.

If you were to ask Janine about any of this, she would tell you I'm crazy. She would assure you that we have a perfectly healthy relationship with my family, and it's not because of me. I'm rude and thoughtless. It's because of her. She has nurtured a proper relationship with my family, and we should all be grateful for it.

ENTRY # 25

SHE DRESSES ME.

Good lord, I'm writing on the toilet again. It's become my passion, or my compulsion. Either way it involves a lot of straining.

But here's what I was thinking about today. I can't buy my own clothes. I haven't for years. Janine buys all my clothes. I get shirts for my birthday, and for Father's Day, and for Christmas. New underwear and socks magically appear in my drawer when I need them. When my pants or shoes wear out, Janine takes me shopping. She picks the shoes, she asks all the questions. I just stand there in the mirror. If I object, she imposes. So it's just better to stand there and shrug. Sometimes articles of clothing just magically appear in my closet and she tells me to try them. They always fit, so I can't complain. Janine really likes that. She loves to tell people that she knows me so well that she can buy clothes for me without having me try them at the store. She makes it sound romantic, like we have bonded to some supernatural extent.

And you've already guessed that Janine tells people that she has to buy my clothes for me because I have absolutely no taste and because I am totally incapable of picking out my own clothes.

Now, no one's stopping me from going shopping and buying clothes for myself. And from time to time I try. If I find some article of clothing that I like, when I get home and show her, she grimaces and says: "Oh good grief no!" And then she takes it back. It's not because the color or the pattern is crazy, or the style is wrong. It doesn't matter what it is, that's exactly the way she will respond.

So I don't dress myself. What's the problem with this?

Janine does a terrible job dressing me. All my clothes are horrible, drab and ugly. I look frumpy. I look like a sad little man. I hate ALL my clothes. I don't even care anymore when I get dressed. I just grab the first thing in the closet, and so things get rotated from the clothes to the dirty laundry. Maybe this doesn't seem like a big deal to you, but it is! It's more than the clothes, it's what it represents.

Janine sees me as powerless and invisible, and she dresses me to be that way.

I have a confession to make here. When I really hate some article of clothing, I purposely stain it, or spill something on it, or rip it somewhere, so that I have to throw it away. I always hope that the ugly garment will be replaced with something I like, but it never happens.

A few times I have even snuck an ugly shirt or pair of pants out of the house and then I've thrown them away in a dumpster at the grocery store. When Janine notices that the article is missing, I just act dumb. I don't know what happens to the clothes! I don't buy them, I don't choose them. I tell her that I don't pay too much attention to my clothes except for helping with the laundry.

I'm lucky that Janine sees division of sex roles. I help with the laundry, but she's in charge of it. So she believes me when I say that I don't notice what happens to the clothes. And why should I? Janine has told me many times that men have no sense of style. We're basically gorillas that would wander around nude, or wrapped in an animal skin if we could get away with it. That's just our nature.

ENTRY # 26

I KNOW EXACTLY WHEN I STARTED FEELING THIS WAY.

Like I've been saying, she's always been this way, but years ago it felt like I had someone watching out for me. It was like she was guiding me. But little by little she started to feel more like a bully. It was only recently that I started to feel like I needed to vent.

Yes, there was one big moment that really pissed me off. Janine is who she is, and I've come to accept that, but this was a moment when she crossed a line.

We were out with some friends. These were some people I knew in college. Jose was there. He's single now, but he's almost like family. It's always fun when we get together. Fast conversation. Lots of jokes, zingers and put downs. Janine got all wound up. This was her kind of fun. It wasn't long before the complaints about me started. I comb my hair wrong. I zone out when I watch tv so I don't listen to her. She has to threaten me within an inch of my life to get me to do the yard on Saturdays. I was dreaming about telling her to just shut up. Then Janine started telling everyone how I often go buy a coke right before bedtime. She told about how annoying it is when she can't get to sleep because I'm off buying a coke. She was getting everybody to agree that it's really a bad habit. It's unhealthy, it keeps me from sleeping well, etc.

I don't care what they think. I know they all have bad habits too. It just so happens, like I told you before, my late night coke habit is one of my few joys in life. I wanted to make everyone laugh before they started staring at us and wondering why Janine treats me like that. I wanted to participate in the zingers and show everybody that I'm not a weakling who can be pushed around by my wife.

So that's when it happened. I said, "I really need a coke before bed time, I really do. That's why I go, because I need to.", and she physically turned around in her seat to face me, rolled her eyes, groaned and said "Why?"

Everyone wanted to hear my reason. They were all on Janine's side. Even Jose was shaking his head at me, waiting to hear what I would say. Before I could answer Janine started in with her punches.

"You don't need a coke before bed time! Why would you say something like that? That's just stupid!"

She kept pushing for a retraction and an apology. It boiled down to the directness I knew was coming. And I knew I would feel extremely cornered when she finally got to that moment.

"Why? Why do you need a coke before bed time?"

And so without thinking about what I was going to say, I said, loudly and to the whole group:

"I need my bedtime coke because I have to live with YOU.

There was a little explosion of laughter at my comment, and then a very uncomfortable silence. Really I was just trying to make a joke, but I think there was tension in my voice and I kind of gave myself away. I immediately knew that everyone was aware of the way Janine treats me. That was it. I was in trouble. Like a naughty little boy. No one made another comment. We all tried to change the subject. And then I saw her face. Funny, she should have been hurt. But she wasn't. There was war on her face. Someone mercifully changed the subject, but Janine kept staring at me the rest of the night. I knew there was going to be trouble.

Now, what would you do if a loved one told you that dealing with you was a real trial in their life? If it were me, I would apologize, and ask how I could make things better. That's not what Janine did.

I never let it show, but it was hilarious to me how Janine could scream at me and rant while asking me how I could ever say that I needed to buy coke in order to deal with her. As far as she's concerned, being married to her is the best thing that ever happened to me! I should be perpetually happy! She makes my life wonderful! She organizes everything! She keeps everything in my life running smoothly! I'd be lost without her! Okay! I'll let her say all those things. As long as I can escape a couple times a week for a Coke before bedtime.

ENTRY # 27

I'M NOT THE ONLY ONE.

Darin Anderson lives on our same street, just about half a mile down. We go to the same church. Darin and his wife are a lot younger than us. They have two little girls.

Darin's wife is mean to him, and that's not a rumor. Anyone can see it. Just walk your dog past their house. You'll hear Darin's young wife yelling at him. They don't sit together in a group. They don't talk to each other. When she does speak to him she always sounds impatient and angry and demeaning. She rolls her eyes at everything he says. She gives him little "death glares". Sounds familiar, right?

Everyone can see the way Darin's wife treats him. Now that I think of it, Darin is the one who got me obsessing about all this.

Darin complains about his wife all the time. He stops by our house if he sees me outside when he's walking his dog. We chat at the fence when I'm working in the yard. He likes to vent about his wife. He vents, and then I vent, and then he starts the whole process over again. That's been going on since before I found this notebook. I think Darin and I are a lot alike. We've both got wives who can be unkind and bossy. Here are some of the things she does from what I've picked up from our little chats:

Darin likes to watch late night tv, and his wife yells at him for waking her up when he comes to bed, so he frequently just sleeps on the couch.

Darin's wife is unnaturally attached to her parents. I can identify with that. Darin was saying how when he gets off work, he knows that his wife and kids will be with her parents. It's a given that Sunday is spent with his in-laws.

I've always thought that Darin and his wife have problems because they got married too young. His wife looks like a spoiled brat to me. And frankly you can just see it when they're together. They don't seem like they're together. He's minding his business, and she's minding hers. They don't look at each other, they just seem tense all the time.

The Andersons figure into this story because of an event that happened last weekend. Janine decided we were going to the Scandinavian Days Fair in Richfield. That's about two hours' drive from here. Janine decided to be benevolent. She decided to reach out to the Andersons and mentor them. Bottom line: She invited the Andersons to go with us.

Fine.

So early Saturday morning we picked up the Andersons and hit the highway. Apparently, grandma was tending the kids, so it was just the four of us. There are so many differences between the Andersons and us. They're younger, they have little kids, they're just different in their personalities and style. It was awkward. We didn't have anything to talk about. Janine started humming and singing. Something needed to be done.

I have family ties to Richfield and the surrounding areas. So, I decided to get the conversation going.

"Hey, let me tell you a little story about the early settlers in Richfield. It's kind of interesting."

That's what I said. And it's true. There are lots of interesting stories about the area, and the Scandinavian people who settled there. Remember, that's where we were going! I thought it would be good to set the stage a little bit.

Darin and his wife perked up and told me that would be great. Then Janine came to life and did her Janine routine.

"No! You're not going to talk!" She said it as if a horrible headache had just invaded her skull. Awkward pause. Silence.

Then Janine started explaining.

"The last thing we want is to listen to Scott talk and tell stories. Believe me. He would ramble on the whole time if we let him."

Awkward chuckles.

"Seriously! Scott starts talking about his family as if anyone cares! Not even his family wants to hear these stories. His ancestors would probably dig themselves out of their graves and run for the hills if he tried to go to the cemetery to tell one of those stupid stories."

Silence. Everyone looked out the windows. Janine continued as if everyone was agreeing with her.

"No. We're not going to let Scott blather and blather about something stupid. He's not the only one on this trip."

Then she sighed and started humming again. When she finally became aware of the very uncomfortable feeling in the car, she turned to Darin's wife and started asking her about the furniture she had seen in their home. Darin's wife meekly told the story of how and where they had purchased their living room furniture. Darin and I just stared out the window at the road.

That's how the whole day went. Janine and Darin's wife did all the talking. I was silent. Darin kept wandering off to look at stuff. Janine actually scolded him like she would a small child and told him to stay with us. It was a disaster. Janine didn't want to try any of the traditional foods offered at the fair, so we were starving. We ended up getting a burger at a horrible little place on the way home.

Janine was disrespectful of the culture at the fair. She mocked everything loudly made jokes about all the Scandinavian things on display. She pointed at the costumes and mimicked the singing. She laughed out loud at the dancing. People stared at her. I wanted to step in and explain things, trying to add a little dignity to the conversation, but she pounded home the point that they certainly couldn't let me comment on anything, or I might kill them with boredom.

When we finally dropped the Andersons at their house, they almost ran to the door. They looked like freed prisoners. I was almost jealous of them. I spend the rest of the night imagining how great it must have felt to be free from us after a horrible day, and I could almost hear the stories they would tell about us to anyone who would listen.

Maybe the Andersons don't have the perfect home life I am imagining.

When I first started thinking about this, I thought that I didn't know any couples in abusive relationships. In fact I questioned, and I still question, if my situation with Janine really qualifies as abusive. Janine's just bossy, and I'm just a wimp. Then I realized that I have met many couples over the years that seem to be suffering from some disfunction in their marriage.

When Janine and I were first married, there was a really weird couple that lived in the next apartment. They seemed really high strung. At first, they seemed kind of paranoid and kept to themselves. Then one day they stopped us in the car port to introduce themselves. They wanted to have a get together with us. That seemed like a great idea, so we set a date.

Almost as soon as they came over, the guy started spilling his guts to me. He said he wanted to show me his car, and said we should step outside. We sat in his car, looking at the stereo, and he started telling me all about his marriage. He and his wife were having some serious problems. They fought all the time.

He said it always started when she talked about movie stars. His wife was in love with every movie star, and it made him jealous. She's so in love with that guy, and this other guy is so hot! He said that she always joked about leaving him in a heartbeat if she thought she had a chance with a famous actor. But then she would take it to another level. She would start to compare this guy with the movie stars. He's not as handsome, he's not as macho, he's nothing compared with them.

Then the yelling starts. The insults, the threats, and all the uncontrolled anger that went with it.

Then she would take it to the next level. Violence. She would start hitting. Then she would start throwing things. Big things. Furniture and appliances. Heavy things.

So this is the story that this guy painted. I've always felt grateful that nothing in my own marriage is even close to this. But this is where this guy's story got really ugly.

He told about how hard it was to endure the hitting and the throwing of the heavy objects without reacting. He said that at this point his wife would mock him for not defending himself. She would call him weak and effeminate and say that this was proof that he was less than her movie star heroes.

I remember so clearly how this guy told me, while crying, that he would always reach a breaking point. He wouldn't be able to take any more. So he would wind up and hit her. He said it was surreal. It was like watching someone else commit the violent act. He said it was horrifying to watch his wife tumble over backwards and fall over the furniture. He would be immediately at her side, apologizing and crying. She would sneer at him, mouth and nose bleeding, and tell him that he couldn't even stand up for himself without crying and apologizing.

I didn't believe his story. And I told Janine all about it. But this guy's wife had done the same thing with Janine. When us guys went out to look at the car, the women started talking. She told the same exact story, and this girl said that it was the gospel truth.

We didn't want to visit with them anymore, or even see them again. I tried to forget their names and everything about them, but that story still haunts me. I ran into him in the carport before they moved, and he asked me what I thought he should do.

I told him to divorce her. I said he should get as far away from the situation as he could. I told him to do it before there were any children involved. He said he couldn't. He didn't want the stigma of being a divorced man, and he said that despite it all, he was passionately in love with his wife.

I hope I never see them again. A friend from high school who lived in the same apartment complex with us told me that this guy and his wife moved to Idaho and he works on a farm. Good. Let them fight it out on the farm. I don't want to hear more about it.

ENTRY # 28

OTHER MEN DESERVE RESPECT.

You'd probably think that Janine's dad is the kind of man that families respect. You'd imagine that he's the king of his castle. But that's not exactly true. It seems like Janine's dad doesn't get to talk for himself in conversations, and he doesn't have a say in family decisions, but he does get left alone. No one asks him to help with the dinner or the cleanup. No one has little task or criticisms for him. That's seems wonderful to me. Sometimes when I see him asleep in his lounge chair with the television on, I want to go tap him on the shoulder and ask him how he does it.

Janine's dad is a retired military officer. He just expects things to run a certain way in his family. They have an understanding. They leave him alone, and he lets them run the household to his specifications. Would I settle for the same deal? I don't know. It sounds pretty good. I can't even imagine what it would be like to be left alone. But at the same time, I'm tired of being invisible.

But I said at the beginning of this entry that other men deserve respect, and I've seen how that works many times.

If we're talking with other people, say, at a party or some other social setting, and some other man like me starts talking about how he's all independent and manly, she can't just let it go. Janine starts taking shots at him. He's exaggerating, he's delusional. The incident with the beard guy is just one of many. Sometimes the wife of the man being attacked by Janine will laugh and go along with Janine, sometimes the guy will even laugh. But sometimes people get offended. Janine doesn't care.

But then at other times, other men can talk about their golf game, and Janine will ooo and aaah and will comment that they must be good at sports in general. Other men will talk about their hobbies, and Janine will comment that they must be very talented and that she admires them for pursuing their interests.

What kind of men are these guys who get to be accomplished and manly? Who are these men who get compliments and encouragement from my wife? They are very handsome or very rich men. It's that simple.

I'm not saying that Janine flirts, but she does flatter. I saw that tonight.

We had to go to the swim team booster party tonight. Sammy is on the school swim team. That means we have to be up to our necks in anything the swim team does. Janine wasn't herself tonight. She was giggling and chatting and fun. I guess it's because she wishes our family was more like the other families in the booster club. Lots of wealthy successful families on the team. And there were lots of handsome men there.

Case in point. There is a girl on the team whose dad is named Taz. Who the hell is named Taz? Taz is tall and muscular and he shaves his head. He's always smiling and friendly. Janine giggles like an idiot whenever he's around. Taz is divorced and he supports his daughter on the swim team very enthusiastically. Janine can't stop talking to him. They're always together at swim team events. Always standing there together laughing and smiling. I've watched them with fascination. I haven't felt jealous, but I have been disgusted at their hypocrisy. My mind is frequently reeling with sarcastic little things I would like to say to them.

"How's it going Taz? Let me know if you need a blow job. I'll talk to my wife. I'm sure she can work something out with you."

But then I actually once did hear my wife ask something amazing from Taz. It was right after practice. I was picking my wife and daughter up at the pool. They were finished. There was nothing more they needed from old Taz. But Janine couldn't seem to tear herself away from him.

"Hey Taz! What do you think about seriously picking a day for that marathon? Have you talked to any of the kids about it?"

A marathon? It's going to be a marathon? How come I haven't heard anything about this? A million dirty marathon jokes started swirling around in my mind. How long could they possibly go at it? Before I could start, Taz turned to me.

"Your husband will come, won't he?"

More horrible jokes raced through my mind.

Janine looked stumped. I don't think she expected me to come up in the conversation at all. In fact I think she had forgotten that I was standing there at all, or even that I existed at all. Then she stammered: "Oh, Scott will come."

This Taz guy suddenly turned to me. I don't know if he was taunting me, or embarrassed for Janine. But he was overly enthusiastic and condescending.

"Is that true? Would you come to a Harry Potter marathon with the team, Scott?"

I was dumbfounded. I didn't understand.

"A Harry Potter marathon? What's that?"

Janine jumped right in as if this were something official and she and Taz were on some committee.

"We're planning to have the team get together some Saturday and watch as many of the Harry Potter movies as we can."

Taz gave me this open-mouthed grin, as if this Harry Potter idea was the greatest idea anyone ever had. Mostly I think Taz and my wife were in love with the idea of lying on a carpet together with a bowl of popcorn. I don't have any idea what Taz was actually planning, but it sure seemed like he and Janine thought they could hide a little flirting behind a bunch of kids watching a movie. I wasn't really interested in talking to the guy my wife wanted to flirt with. He barely got a mumble out of me.

"I don't know if I can. Weekends are pretty busy for me."

Taz pushed my shoulder and winked at Janine.

"Oh boy! It's another honey-do! I think Scott's saying that the little woman's got jobs for him to do on weekends! Am I right? Got a lot of 'honey-do's' waiting for you?"

I barely shrugged. But inside my mind my jaw had just hit the floor. Was our situation that transparent? Could other people see what was going on in my life?

"Well, she's got things for me to do."

Janine was glaring at me pretty good. She folded her arms across her chest and leaned her shoulder toward me as if that would keep old Taz from hearing her or picking up on her attitude.

"What is your problem?"

She said it as if suddenly a wall had surrounded us for a moment and no one else could hear her. I magically made the wall disappear and invited Taz to rejoin our conversation.

"I'm just saying that I don't think I'd have time to watch a bunch of movies back-to-back on a Saturday. You know what I usually do on a Saturday."

Janine stared at me in motionless fury. Veins were popping in her neck and on her forehead. She looked like she would start to shake, and maybe erupt. Then she started to slowly shrug her shoulders in an exaggerated display of innocence. She slapped her thigh and then the side of her head. When she spoke she sounded mean and sarcastic. She leaned into me and tilted her head menacingly. It was funny to me that she didn't seemed to be concerned with the impression this scene was making on Taz.

"I don't know what you do on the weekends. Sometimes I'm looking for you on a Saturday, and I don't have any idea where you are. Then I find you in the yard. And sometimes you're not in the yard. Sometimes you've left with one of your friends."

I had her cornered. We both knew she was full of crap now. I gave a little laugh of silliness as if I thought we were all just teasing.

"Sometimes I'm with my friends? When? Who are these friends I go see on Saturdays?"

Janine tipped her head like an aroused pit bull. Taz looked frightened. I smiled nervously and made a sarcastic suggestion.

"Maybe you guys can get started with the Harry Potter movies, and I can come over later and the grownups will do a Sons of Anarchy marathon. How about that?"

Taz looked like he had bit into a lemon.

"Sons of Anarchy? The show about the motorcycle gang? Isn't that a little violent and vulgar?"

Suddenly I was Clay Morrow.

"Oh, I see. You'd rather have teenaged girls lying on your rug in front of the tv watching teenybopper movies? Do they like watching with you?"

That seemed to startle old Taz.

"Whoa! Hey! What brought this on?"

Janine started sucking her breath between her teeth.

"What. Is. Your. Problem?"

I was winning and I gave her a confident smile. Taz was just amused by the whole thing.

"Nothing. I'm just responding to the invitation that was issued to me. Unfortunately, I'll probably be occupied on any given Saturday. I spend my Saturdays in the yard, doing the yard work."

This time Janine's hands went to her hips, which I hate even more than the arms folded across her chest. She nodded her head rapidly and sarcastically. She needed to redirect the conversation away from the little shot I had taken. She needed to protect Taz and put me in my place.

"Don't I ever help you in the yard?"

I leaned toward her and squinted. My voice came out heavy and breathy. I was still feeling like a biker from 'Sons of Anarchy'.

"Are you asking me if you ever help me in the yard?"

Janine's nostrils flared so much you could have put hot dogs in them.

"What. Is. Your. PROBLEM?"

I pushed it a little far this time. And I got a little lost in the thought of pushing hot dogs up Janine's nostrils. But I refused to say one way or another if I'd show up for a Harry Potter marathon. But just so you know, I wouldn't.

Entry # 29

We actually have a pretty good sex life.

Wow! That threw you for a loop, didn't it? That was totally out of left field, totally unexpected and totally opposite of everything else in this notebook. Isn't this fun?

As long as this is going to be a very private notebook, and since I am writing this in the bathroom under the guise of taking a crap, you probably would want to hear about steaming, or steamy things like this.

Janine is really pretty uninhibited in bed. She considers herself to be an open-minded woman. You'll find this ironic, but I'm aware that I'm lucky in this regard. I've heard other men talk about their sex lives. Some guys joke about how after I don't know how many years of marriage, there is now no sex at all in their lives.

I've heard people say that if a couple put a jellybean in a jar every time they had sex during the first year of their marriage, and then took a jellybean out of that same jar every time they had sex after the first year of their marriage, the jar would never be empty.

That doesn't even make sense to me.

You know, maybe I can take some credit for this one. I've always tried to keep myself in shape. If Janine is open minded, then I'm dirty minded. Even after she's been belittling me, nagging me, and insulting me, it's not hard for her to convince me to do the horizontal mamba.

Seriously, the sex is good. I guess this is evidence that she doesn't hate me. Yes, I suppose that's true. Janine doesn't hate me, she's just cruel to me. And in the bedroom, cruel can be very interesting.

So some illustrations would be appropriate here. I'll just take a little arousing walk down memory lane. You're going to think I'm insane. This is the same woman I'm complaining about in this notebook. This horny woman with perky breasts. Now things are a little different. Now she's an angry, complaining, bullying woman with perky breasts. But here goes.

Our favorite romantic getaway was always an over nighter in a hotel in town. Janine would do it up right. She'd wear something really tight and really low cut with no bra. That may not sound very daring, but real life isn't like the movies or tv. Women in real life don't usually walk around like that. We'd stop at a store, or wander the mall, or go out for dinner, and Janine would cause heads to spin.

There she'd be, in a clingy top showing tons of cleavage, and it was very arousing. She'd bend to examine something on a counter, and people would stop talking and bluntly stare. Frequently people would get a view that wasn't completely legal. And there were always pokey nipples. I just loved those pokey nipples! Of course along with this there would be a miniskirt or a skirt with a slit way up on her thigh. Janine really had fun with it. It was always very arousing for both of us. By the time we got to the hotel, she was on fire.

I particularly remember one summer evening when we'd been married about five years. Daniel was a little guy, and we left him with Janine's parents. Janine was looking good then, better even than she had looked in college.

When it was time to go, Janine came out to the car in a big, oversized men's tee shirt. And nothing else. Oh, she had on some cute tennis shoes, but it was clear she wasn't wearing anything other than the tee shirt. She had the sleeves rolled up over her shoulders. I can't explain how sexy she looked.

She didn't do anything. She just sat there in the car and giggled. It was incredible. We drove around for hours. We stopped for gas and everybody was staring at her. She bought a lollipop. We kept on driving and when we would pull up to a stop light, she would pretend to offer me a taste of the lollipop. But just as it was almost in my mouth, she would stick it to some part of my face. Other drivers noticed and were very distracted.

Finally, at the last light, she was commenting on how sticky my face was, and she got on her knees and started licking my face. You should have seen the faces of the other drivers at the intersection.

On our way to the hotel, we were passed by a car full of boys. Janine noticed and yelled to them and waved. They pulled alongside of us. Janine said, "Watch this." Then she started wiggling her bum side to side and pulled the tee shirt up past her stomach. The sight of her bare bottom made the blood rush from my head. Then she climbed onto her knees and waved at the boys in the other car again. Then she flashed them. You should have heard the screaming and obscene propositions. Janine laughed and laughed and flashed them two or three more times. I thought she was going to cause an accident. I can't explain how erotic the whole experience was.

When we got to the hotel, Janine was all kissing and groping on me as I tried to arrange for a room. I thought the desk clerk was going to call the cops. I bet they thought Janine was a hooker. The sex that night was so hot I was worried about one of us getting hurt.

So now let's jump five more years down the road, and talk about our tenth wedding anniversary. Our anniversary is in February. Janine still looked amazing. High school girls were jealous of her body.

Janine told me she wanted to have dinner at Ruby River Steakhouse. We love that place. What an evening! Twice as formal and mature as that night five years earlier, and one hundred times more sexy and erotic.

Janine came out to the car that night wearing her long, formal coat. It was tan with furry lapels, and it was knee length. Very beautiful. As we were driving, Janine asked me if I knew what I had on under her coat?

I had no idea. She smiled innocently and told me.

Nothing.

That's great! I told her it was great. So she undid two buttons and showed me. It was clear that she had nothing on under her coat. I just smiled and nodded like an idiot. We got in the car and Janine sat smiling at me. We didn't talk. I had to force myself to concentrate on my driving. Janine softly undid two buttons on her coat, and her right breast slid out into the night air. It was intense.

When we got to the restaurant, the guy at the door offered to take Janine's coat.

"Thank you very much!" Said Janine, and she undid three buttons. I could see all the way down to Janine's navel. I thought I was going to faint. Then she shot a big grin my way.

"On second thought, I feel a little chilly. I think I'll keep my coat."

"That's fine." Said the man, and he ushered us to our table.

I could hardly think of anything to say while we ate, and Janine just ate and smiled at me. When it was time to go, we walked to the car. I opened the door for Janine, and she gave me a kiss. Then she took off her coat and laid it softly on the seat of the car.

For a brief three seconds on that cold February night, Janine stood completely nude in that parking lot, except for a pair of very nice high heeled shoes. I've never seen anything like it, and I don't think I ever will again. I don't know if anyone else noticed, but the image is burned in my memory.

We made love three times that night in the car alone. We found amazing new positions to make it all possible. It was all a blur of excitement. We didn't talk, we didn't argue. We were just lost in the moment. I miss things like that so much.

All that was a long time ago, but things are still good from time to time now. Yes, sex is good when it's Janine's idea. When it's my idea something frequently goes wrong, but sex is still a good part of our marriage.

Maybe you'll come to the conclusion that our sex life is what has kept us together. I've thought of that too. I don't know.

I also know that those memories completely crash, head on with the reality I'm living now.

Maybe I'm not as big of a loser as I sound.

One thing's for sure, she takes my athletic condition for granted.

She's always putting things in the room where my weights are. She hangs things on my barbells and stacks things on my bench. I'll go in there to work out, and all my weights and work out equipment will be covered or moved.

She complains or mocks me when I work out. "Are you still doing that? What good do you think that does?"

Typical of me, I don't answer her. Even if she's not mocking me, she's impatient for me to quit.

"Are you done yet? I've got things I need you to do!"

At those times I try to give her a very straight-forward answer.

"I'm working out. I'm in the middle of my routine."

And she always answers with a condescending sigh or a laugh.

That's not the way a marriage should be. I'm sure of that. I'm not perfect, that's for sure. But I've always tried to complement Janine when she's accomplished something special, or when she looks pretty.

Would it kill her to encourage me a little bit, instead of mocking me?

ENTRY # 30

I HAVE A NEW ALLY.

I was emailing back and forth with my sister Kay today, and I starting thinking about this notebook. So I decided to ask my sister some questions about my marriage. I could immediately sense that the subject made my sister uncomfortable. I'll share some of our actual email exchanges here.

"Scott, sometimes I see the way Janine is with you and I just can't believe it. I understand that sometimes people get frustrated and take it out on the people they love. But the way I see Janine treat you, well, sometimes it makes me really angry."

That left me speechless. I didn't answer her for a long time. Then I admitted that there was a problem.

"Have you ever confronted her about it? Have you ever talked to anyone else about it?"

I told her that things in our family have been building for so many years, that it's hard to talk about it. It's hard to put a finger on exactly what the problem is. My sister thought somehow the problem was her fault, or my parents' fault.

"We've always thought that we did something horrible to offend her. Something we've never told her. We've never said anything because we were afraid of driving your family completely away."

I assured my sister that they've never done anything to offend Janine. Then I really had to think carefully about what to say next. I told my sister that Janine has just developed this attitude that she can push everybody around. I told her that Janine is angry all the time, and I don't know what to do about it. It's like living with King Kong. Did I just make another ugly animal reference? Kay was very understanding. I begged her to let me deal with it.

"Of course, I'd never say anything about it. Not to Janine, not to anyone. I really don't feel like it's any of my business."

But I didn't want to let go of this life raft that my sister was offering. It felt like I was lost at sea, and someone who loved me was finally there to rescue me. I just can't explain how good that felt. So I didn't let the subject drop.

"So, any thoughts? Any advice? What should I do?"

I could hear the frustration building in Kay's voice.

"Well, frankly, I think you are just too nice, and you're willing to put up with it too quietly. It's like when we were kids, and you took all of Dad's anger for all of us."

That's true. I did do that. When my dad found something that angered him, a mess in the kitchen, a neglected chore, something broken, he'd start demanding to know who was responsible. I hated to see my dad when he was angry. He became a monster. No one ever wanted to admit their fault when Dad was angry, and I hated to endure his tirades. So I would always step up and say it was my fault and I would take care of it.

Kay was trying to be helpful, and she was helping. But she was pointing out reasons why this was my fault, and although I could see that it was true, what I really wanted to do was complain about Janine. And we did a good amount of that together. It felt good to talk to my sister.

ENTRY # 31

I WENT TO A FUNERAL TODAY.

I hate funerals. Funerals and weddings. I never go if I can help it. But I went to a funeral today.

Remember when I was talking about being a scout leader when my son was younger? Well, one of my scouts died this week. But he's not a kid anymore, he's grown up. He has been away at a university in another state. Apparently, he went to some lake with his friends, and he drowned in an accident.

I'm writing about it here in my bathroom book because his family called me and asked me to speak at his funeral. They said he would have wanted me to speak, because I was someone who was a great influence in his life.

What?

That really set me to thinking.

This kid was not a good scout. He was a problem kid. His family was in a lot of turmoil when he was in my scout troop. Frankly, he used to drive me crazy. He couldn't sit still, he couldn't shut up. He never showed up on time to scout meetings, but he was always there.

One day, I walked into our family room, and he was sitting there watching tv. He had just let himself in the house. I didn't think it was a threatening act, but I wanted him to know that it was inappropriate. I talked and talked, but he didn't seem to get it.

So I worked with him. While other boys were learning to tie knots and build campfires, I was talking with this kid about the importance of knocking on a door when you visited someone, and then telling everyone goodbye when you left, and how to participate politely in a conversation.

It occurred to me as I prepared to talk at this kid's funeral, that the skills I tried to teach him were things that everyone should learn. Getting along with others, social graces, thankfulness. Traditional scouting skills are good, but they're very specific to scouting. How many times in your life have you needed to tie a bow-line knot?

What does any of this have to do with Janine?

Well, think about it. Janine wrote a talk for me to give and told me how to do it and what to say.

I didn't follow her instructions. She was really mad. She said I ruined the whole funeral. She couldn't see that it's not about the funeral. It was about my relationship with that kid, and the difference we made in each other's lives. Why can't people see that?

Entry # 32

Never thought I'd see it.

I came home from work today and Janine was puttering around in the yard. She had an apron on and some lime green gardening gloves. She was carrying a little bucket and a pair of grass clippers.

When I shouted to her, she ignored me. So I went into the house and got a cold drink.

About a half an hour later she came in and saw me stretched out on the couch, watching television. She just stood there, looking at me for a long time. I knew she was really annoyed. She was waiting for me to get up and stand at attention. She was waiting for me to at least look at her. Finally she did her sigh of frustration and then groaned at me.

"There's a lot more to do out there."

I didn't even look up from the tv. I was watching Sons of Anarchy. I just took another drink of my soda.

"Then I guess you'll be out there for a while longer."

I could feel the anger radiating out of her. She took a step toward me as if she thought that would scare me.

"Just get out there!"

I still didn't even look up at her.

"I'll be out there all day Saturday. I'm not going out there tonight!"

Janine stood there for a long time as if she didn't know what to do. She sniffed, and she wiped her nose. Then she put her gloves back on and left. But she slammed the door so hard that I thought the window would break.

Good for her.

ENTRY # 33

I'VE REALLY DONE IT THIS TIME

I'm hiding in the bathroom, and I deserve it this time. I saw my niece downtown yesterday, and I emailed my daughter to tell her about it. Lauren was with a new guy. There's nothing wrong with that. I hope she's happy. But I just fired off a short email to my daughter, saying Lauren must have dumped her old boyfriend. The problem is that I didn't just send it to Sammy. Turns out I accidentally chose the family group email from my contact list, instead of just Sammy. Everybody in the family got an email from me, making a snarky comment about Lauren.

I was very embarrassed, and I felt really bad.

Janine was so mad! She yelled for an hour straight. I felt like a naughty child. I humiliated her! I disgraced our family. I'm an idiot! I'm showing everybody just how stupid I am! And then she started something new. She told me she is tired of all this. She told me that I've been humiliating her for years. She got right in my face and told me that I've been screwing up over and over again. I don't believe it. I'm not stupid. Yes, sometimes I have a bad run of luck and make some mistakes, but doesn't everybody? I guess I have had a few blunders in a row, but this time I wanted to scream back at her. Sometimes people make mistakes! I didn't, though. I just sat there and took it.

But then it got better. Yesterday Lauren suddenly called me to tell me about her new boyfriend. She said she thought my email mistake was funny. She was flattered that I had taken an interest in her and didn't think I even noticed the boy she was dating. We actually had a great talk. She said my sister, her mom, loved my little mistake, and that they all had a good laugh. I still apologized several times, and each time Lauren told me to forget it.

Janine was ready to get things all fired up again as soon as I walked in the door this evening. She had it all figured out. Janine was more animated about this confrontation than she usually is. She was truly abusive tonight. She wasn't leaving me an inch to defend myself. I told her I had already talked with Lauren. Janine says that Lauren is lying. She said that everyone in the family knows what a screw up I am. They're just sick of dealing with me. Lauren's just trying to calm the situation down. I don't think so.

Sammy suddenly yelled at her mother. She told Janine to leave me alone. We were both shocked. I thought that Janine was going to lash out. I could see that "boiling over" look brewing on Janine's face. I didn't want her to aim her anger at Sammy. I blurted out that I knew it was stupid of me but I wanted to drop the subject before it turned into a family fight. I pretended to glare at Sammy and Janine stormed upstairs.

Sammy and I sat down and had a talk. I didn't tell her about this notebook. But I did open up for the first time about how I feel about the way Janine treats me. I was surprised that Sammy had feelings about all this.

Sammy said that she thought that the whole Lauren thing was an honest mistake, and that I should never have felt so bad about it. She said that she had talked with her cousin, and that it was true that Lauren just thought it was funny. Then Sammy offered a timid opinion. She said she thought that her mom was frustrated with her own life a little bit, and that was the reason she is so nasty to me all the time. I'm just the logical target. And it helps that I take it without complaining. I asked Sammy what she thought Janine was frustrated about. What could be happening in her mom's life that would cause all this? Sammy sighed and said she didn't know.

But our talk wasn't about Janine. It was about me. This has never happened before. First my sister, now my daughter. I can't explain how much it meant to me to hear someone in my family tell me that they notice all this stuff that is happening to me. It was like having the weight of the world lifted off my shoulders. It made me feel less crazy.

Then Sammy hugged me. My little girl actually hugged me. She hadn't hugged me in a very long time. I instantly remembered holding her when she was a tiny little girl. It felt familiar, as if she had been a little girl only yesterday. I gently kissed her cheek and I instantly remembered the sensation of kissing her when she was a little girl. I was suddenly overcome by bitterness. I was a fool. I regretted that at some point I had stopped holding and kissing her. How much have I missed? How many special, tender moments like this? When did I stop hugging and kissing my daughter, and why? Quite a deep moment, don't you think?

All this communication stuff is good and bad. For years I've flown under the radar. I've swallowed all my feelings, and no one has known what's going on in my life.

But now, as I'm writing all this down, things seem to be happening. I'll bet most of what happens because of this notebook will be bad, but I don't care. If disastrous communication will bring my Sammy to me for a great talk like we had today, then it's all worth it. I don't care who is embarrassed or offended, if I get a hug from my daughter, I'll do it again.

Even while I'm feeling so warm and fuzzy, I'm reminded that Janine makes a fool of herself with the family all the time.

Last year Janine found a job for my brother's son. She arranged everything. She told this guy who was hiring that my nephew had agreed to take the job, but she hadn't even talked to him. She was excited to give them the big news.

Problem? My nephew didn't want the job. It was awkward all around. Janine was angry and offended. She started throwing around terms like 'ungrateful' and yelled about how much effort she had put into helping disadvantaged family members. Then my side of the family was angry and offended.

Who got in trouble? I did.

I was told that everyone was angry because the suggestion was so intrusive. But I didn't make the suggestion. It was all Janine's doing. I was told by Janine that my family is uneducated and rude. It was a mess. I don't know how to manage things like that. It feels like I'll never get out from under this.

ENTRY # 34

MY GRANDMOTHER IS DYING SOON.

It's cancer. My grandmother has cancer. Lots of people lose their grand-parents to cancer. I'm about to be one of them. This isn't the first time I've lost a grandparent, but it will be the last. Grandma Macon is my last living grandparent. Maybe I'm a little old to be complaining about losing my grandmother, but it's as hard now as it was when I was a kid.

Grandmother called a few weeks ago and asked me to go to the doctor with her. My parents had taken her before that, but this time she wanted me to be with her. The doctor sat with us and broke the news. I'm just like my grandmother. Neither of us showed much emotion as he broke the news to us in a very professional manner. But Grandmother did reach over and hold my hand.

I've never been close to anyone in my life like I've been close to my grandmother. I've been closer to my grandmother than I've even been to my own parents. And that was true about my grandfather when he was alive. He was my hero. I was closer to my grandfather than I am to my own father. Grandfather passed away when I was a teenager, and I felt like it was my personal responsibility to look after my grandmother after he was gone.

The fact that I've basically divorced myself from my family for Janine makes my relationship with my grandmother extra special. I've allowed Janine to say whatever she wanted about most of my family, but she's always respected my grandmother. This is something that I have fought for.

I remember as a very little child, sleeping over at her house when my grandfather was away driving truck. Being a trucker's wife was lonely for her, and she would have me sleep over and I slept in her bed with her and she would tell me stories. We would lay in bed on Sunday nights and listen to the Grand ole Opry. I remember the old clock radio on her nightstand and how it would glow as we listened.

I remember taking the bus downtown with her to buy shoes. Every fall we went to buy shoes. It was our tradition. We would stop at the lunch counter in Auerbach's for lunch.

She's a tough old bird, my grandmother. She's been making jokes about her cancer. She says it's perfect timing. She has had enough of all of us. She misses my grandfather. She says we're all a motley crew for acting like this is all some kind of big news. I don't think she meant the band. I don't think she even knows that there is a rock band with that name.

Grandmother has actually been sick for quite a while. And she's very old. She's ninety-six. No one can say that this is a shock or a surprise. The frustrating thing has been her hate of doctors and hospitals. She begs us not to take her to see the doctor. She won't admit when she's not feeling well. Heaven knows what all is wrong with her.

Grandmother has been telling me that I need to work on my relationship with Sammy. Grandmother says that whatever else has happened in our family, we have a tradition of raising good kids. It's something that she's given me that she wants me to pass on. I've never told my grandmother about these feelings I have about my relationship with my wife. But I think she knows. That makes me feel ashamed of myself.

But words cannot express how hard this is going to be for me. You might be wondering if Grandmother's condition is part of the reason I'm having trouble with my wife. It isn't.

Entry # 35

Who am I?

I was watching Les Miserables on tv. Tonight. Not the movie, but the concert they play on PBS.

They got to the part where Jean Valjean is singing about "who am I". It's when Javert has found another fugitive that he thinks is Valjean. He tells the Mayor, or the real Valjean, that the prisoner is going to be tried and executed. I don't know why, but it really moved me. I mean, I've seen it before, but this time I was just mesmerized by the scene. I sat there and almost cried. Here's a guy, asking himself why he thinks he deserves to get away from justice by letting someone else be punished for his crimes. Yes, I thought the music was very beautiful, but it kind of made me feel ashamed. I don't know that I can answer that same question. Who am I?

I was just sitting there with my daughter watching this concert, and I don't know if she noticed that I was getting emotional, but when she got up to go to bed, she did something strange. Sammy kissed my forehead and said, "You're Jean Valjean, daddy. People just don't see it. Mom doesn't see it. But that's what you're like."

Wow. That was a moment in my life that I'll always remember. Sammy has given me a lot to think about. But 'Who am I?' is only the first question.

What am I? I'm a good person. I'm strong and faithful and patient and forgiving. I can be trusted.

Where am I? Weird, hippie question. I know. But I don't know where I am. I'm lost.

Yes, sometimes I'm hunched over here on the toilet, writing down weak things in this notebook, but that's not who or where I am.

I think I'm just kind of standing still. That's where I've been for years.

ENTRY # 36

WHEN IT RAINS IT POURS.

I think I'm starting to get an idea of how much this notebook means. I'm learning. I'm seeing the world and my life in a whole new light. And everything started when I picked up this notebook and started looking at my marriage.

We went to a funeral today. I didn't want to go. I've got enough on my mind, and a funeral doesn't help me think about my grandmother's situation. But Janine didn't give me any choice in the matter. Did I think she would? A neighbor's mother died. A good neighbor. Friends of ours. I still didn't want to go to the funeral.

But there was an interesting story told at this funeral. The speaker was one of the lady's daughters. She was talking about how her parents were very much in love. Janine's friend and her sisters had always wanted to have a portrait taken of their parents. But the parents resisted. Mostly the father resisted.

Now don't get ahead of me. This guy apparently wasn't like me.

So anyway, this lady had the actual portrait of their parents to show us. It was a great big, framed portrait. Very nice. The couple was facing each other, as if about to embrace.

And here's the story: This couple didn't want to have their portrait taken, because the father could not look at his wife, without tearing up. From the start of their marriage, and for forty or fifty years after, or whatever, this guy couldn't look at his wife in the face without tearing up. All the time, every time, year after year. I'm not kidding. The lady speaking said that no one could remember a time when this wasn't the case. This guy would look at his wife and get all misty eyed. Always. Every time.

At first I wanted to snicker, but the story got good.

The daughters in this family, and there were four of them, had all seen this all through their lives, and it was something very special to them. When they became adults, they asked their parents if there was a reason behind this phenomenon, and if there was a story they could hear.

The mother told them that yes, there was a reason behind their father's tears. The reason was gratitude. And she told them that the story was none of their business, and to please not ask about it again. So their father went on crying every time he tried to look into his wife's eyes. Grandchildren came, retirement, old age, and he still kept crying when he looked at his bride.

Now, you might think this is all kind of silly, but remember, no one's asking you. It is what it is. That's what happened in this couple's marriage for decades. The guy got all teary eyed whenever he looked directly at his wife. Love it, hate it, that's what happened.

His daughters decided to stick their noses into their parents' business one more time. They insisted that they wanted a portrait taken of their mom and dad, looking into one another's eyes.

At first both mom and dad were upset, and utterly refused. But each daughter expressed their awareness of the miracle of the tears, and insisted again that they wanted that picture. After months of begging, the parents gave in.

So this was the actual moment when the speaker pulled up the actual picture. She had the portrait of her parents, the one that she was talking about, right there with her. It was big and had a really nice frame. It was quite a picture. It actually got me choked up.

The big, nice portrait shows a happy, loving old couple. The pretty lady is smiling up at her husband, and tears are streaming down his face and off the end of his nose. An absolutely unforgettable image.

Are there really married people who love each other like that? It's hard for me to believe. I get all teary eyed when I find out Janine isn't going to complain about something, but has rented a movie and wants to watch it with me.

Entry # 37

We had an actual argument today.

We actually fought in front of other people. Janine was shocked that I would talk back to her right there with friends listening to us, and I knew that there would be consequences when we got home. She's been ranting at me for an hour.

Here's what happened. Our neighbor in the cul-de-sac put on a birthday party for her little girl. All the neighbors were invited. Of course, I didn't know this beforehand. I learned about it when Janine told me it was time to go. So, without telling me about it, Janine dragged me over there about seven o'clock. We were sitting there in a little group of parents. We were all having a nice chat.

At one point we were talking, apparently, about manliness. Again. I never even noticed how the subject came up. The ladies in the group were comparing notes on how macho their husbands were. Some said their husbands were very macho because they watched a lot of sports on tv. Others commented on camping and hunting hobbies. One of the ladies started talking about how her husband wears a lot of camouflage and hunts and fishes all year round.

Janine brought up the incident with the beard guy. People gave timid opinions about beards, and most surrendered to Janine's hatred of facial hair. Some of the ladies timidly mentioned how their husbands didn't like sports, or liked flowers, or other unmanly pursuits. They all seemed to want to point out that their husbands were wonderful men without being overly macho.

Then Janine made a comment. She brought up Sons of Anarchy. She got everybody talking about how terrible that show is. Everyone seemed to agree. Shows like Sons of Anarchy do not represent proper manliness. They should be shunned and men should understand that this kind of bravado was unacceptable. Whatever. Then she told everyone that I was watching Sons of Anarchy. She told everybody how stupid I was for watching that show. Then she started making comparisons between me and the kinds of guys depicted in that show. She said that I was about as far from macho as a guy can get. And yes, she said it with a big eye roll.

Really? How do you all agree in one moment that the guys in Sons of Anarchy do not represent manliness and macho, and then turn around in the next moment and compare me to them and say that I'm on the opposite side of the scale, and then laugh about it? By their own logic, shouldn't I be wonderful for being the opposite of the guys on that, fantastic show? Shouldn't they congratulate me, and tell me I'm doing a good job? Shouldn't they tell me I'm a real man?

I wasn't going to let it go. So I popped into the conversation. I instantly started getting "the treatment" from Janine, which made my heart start to race this time. Janine was patting my knee, laughing, calling me 'honey' and looking at the ceiling. I tried to remain calm and resist Janine's attempts to silence me.

So I told them all that yes, I've always dreamed of owning a motorcycle. I have. That's what I like about the show. The beautiful Harley Davidson motorcycles. One day I want to have some kind of low slung, really cool road bike. I turned and gave Janine a big friendly smile as if we were on the same page. That must have looked funny because Janine looked like she was playing the bongos on my knee. I looked back at the group and made a menacing face. I said I was hoping that Janine would be on the back of that bike when I go riding. I winked and suggested that maybe she could go braless. But with or without her, one day I want to hit the road on my own bike.

You can imagine how she reacted.

You can imagine, but actually you'd be wrong. Yes, I felt the explosion that happened between us. I saw it in her eyes. But I don't think that anyone else even noticed. Janine calmly stopped hitting my knee, and calmly crossed her legs. Then she started to talk. She was very controlled and deliberate. I thought that nothing could be more painful than her insulting explosions, but I was wrong. I sat there like a whipped dog as she put me in my place like a little girl laying down the first row of Legos in the cute little toy cottage she is building. She was matter of fact, she was just explaining how things are and who I am and how I picture into my own life.

It wasn't so much that she said that it would never happen, it was the way she said it. It was as if I was nine years old and saying that I planned to get a Labrador. I was delusional and immature. I was embarrassing myself.

And even worse, there was a moment when she was imagining me with a motorcycle, and she laughed. She said, "You can't even ride a motorcycle!" And when she laughed, everyone laughed with her. It was as if everyone knew that the thought of me on a motorcycle was utterly ridiculous.

Now, is this really an unusual reaction from a spouse? I realize that it is not. Couples disagree all the time about how to spend money. I remember a neighbor who bragged that one day he was going to go to Vegas and play Texas Hold'em. It was his dream. His wife told him to forget it. She was never going to let him lose all their money gambling.

An uncle of mine dreamed of having a fancy truck and a long travel trailer. But they were humble people and his wife always told him that it just wasn't possible. Funny thing, my aunt ended up buying a church organ for their home. It was an odd thing, and I remember how hurt my uncle seemed. They fought about it a little bit in front of my dad and me when my uncle asked my dad to intervene. But what can you do? A couple does what they are going to do with their money. Sometimes they cooperate and have the same goals. Sometimes they fight and one wins and the other loses. That's kind of where I was the other night when Janine and I were talking about motorcycles in front of friends.

Well, I did something that I haven't done very much before. I raised my voice to Janine. I told her that it wasn't up to her. I'm a grown man and I can buy a motorcycle if I want to. I said it angrily. You should have seen the look on her face. People started to ooh and aww. Even worse, some of them laughed. When they laughed, her face cooled instantly, and she started to laugh with them. That's a neat trick. Janine can't lose. She'll never be caught on the wrong side of an emotional surge. She'll manipulate it and turn it around in the direction she wants it to go.

What did I do? I didn't laugh with them. I was determined not to laugh with them. But I squirmed uncomfortably. That made them laugh more. They poked me and prodded me to say something, but I just pouted like a little boy.

I hate that she can influence what others think about me. It's not fair. I don't do that to her. I can honestly say that I don't talk about her behind her back. Well, I do here in this notebook, but I don't verbally say mean things about her to others. But I sometimes wonder if people can see how she is and draw conclusions about her on their own.

After everyone calmed down, she stared intently at me, said that it WAS up to her, and that I was NEVER getting a motorcycle. Funny note: danger wasn't the biggest reason for her objection to motorcycles. Yes, she thinks that motorcycles are unreasonably dangerous. But more important than that, she doesn't want a motorcycle in her garage. It's unseemly, it takes up space, and it's not the image she wants for our house or our family. The image of a husband tooling around on a motorcycle is just embarrassing. And it would mean clutter. It would take up space that she wants to use. In third place is not wanting me to have a new activity that wastes my time.

It wasn't just a motorcycle, either. For ten years it's been a pool table. When we moved into our house, I noticed that there was ample room in the basement for a pool table. She laughed, rolled her eyes and told me to forget it.

Now here's an example of how I react. I just realized that I've given the impression that I'm a real pussy about all this. Not so. For ten years I've brought up to several people, on several occasions, the fact that I love pool. Janine will always interrupt me and sarcastically say: "He thinks he's getting a pool table. He's not". At that point I say with a steady voice: "There's plenty of room in our basement for a pool table, and if I do get one someday, I'll invite you over to play."

A comment like that ramps the situation up, and Janine gets embarrassingly assertive, telling me, and everyone listening, that there will never be a pool table in our basement.

For longer than the pool table has been an issue, it's been golf. I actually own an old set of golf clubs. Janine has embarrassed me several times when the subject of golf has come up with other men. Someone will mention a recent golf outing, or some lady will mention that her husband was out playing golf the other day, and Janine will heave a frustrated sigh and declare: "I would NEVER let Scott play golf!"

That's always embarrassing. She never mentions that I own a set of golf clubs and that I used to play quite a lot.

Does Janine have some big, personal, expensive hobby? Yes and no. No, she doesn't have an expensive hobby. But yes, she spends money as she wishes on the house. She's always buying things she thinks we need. She came home with an expensive leaf blower because she decided it would make the yard cleaner. I've used it once. She found a dish that didn't seem clean to her, and so she announced that we needed a new dishwasher. She picked an incredibly expensive model. She decided the rain gutters weren't doing a good job, and so she contracted the most expensive service she could find to replace them. It's the same with the hair salons she picks, and cars that are fancier than we need, and constant decorating of the house. She says everything she spends is in the best interest of the family, but it's Janine's choice, and Janine controls it all.

That's the bottom line, isn't it? It's all about control. Controlling what I do, what I wish I could do, what I want, what I think. It's a game. It's a game that takes place over decades. It's not that she wants to mold me into the husband she wants me to be. I'm more like a hunting trophy. I'm a man that she bagged, stuffed, and hung on the wall. She's proud that she ripped all the things I ever wanted, no matter how small, right out of my guts and she's got it all where she can proudly show people the carnage she's caused.

This entry is as dramatic as a real good session of constipation.

Addendum:

She's concerned. This happens from time to time. She just gently knocked on the door and asked if I was okay. I went out and she asked if maybe one day I would like to have a scooter. I flatly told her that scooters and motorcycles were not the same thing. She raised her voice and said that of course they were. I was silent. She sighed. Then she left the room and said that I was never getting a motorcycle.

I'm brushing my teeth now. I'd like to point out that I picked my own toothbrush, and I picked the toothpaste we use. Neither were the cheapest brand.

Entry # 38

Other couples are in love.

There are two couples we've known for years that are friendly with us. Even all of our kids have always gotten along. We get together as a group of couples and go out to a movie about once a month. Usually, we go to a restaurant before or after the movie.

But two of the couples who are in our group are very interesting. Both of the wives are really heavy. That's important to what I'm about to tell. I'm not just being shallow. I thought I'd take a minute and describe what I see in these two couples when we all go out.

The first guy, Rich, ignores his wife. She stumbles along behind him. He doesn't hold the door for her at the restaurant or at the movie theater. He doesn't talk to her, and she doesn't talk to anyone else. She looks drab. She looks like she never feels well.

The second guy, Wayne, loves his wife so much! They hold hands and tickle each other and hug and kiss in public and they whisper and giggle. And she always looks very nice. She's a really sharp dresser. She's in the middle of the conversation and she always has everyone's full attention.

One day last summer I got together for lunch with just the guys, and we started talking about our wives. The guy with the sad wife got kind of emotional all of the sudden. He addressed himself to the other guy, the one with the happy wife.

"Can I ask you a personal question?"

Wayne shrugged his consent.

"Why is your wife so different from mine?"

Wayne squinted his eyes as if to try and understand the question.

"Different in what way?"

"I hope this isn't too personal, and I don't want to offend you. But I've known you and your wife for a number of years now, and we both know that our wives now have something in common."

Wayne smiled and tipped his head playfully.

"They've gained some weight?"

Rich was taken aback by Wayne's blunt response.

"Well, yes. But that's not what I'm talking about. Your wife is beautiful! She's fun, she's outgoing, she's radiant!"

"It's not because I'm a good husband, I'll tell you that."

Rich was asking in earnest.

"Seriously. What do you think the difference is?"

Wayne was reluctant, but he started to tell his story.

"A few years ago, my wife started gaining weight. I didn't say anything about it, but not for the reason you think. Finally one day, she came to me to talk about it."

"I'm so ashamed! I don't feel attractive anymore!"

This good man put his hand on his wife's shoulder and spoke softly.

"Then you don't know how you make me feel."

She was baffled, and begged him to explain.

"Whenever we go out, I love holding my head high and strutting. I feel like shouting to all the men and boys that I see, 'Look at the chick I'm with!'"

His wife was moved, but still didn't understand.

"I love hearing you say that, but I don't understand why."

"Sweetie, don't you know me by now? I'm a breast man!"

So that was it. No knight in shining armor, schooled in gallantry and feminism. The guy just liked big boobs. But how did that make the difference in the two couples? The difference between those two women is the way they are loved. What does that tell me about Janine? Is it the way she's loved? Is all this, my life, our marriage, everything, my fault?

Entry # 39

I'VE GOT A NEW HOBBY.

Janine's always trying to get me to start a new hobby.

This new hobby is perfect. I'm happy to say that Janine approves. What is this new hobby?

It's walking. Just going for walks. By myself. Janine says that maybe it will be healthy for me and keep me from getting fat.

I don't know how to feel about this. On the one hand, it's great! I can make my walks as long as I want, and while I'm walking, Janine's not hassling me! On the other hand, I'm leaving the house and taking a walk, because she told me to.

She bought me some new walking shoes, and some exercise pants, and some cargo shorts, and some appropriate tee shirts, and a funny canvas hat. She got me a compass, and a water bottle, and a fanny pack. So I go walking. Almost every day.

I walk in the evenings after work, and I walk on Saturday and Sunday. My walks take me all over the city. I walk down Main Street and window shop. I stop sometimes at the art gallery and look around. I walk through neighborhoods from my past that make me feel nostalgic. A couple of days ago I walked past the home of an old friend from high school. It felt like such a short time ago that I was sitting with Don under the big shade tree in their yard, talking about all our plans for the future. Don is gone now. Not dead, I hope, but I haven't heard anything about him in years.

I stop sometimes at the hospital, just to sit in the lobby and relax. Why the hospital? Well, for one thing Janine isn't there. The hospital lobby is quiet and air conditioned and no one bothers me. I can sit and read the magazines and listen to the soft elevator music.

I just sit there for a while. I don't know, maybe just a half an hour. I think maybe once or twice I've been there as long as two hours.

When I'm done relaxing, I finish my walk and go home. Janine never questions me about where I've been or what I've done. I was obedient. I went for a walk, just like she told me to. That's all that matters.

Entry # 40

Friendly advice.

Lots of people I see every day have advice for me. I've started opening up to people I interact with in the different places I go. I've never done that before, but since I started writing this, somehow it's been easier to talk to other people. People give advice, and they tell me about their own lives. I have to admit that I've heard horror stories.

The first thing that happened when I decided to open up about the problems in my marriage was that I started talking in the office, to coworkers. I guess that's common. You hear a lot about office gossip. I just really needed to talk to someone, to get all this off my chest. This notebook is great, but it's not a person who can give me feedback. So I started talking at work. Everybody had an opinion.

Nate has been through a divorce recently. From what he says, it was really rough. He says he shares in the blame, but he has some amazing stories about his wife. He told me she was completely without affection for him. If he wanted to have a night of "romance", he had to take her to dinner, buy a really expensive bottle of wine, and have a gift for her.

Nate had one of those relationships with his wife where they kept their finances separate. Their paychecks went into their own, private checking accounts. Each one was responsible for their own spending and their responsibilities were separate. But separate does not mean equal. Each spouse kept their own money, but Nate paid the mortgage and the car payment and the grocery bill. His wife's financial responsibilities were a little more vague. Lunches and such for the kids, miscellaneous, etc.

When they decided to get a divorce, Nate was waiting to hear about an affair. He had even suspected that his wife was a lesbian. But the only reason his wife gave for wanting a divorce is that she didn't want to be married to him anymore. That was it. She just felt that she was finished with him. Bored. Didn't like him anymore. He said that it really hurt him.

She said something classic. She said that she loved him, but that she was not 'in love' with him. She said that she didn't find him sexually attractive, and that she wanted to find someone who would sweep her off her feet.

The lowest point for Nate was when his wife confessed to having had a miscarriage. She said that she was glad about it, because she wouldn't have wanted to have had children with him. That's horrible. That's the kind of thing I couldn't even dream of Janine saying to me.

Nate said that after a few days his ex-wife apologized for some of the things she said. She blamed it on Xanax. She said the divorce was taking a toll on her as well.

Nate says his relationship with his wife was demeaning, and he's glad it's over. But he also says that divorce is a horrible thing, and that I should avoid it at all costs. He said that he can feel that the solution is to just disengage from her. He doesn't want revenge, or any other kind of bad feeling about his ex-wife in his life. He just wants to be away from her.

Drew has been married twice, but he's been single for quite a while now. I told him about the problems I have been experiencing, and he just smiled at me and slowly shook his head.

He said, "You see, that's why I'm not married!" And I get that. Any story about my relationship with Janine could serve as an advertisement against marriage. Drew says he's been through all that, and he's done with it. But sometimes he seems lonely to me. Come to think of it, I feel lonely myself.

Bad marriage wasn't the only thing we talked about. Everyone was eager to talk about sex. I think men like group talks like that to see if they can get a feel for what is normal, in marriage and especially in sex. Things got especially awkward the other day when Brent wanted to talk about smutty language.

"We like to talk dirty. Do any of you ever talk dirty?"

"I think everybody talks dirty when they have sex."

"Well, I'm not talking about saying sexy things."

I didn't want to hear more, but some of the guys thought it was funny.

"Just tell us. What kind of dirty talk do you and your wife do?"

Brent seemed relieved to get all this off his chest, and he launched into information that should have been kept private.

"We call each over names, and we swear at each other. We insult each other with really vulgar terms."

Maybe it was the shock of what Brent had told us, but everyone was ready to change the subject and get back to insulting my wife.

"Well, Brent, the things you and your wife say to each other in bed is probably none of our business."

Brent didn't want leave the subject alone. He seemed anxious. He was clearly looking for validation.

"But do you guys ever do that? I mean, I call my wife a dirty whore, and she tells me I'm a cock sucker with a pathetic little prick. I tell her I'm going to screw her lights out because she's a worthless slut, and she tells me she'd probably vomit if a disgusting little fucker like me even touched her. I tell her she's fat and revolting, and she tells me I'm greasy and, well, she usually takes shots at my small penis and lack of manliness. It always ends up in some pretty hot sex, but I've always wondered if there's something wrong with it all."

It was more than any of us had ever wanted to know about Brent and his wife. Some body needed to make him stop.

"Brent, it's time for you to stop talking. I don't think your wife would want us to hear all this."

Brad told me that he was glad he wasn't in a marriage like mine. That struck me as odd, because I've always shuddered to think about what his marriage must be like. Brad never brings his wife when people at work socialize. Whether it's a company party, or just some couples going out to a movie, Brad comes alone. Even Janine joins me when someone suggests we have a work related get together. Janine always says that it's good for my career. But Brad doesn't ever bring his wife.

Every once in a while, Brad mentions something about his home life that would make your jaw drop. When we had our office bathroom remodeled, some of the ladies asked if we could make a rule that the men have to sit down to urinate. We all laughed pretty hard at that. But Brad said he thought that it was fair, and he said that he has had to sit down to urinate all his married life. If he could do it, we could do it. That was something we all didn't need to know about Brad.

Janine has never said anything about wanting me to sit down to urinate. Should I feel lucky that she lets me pee like a man?

I've never talked about Janine before, and it was a weird feeling to ask for advice about my marriage. I was surprised to see that the people in my office weren't surprised.

The term "whipped" was thrown around a lot. I'm whipped. I've given in. I'm letting myself get pushed around and bullied by my wife. I no longer have the courage to stand up for myself. This implies that it's all my fault. Maybe it is. I don't feel whipped, but by every measure of the term, I am.

Some of these people at work know Janine. Some of them have attempted to socialize with her, or have just interacted with her when trying to interact with me.

"Scott," one of them said, "I don't mean to be offensive, but your wife has been so rude to me!" Apparently when someone calls on the telephone to our house looking for me, Janine treats them with the same contempt as she treats me. Nobody disagreed. The consensus was that Janine is a difficult person. I was almost tempted to jump to Janine's defense. She's my wife, and I don't feel like giving them all license to insult my wife. After all, they don't know that whole story.

Entry # 41

Walking Story

This kind of feels like a commercial break in my writing, it really has nothing to do with Janine, but I had to share this experience.

I was out on my walk the other day, and I stopped at Costco to look around. We shop there from time to time. I didn't really want to buy anything, I would just out exploring and walking.

I went over to the food court area, and considered getting a hot dog, but I decided I wasn't hungry, so I just sat on a bench that was there by the wall.

I sat there for about ten minutes, when I noticed a strange looking man walking past, and looking at me. He walked past me about three or four times.

I say he was strange looking because of his demeanor, not the way he was dressed or the way his hair looked or anything. He looked like a normal guy, except for the way he was shuffling, and that look in his eyes that told me, "Oh boy, here we go."

I knew he was zeroing in on me. Not in a gay way, he was just building himself up to approach me about something. He was carrying a legal pad, and he kept looking at it by holding it really close to his face, and then he would write something on it, and then read what he had written. I assumed he was writing something about me.

Finally he sneaked up to the bench where I was sitting. I didn't mind. I said hello, and he shook his head at me. He didn't want me to talk. And he didn't say anything. He sat down, and carefully put the legal pad down on the bench between us. Then he set his pen down next to the pad. He was looking away all the time, as if we were making a secret transfer of sensitive material. Then he got up and walked away, leaving the legal pad.

I was amused.

I picked up the pad and looked it over. He had written a few lines of what looked like gibberish. But the last line said, "What is your name?"

I took the pen and wrote, "My name's Scott. It's nice to meet you."

I didn't know if he was maybe a deaf mute, or just crazy. But it seemed harmless, and I think things like that are fun.

He took the pad and wrote: "Thank you."

That was nice, and he now seemed harmless. So I took the pad and wrote: "What can I do for you?"

He was keeping his back to me, pretending that we weren't together, or communicating. He wrote: "I seek the angel that is sitting on the other side of you."

Funny. I didn't know how to answer that, so I wrote: "I see."

He grabbed the pad and stood up. I thought he was going to go away. But he hovered just a few yards away. He scribbled something quickly on the pad.

After circling a few times, and avoiding eye contact, he finally came back and sat on the bench. I tried to say hello again, but he shook his head nervously at me. He pushed the pad across the bench toward me.

"Who are you?"

That was really fun. He hadn't offered his own name or anything about himself. No explanation about why he was doing all this. He just wanted to know who I was.

I knew he was looking at me, even though he was trying hard to make it seem like he wasn't. I tapped the side of my head with the pen and then wrote:

"One who knows."

He came back, but didn't sit down. I handed him the pad, and he put it right in front of his face, read my message, and gasped. He didn't walk away, but stood there carefully examining my message. He underlined something he had written previously, and then he circled the word "one" that I had written. Then he drew a line from the circle and turned it into an arrow, and wrote: "Holy of holies".

He showed me what he had drawn, and then took the pad back and walked away.

When he came back, he stood right in front of me and handed me the pad. He had written: "Can we talk again?"

I took the pad and wrote, "Sure."

He wrote: "Thursday, Taco Time on 5th, 4:30."

I wrote, "Fine."

He walked away, with wide eyes, as if he had met an alien.

So.

I thought about meeting him to visit again, but I decided it wasn't a good idea to pursue the whole thing. So I didn't go. I don't know what his story was, and I didn't think I'd ever see him again. But then a few days later I was at the grocery store with Janine. I was alone near the bakery. I had been assigned to pick some pastries for dessert. Suddenly I see this guy walking toward me briskly as if he had been expecting me. He had his pad with him again, and he handed it to me as soon as he was close enough.

"You weren't there. I was very disappointed."

I wrote: "I'm sorry. Something came up."

He wrote: "Don't worry, I wasn't there either. I had someone there representing me."

I didn't know what to say, so I didn't write anything. I just gave him back his pad. He looked at me with the saddest eyes you ever saw. He wrote more.

"I could be the most faithful friend you ever had."

I didn't write anything. He wrote more.

"Will you come to my house?"

Now it was becoming uncomfortable. I took the pad.

"There's just too much going on in my life write now. I don't think it's a good idea. My family needs me."

I could tell by looking at him that this could get out of hand at any moment. He wrote something at the bottom of the pad and tore off the bottom half of the page and gave it to me. Then he quickly walked away. The scrap he gave me had his address on it.

Wow.

Last night I left the house to get gas in the car. I decided to drive to the address this guy had given me, and just see what was there. It was definitely the kind of neighborhood where you might expect to find a guy like this. When I got to the address, I found a little house. It wasn't dirty or run down. I could tell that whoever lived there took care of the house.

Then I noticed through the window that someone was sitting in a chair in the front room. It was my silent friend. He was sitting very straight, just staring off into space. I pulled my car over at the curb across the street and watched him for a minute. Every so often the little silent man would swing his hand in front of his face as if he was trying to catch a fly. Then he would look all around him, and snatch at the fly again. Then he would sit very still and stare into space.

I drove home, knowing that our little encounter was finished.

Entry # 42

OTHER WOMEN BULLY ME

I was thinking about the office today, because I was writing a while back about the guys at work.

There's an office manager at work who pushes me around pretty good. Denise at work is a hard drinking, heavy smoking, pro wrestler type of woman. She's pretty blunt.

Years ago, when things were sexy with Janine, on a Monday everyone at work was talking about their weekends. I mentioned that my wife and I had spent a very romantic weekend. That made Denise pull a face like she had bit into rotten meat.

"What did you do, tickle each other with feathers?"

I understand that I had offered up my private life so she could take a shot at it, but I was suddenly overwhelmed with a sense that it was none of her business.

"I'd rather not get into details."

That made her laugh and sneer.

"I'll bet you don't even know what sex is. I'll bet you were a virgin when you got married. You'd probably die if you had to go to bed with someone like me!"

Now isn't that harassment? Why does Denise get away with it? Is it because she's so manly and butch? I wanted to lash out at her. I shouldn't have done it. But I couldn't resist. I could have dropped the subject right there, but I had one more comment for Denise. One more comment about whether I not I could endure sex with her.

"Now, I wouldn't want to take it up the bum for anyone!"

I got in trouble for that one. I had to spend a half hour in the manager's office, discussing sexual harassment. He told me he was only doing what he had to do, and wouldn't even listen when I tried to talk about the horrible things Denise has said to me. That's just the way it is still between men and women.

It wasn't the first time I got lectured for saying inappropriate things to Denise. More recently Denise was speculating that I might be a homosexual.

"I don't see you going out drinking with other guys from the office."

"You don't swear like the other guys in the office."

"You don't get involved in the arguments about sports."

Those are the clues that expose a homosexual? But she didn't stop there.

"Even I'm more manly than you are!" She said it. I didn't ask her to, she said it all by herself. And she didn't stop there.

"I'm stronger, more assertive, I know more about sports,"

I knew she would never be chastised for a comment like that. Women seem to have more leeway in what they can and can't say in an office setting. No one was going to tell her she was inappropriate. I had to take matters into my own hands.

Actually I wasn't obligated, I couldn't resist. She was literally asking for it.

"Yep, you even grow a better moustache than I do."

The shock on her face was like an earthquake. The silence in the room was deafening. When she stormed out of the room, I almost wished I could take the words back.

Yes, Denise can say what she wants to me, but when I make a comment, I get threatened and reprimanded. I spent another hour in the supervisor's office listening to him yell about how he can't believe that in today's culture of politically correct speech I could say such insensitive and stupid things. I'm not even going to say that it's sexism. It's just the way things always go in my life.

Entry # 43

I had lunch with Jose today.

Jose is a friend from high school, and we've always stayed close. We get together for lunch a couple of times a month.

We used to get together a lot with Jose and his wife, until they got divorced. It's only been a few months. None of us even knew there was a problem. We still don't know what it was. Jose tells stories that really make my stories look silly. Jose has really had trouble with his wife. Apparently she's been very cruel about everything, and just suddenly sprang this divorce on him out of nowhere. She refused to give a reason, she refused to talk it over with him, and now she refuses to let him near his son. That's the way it's been in Jose's marriage. We just never knew.

One day, Jose came home, and his wife was cleaning out their apartment. She was leaving him. Her father and brother were there helping her, and they threatened Jose with violence if he interfered in any way, or if he even tried to approach his wife. Jose is devastated. He just doesn't understand what happened. Jose brings it up all the time. We all feel really bad for Jose, but there's not much we can say to him. None of us knows anything at all about why his wife left him. Janine has mentioned to me a few times that Jose's situation should make us feel blessed to have such a stable marriage. I have to admit, it sometimes feels that way.

Anyway, it's funny how I'm listening to him in a new way since I've been thinking about all this. Jose's wife left him all of a sudden like. We were all sad. Who can explain why a wife would treat her husband that way? Janine reminds me that we should be grateful for our stable marriage.

So what does life have in store for Jose?

Jose's really friendly. Women seem to love him. He's got that Latin look going for him. And he's no push over. I couldn't imagine Jose letting himself be bullied.

Janine was really touched by Jose's situation. They talked a lot for a while. When they were on the phone, I would listen to Janine's side of the conversation. She understood. She really understood. She knew what it was to have a challenging spouse.

What the hell?

Jose was always really receptive to Janine's advice. That made me wonder if Jose might be in the wrong. If he can see my marriage and think that Janine has the short end of the stick, then he's either blind, or sick in the head. But what do I know, Jose's the one who's been through a hard divorce, not me.

ENTRY # 44

IN MY FACE.

My walking hobby blew up in my face today.

Remember my walks? And my visits to the hospital? It's all been blown to crap.

There is a lady at the hospital who is one of the administrators. Apparently she knows Janine, but I don't know her, or at least I didn't recognize her. Anyway, she has seen me sitting in the hospital lobby, and she called Janine.

We've been through this a thousand times, haven't we? You all know what happened.

Janine sat me down like a naughty child and told me how much I embarrassed her. Then she asked me what craziness is going on inside of me that would make me just go sit in the lobby of a hospital and read magazines.

At first that sounded like a good question. But then I resented the question itself. Why is sitting in the hospital waiting room a crazy thing to do? Is it just because I decided to do it? I understand that the people there thought it was a little unusual and were concerned, but it was something that I enjoyed. I wasn't hurting anyone.

I'm wrong so often, or at least I'm told I'm wrong so often, that I feel like I don't know which way to turn. I feel like I'm perpetually standing in the wrong spot, and always in somebody's way.

ENTRY # 45

MAYBE I SHOULD BE GRATEFUL.

A lot of people have things a lot worse in their marriage. Some people really have horror stories. Marriages suffer through alcoholism, drug abuse, physical abuse of all kinds, crime, cheating, and hateful actions of all kinds. It all makes me feel like a cry baby.

I've got it pretty good, if you really look at my situation. We've got a nice home, and a nice life. Our kids are great. We've had our challenges as a family, but we've never really faced any tragedies. I realize that I've just about filled this notebook up with my whiney assed complaints, but believe me, I know I've been a lucky man.

Earlier today Janine gave me a free pass. I could hardly believe it. She said I was a dead-beat father. Doesn't that sound like a free pass? She told me I should spend more time with Sammy. She said I should invite her to go out and do something with me. See what I'm saying? I've got a loving, caring wife. I think she's worried about the whole hospital lobby thing, and she's worried about me. She's so sweet.

So I invited Sammy to spend the day with me. And she accepted! We went to lunch. It was wonderful! Sammy told me about this great little Italian place downtown. It was go great. The waitress thought we were in a 'may-december' relationship, and Sammy wanted to play it up. The waitress said we made a cute couple. Sammy called me 'sweet-heart' and took my arm when the waitress showed us to our table. We got to sit at a little table in the window, where we could see the people walk by. I saw my life in a whole new light. I was spending a happy afternoon with my beautiful daughter. We laughed and talked and made jokes about her mother.

Afterward we did something that amazed us both. I took her to the driving range and showed her how to hit a golf ball. My old clubs seemed like treasures to me as Sammy asked me to tell her about what golf had once meant to me. She did really well, too. We both did. We were really smacking them out there.

When we got home, Sammy told Janine all about our day. I wondered how she would react to the golf, but she didn't say anything. In fact, she didn't say anything to me at all. She talked with Sammy about our day and told her how glad she was that she had a good time. But she didn't say anything to me about it. That's okay. It was a special day to spend with Sammy. Janine wasn't even invited anyway.

I have been getting closer to Sammy. We've had some great talks. I haven't told her about this notebook, and I don't think I ever would. But she wants to know what's happening between her mother and me. She says that it's been bothering her for years. She said she's not on anybody's side, but she's not happy with the way her mom talks to me, and she's not happy that I don't act more assertive. If I'd had known that she was watching, I think I would have changed things with Janine a long time ago.

I just felt invisible at the time. It's hard to explain. I didn't think anyone was paying attention to what I was going through. But it turns out my kids were very aware of the situation.

I decided to call my son and ask him directly if he noticed how things were between his mom and me, and offer any opinions if he wanted to. I couldn't tell if I was surprised or not to find out that it was very obvious to Daniel the way his mother treated me. I guess I was mostly shocked to hear it spoken out loud.

"How long is this going to go on, dad?" That's what he said to me.

The truth? Longer than I would like to think. Maybe till the day that death mercifully knocks on my door. Is he asking me to fix things with his mom? Is he suggesting we split up?

"Why do you allow it? What's wrong with you?" That's the question my son asked me. That's what I've been thinking about all day. That's what lead me to the crapper this afternoon.

What's wrong with me? I've now got a substantial notebook here in my bathroom, full of the things that I think are wrong with my wife. And it all leads to one question.

What's wrong with me?

Entry # 46

It's funny how things are working out.

They say that when your wife is pregnant, you seem to notice pregnant women all around you. Or if you buy a certain kind of car, you'll suddenly notice cars exactly like yours everywhere you look.

That's kind of what's been happening to me. I'm talking to everyone about marriage problems. Everyone but my wife. Oh well. Remember Darin and his wife who went to the Scandinavian festival with us? Darin was walking his dog again, and boy did he have some good stuff about his marriage to share today. I'm wondering how his situation is going to work out. It's just the kind of thing I can't follow up on. How would I even ask about this?

Anyway, Darin has an amazing story. His father and brothers invited him to go duck hunting last weekend, and for some reason, his wife told him that it was fine, and he should go. Well, now he knows why, but when she let him go, he was amazed.

But the hunting trip didn't work out. There was trouble with the truck, so Darin came home a day early. When he walked into the house, he said there was clothing scattered everywhere, as if someone had been trying on everything in the closet. The stereo was blasting too. There was no sign of his children anywhere. Darin carefully made his way through the house, looking for his wife.

He found her. In the bathroom. She was furiously masturbating. Just naked in the bathroom masturbating. Think of that for a moment. Of course she screamed bloody murder when she saw him. He ran to the living room, and she ran to the bedroom, slammed the door, and put on some sweats. She was crying when she finally came out to talk to him.

Quick side note: Darin said it was the sexiest thing he had ever seen in his life. But he didn't tell his wife that. At least not right at first. He didn't tell me how she was masturbating, or with what, or in what position, and I decided that it would be rude to ask. But he's still a bastard for not being more considerate with details.

But back to our story:

So she plopped down on the couch in her sweats and started crying again. Darin sat nervously on a chair from the kitchen table. She asked him if they should make an appointment with their pastor, so that she could confess and he could accuse her. And Darin said no. And then she asked if they should talk with her parents and his parents, so they could tell them what a pervert she was. He said it was none of their business. Finally she asked him what he was going to do about it, and he said that he was just sorry that he had bothered her in such a private moment.

At this point something really interesting happened. She got angry. She was shocked that he wasn't offended and repulsed by what he had seen. She yelled at him and asked him what was wrong with him if he wasn't angry about what he had seen?

I liked this part: He said to her, "Believe me, I understand."

Women wouldn't understand why that's funny, and it is. It's very funny. But applied to the situation, it proves that a little communication and understanding could go a long way in a situation like that.

Then suddenly Darin's wife snarled at him and told him that it wasn't the first time this had happened. Does that sound unusual? I don't know. I guess she meant that she was frustrated and confused, and that had turned her into a habitual masturbater. How would you react to news like that? What did she want her husband to say?

Well, apparently she yelled and cried for a while, and they talked about their marriage, and sex in general. Darin asked his wife why she had never talked to him about her sexual feelings before. She said that she didn't know which ones were right and which ones were wrong. He told her that there was absolutely nothing legal that she could talk to him about that would repulse him. If she was curious, he'd try it with her. It was better that way. Maybe one day an afternoon of masturbating wouldn't be enough, and she'd look for satisfaction with another person.

He said that seemed to make her think. Apparently they worked it all out, and Darin was very happy when his wife saw the point he was trying to make.

I wonder what that feels like. I mean having your wife understand what you are trying to say. I don't mean masturbating. I also wonder why he told me all this. Do you have any idea how uncomfortable it was to hear such personal things about his wife and his marriage?

ENTRY # 47

MY COUSINS SUCK.

That's not a very good thing to say about people on the day of my grand-mother's funeral. But my cousins have already ransacked my grandmother's house.

There was so much there I wanted to see one more time. The old desk. Grandmother had a beautiful roll top desk. I realize that I'm not the only person who had a right to it, but I would have at least liked to have discussed it. Or even to have seen it. And she had a beautiful cherry wood bookcase. I used to arrange the books in her beautiful bookcase, by size and color, so that they looked like books in a fancy house. Grand-mother's books and her bookcase weren't just for show. My grandparents loved to read. There were a lot of great books in that house. Some of them were probably collectible. But they are all gone now.

The pictures on the wall are gone. We're talking about priceless pictures that cover decades. Pictures of Grandfather and Grandmother when they were courting, and when they had a young family. There were pictures of important ancestors. Absolutely priceless pictures. I think I should have been able to have at least a few of those.

And the paintings. Holy cow. All the paintings Grandfather did are all gone. I don't even get one of them. Beside the wonderful paintings he did himself, there were a number of paintings that he had collected by wonderful artists that he had known. I'm sure they were all very valuable.

Another thing Grandmother had was a fun shelf that Grandfather built where she kept her little porcelain figurines. Grandmother collected fig-urines from all over the world. She had collected for decades. But now they're all gone. All the antiques, important books, lots of things. All gone. I wish we could have talked about it. I think my feelings deserve consideration. There are a few things I would have liked to have, things that held great significance for me. But my cousins took it all, and left nothing but garbage that will need to be hauled away.

160

How much of a fight should I put up? I've called a few of my cousins, and the conversation gets heated right away. Lots of denial and ignorance and justification. I guess I could get mean and ugly and really cause a big fight.

The most frustrating part for me is that I don't think my cousins really cared about the things. The just took it all because they got there first. They weren't looking for desks and chairs and art and nick nacks. They were looking for money. I'm sure they found it. Envelopes stuffed with bills here and there, labeled with the things grandmother was saving for, like vacations and wedding gifts and cars. And there were mason jars filled with change, coins for a rainy day.

Grandmother was eccentric, and she had money. But you have to understand that my grandparents weren't society people. They didn't own a business. They didn't belong to a rich family. Grandfather was a machinist for a mining company. Grandmother was a secretary for the shop in her younger years, but never worked outside the home once she had a family.

My grandparents lived a very simple lifestyle and had no extravagant hobbies or tastes. Yet they always had money. They were very generous.

No one really knows all the details, but it had something to do with a silver mine that my great grandfather owned, and that my grandmother and grandfather inherited and managed for a time. They didn't work with the mine for more than about ten years, and they never talked much about the experience of owning and managing a mine, or the mining industry in general. At some point they sold the mine, and they never talked about that either. But anyway, Grandmother didn't trust the banks. When I would visit her and she would give me a little gift, she would go to her desk and pull out an envelope. She would carefully choose a few bills and then tell me it was for school, or for my upcoming plans with friends, or to take out a nice girl.

I always noticed that the bills were old. Old but crisp. It's hard to explain but it was the coolest thing you ever saw. Old, crisp five, ten and twenty dollar bills. They felt so good in your fingers! And they smelled like treasure. It always made me feel rich when I had those bills in my wallet. I figured that it was money she had held onto for a long time. Grandmother was always very generous. Lots of people in the family suspected that she and Grandfather were rich, but I always just liked to think of them as generous. If you had an unexpected expense, like a car repair, Grandmother would send you an envelope of money. On birthdays, graduations, and other special occasions, you got an envelope of money. When each of our children were born, we got an envelope of money.

And not just twenty or thirty dollars. It was always more than a hundred dollars. If someone had a car repair or a hospital bill or other serious expense, the envelope had hundreds of dollars in it. I think people were reluctant to admit how much grandmother had given them on very dire occasions. I know it wasn't just our family. Grandmother gave money to my cousins, and I know she gave money to many of her nieces and nephews. No one wanted anyone to think that they were accepting huge amounts of charity money, but I know grandmother gave some huge amounts at certain times.

I know my own parents must have received a lot from grandmother and grandfather when we had our house fire when I was in grade school. We lived in a hotel for more than a month. We ate in restaurants, and the house was rebuilt better than it was before. My dad always talked about the fight he had with the insurance company and how they resisted paying what was needed. But somehow we had everything taken care of and then some.

Oh by the way, Grandmother died last Thursday. I knew it was coming, but I still just feel numb. My wife, my kids, it has affected them all. It's kind of like a truce has been called in our house. Janine is quiet and polite. Sammy is being respectful of her mother. I don't feel calm, though. I feel like a volcano is building up inside of me. When Janine talks to me, I rub my temples and sigh. It shocks her.

So, I've been to a lot of funerals lately. But this one was hard for me.

The funeral service was very nice. My grandmother had asked me to speak at the services, and my father also spoke. We painted very different pictures of my grandmother.

My dad loved his mother, but he thought my grandmother was just a foolish old lady. There was something about the way he talked about her that was dismissive. He made her sound loving, but silly. He talked about her odd habits, and how she always seemed old fashioned and behind the times. He made it sound as if Grandmother couldn't get along without her children, when so many times it was the opposite. It has always bothered me that my dad didn't have more respect for his mother.

During the whole funeral, I wanted to shout at everyone: "You didn't know her! You didn't care enough to get to know her! She was MY Grandmother! She was MY friend! She wasn't behind the times, she was timeless. She was classic, she was elegant.

That's the way things seem to be in my life. I see things differently. But I can't seem to just agree to disagree. I think other people are wrong. I don't think my dad knew his own mother.

Entry # 48

Things have been quiet.

If you're reading this, you might think that my wife is a monster. I'm sorry about that. I'm painting a very ugly picture of my wife here. It may be hard to believe, but that was never my intention. The last couple weeks have made me think that maybe I complain too much. The truth is that my life isn't a constant stream of vicious attacks from my wife. Most of the time life just works itself out. I have routines. I have structure. I have responsibilities. I do my thing and Janine does her thing.

Janine's not the only annoying person in the world. A few years ago there was a guy at work who was getting on everybody's nerves. He was short, and loud, and he never shut up. He was a "know it all". He stuck his nose in everybody's business. And it wasn't just his poor conversation skills. He was dirty, and he was always snorting and trying to clear his nose. It felt like he left phlegm all over the office. I don't know, the whole thing just bothered everybody who worked with him.

A bunch of us in the office started making jokes about this guy and complaining about him. We cleaned everything with Lysol if he had touched it. Soon it seemed unbearable to have him around at all. Then Drew made a comment about the situation that really made me think.

Drew is kind of saintly. Drew sees the good in everybody. Drew said that we needed to "grant him being". This meant that we needed to accept that this guy was who he was. Could he change? Could he improve himself? Sure. But it wasn't our job to wish he would change. He had a right of being just the way he is. Our responsibility was to grant him being. Let him be himself. The more I thought about that, the less this guy bugged me.

Can I do that with Janine? I feel like this is what I've been doing all along. But it's different with Janine. She's not just annoying, she's a bully. She's focusing on me. She seems to want to head butt me at every turn. I can't seem to understand why. I really want to understand Janine. That's part of the reason why I haven't left.

There's a lot about Janine that I do understand. I sometimes feel a desperate desire for other people to understand her. Loving Janine is a lot like loving a really mean dog. Lots of people have a large, vicious dog in their yard, and everybody thinks it should be put down. But the family loves it. They understand the dog, they know how to manage the dog's violence and outbursts.

There I go comparing Janine to a dog again.

But that's very much like the way I love my wife. If Janine died, to use an extreme example, I would feel a great desire to control what was said at her funeral. No one really knows her like I do. I understand what she's been through and how she thinks. People would try to cover up all the truths about her. I would hate to hear people talk about her at a funeral. I wouldn't want people saying deep, spiritual things about her that aren't true. I wouldn't want someone trying to make things up about her to hide what she really was.

At the same time I wouldn't want anyone to stand up and say mean things about her. People might have a glimpse of some quirks in Janine's personality, but they don't understand. I would want to try to make everyone see the good things about Janine, and I would want to stop other people from saying silly things about her in an effort to make her look like a gentle person who had lived a sweet and good life.

We were sitting watching the news the other day. Janine asked about my friend James at work. James is a work contact that I met fifteen years ago. We've remained good friends. Janine thinks that I need to stay close to James because she thinks one day he will provide a connection to some big career opportunity. She even lets me play golf with James, and he invites me three or four times a year.

Janine is also aware that there's been some drama in my friend's life in the past couple of years. James' life and marital status have both been a long, strange trip. James has been a good friend to me, and we've talked a lot about wives and life and family.

James married his first girlfriend, right out of high school. He's told me many times that he realizes that he knew nothing about girls or love or marriage or sex when he got married. James and his wife have had a very tense marriage. Or had. We all knew they were headed for divorce. They kept separate bank accounts. They didn't do anything together.

Finally she asked him for a divorce. He didn't know what to think, but he had been expecting it. He wondered if she had left him for a doctor. He even wondered if she had left him for another woman.

Things went back and forth. His wife's family was devastated and begged him to try to fix the marriage. They invited him to visit as if he was still married to their daughter. James had to put a stop to it and make sure everybody understood that the marriage was over.

James started dating again soon after his divorce. Everyone he knew tried to talk him out of it. They told him not to get mixed up with another woman. They told him he needed some time to himself. Time to do guy things with the guys. James told me once that he felt that having a wife and a family was the greatest wealth on this earth. Even though his first marriage had turned out to be so painful, it was still what he wanted.

James did the club circuit. But he regretted that immediately. He didn't like the one-night stands. I couldn't believe that. Here was James, in his thirties, free from a bad marriage, and pretty girls in clubs wanted to hook up with him. He said it got old really fast.

Then James met Victoria. Victoria was born in South America. She came here when she was a little girl. She was in a rough marriage and was a single mother of two beautiful little girls. Victoria left her abusive husband and was raising her daughters as a single mother. Then she met James. James was thrilled with her company from the very first date.

While they were dating, James' wife suddenly wanted to come back. James was prepared for this. He knew it was a possibility. He told his ex-wife that their marriage was a chapter in his life that had ended. He said she cried really hard, but he told her that the door was definitely closed. It was a difficult position to take, but he felt it was the right thing to do.

When James married Victoria, he didn't tell any of his friends. They just went to the courthouse with a small group of family and had a quick ceremony. Everyone thought he was in trouble. Janine thought it was the worst thing she had ever heard. That's why she asks about him. She's sure that there's a horror story lurking in James' life.

I took James to lunch the day I found out that he had married Victoria. It was a very cold and snowy day in February. We didn't talk much. But he told me something kind of amazing. It was something that has stuck in my mind ever since. It was something that I'm not sure how I feel about.

James told me that my marriage and my children made me a very wealthy man, and that I should never let anything happen to my family.

Then he told me about how his day had unfolded. When he had gotten up and had breakfast and was ready to go to work, his wife met him at the door to say goodbye. James gets to work before six a.m., and it was still dark and snowy outside. His wife asked him to hold her in his arms for a minute. She said that she couldn't let him go out into the cold and dark unless he did. She felt that hugging him for a couple of minutes would keep him warm on his way to work.

He was almost emotional. He said, "Can you imagine that? I couldn't. Never in my life would I have ever imagined that a beautiful, sweet lady would want to warm me by standing there in my arms for a minute, trying to make me warm and safe before I left for work. I literally never dreamed someone would treat me like that in a million years."

I can't get that image out of my mind. Is that what marriage is supposed to be like? Was my marriage ever that way?

When I talked to James about his new happiness, I kept pointing out that he has overcome great trials and heartache. I wanted to know how he made it through all the hurt, to finally find so much joy in life.

James seemed really casual about it.

"You're forgetting I was in the Marine Corps."

Then he shrugged his shoulders at me.

"Adapt and overcome. It's what I've always done."

That hit me like a ton of bricks. I'm not a Marine, but that has to become my new motto.

Adapt and overcome.

Entry # 49

Janine got me a gift the other day.

Now how can I say such mean things about a lovely lady that would bring me a gift? Tickets to a concert. Blues in the park. It was part of a concert series they hold every year at the Red Mountain Amphitheater. I love blues music. Janine didn't care about, or know about blues music when I met her. Now it's something we both love. Janine didn't say anything about why she gave me the tickets. Maybe it's because she knows I'm feeling bad about my grandmother. But I honestly can't tell.

We got to the venue early, because the seating was open on the grass. It's not as bad as it sounds. The audience area is on a beautiful hillside. But it's first come first serve, and that means that Janine wants to be absolute first. It was okay. We sat and ate a picnic lunch while we waited.

We really had a lovely weekend. The night after the concert we went to our favorite restaurant up in the canyon. We hadn't been to The Oaks in months, maybe years. They still make the Rueben sandwich I loved. We sat outside on the patio and enjoyed the view of the river.

Does this mean she didn't gripe at me? Not at all. I parked wrong, I sat down in the wrong place. I got grass in the bag where the goodies were. I brought the wrong goodies, I dressed wrong.

But as hard as this is for me to understand, it would be even harder to explain it to Janine. She just does things that bother me. Not like an annoying habit, but things that she thinks are encouraging, but make me want to scream.

She just assumes that I'm lost. She assumes that I'm ignorant about art and literature and politics and current events.

Janine tries to get me started with hobbies. She used to tell people it was her idea that I go out for a long walk a couple of times a week, until that incident with the hospital.

Janine bought a set of cheap watercolor paints and told me to go out to the back yard and paint flowers. She says it should come natural to me, because my grandfather painted with watercolors. We have a number of his paintings in our house. But I don't know that first thing about painting. Still, she gets books from the library about painting, gets the paints out, and tells me to paint.

She brought up the motorcycle again. She suggested again that I get a scooter. It's the same thing, right? I guess I snapped a little. A Scooter is not a motorcycle. She just didn't understand that. Last time she had made it clear that the subject of a motorcycle was closed. I think that bringing it up again was her way of saying that she cares about what I want. As long as what I want is pre-approved with her, or suggested by her.

But worse than that is the fact that she wants to make decisions for me about what I want and don't want. I know what I want and what I don't want. I don't need anyone to decide for me.

For example, I don't want Danny to come over and visit. I guess that's a bad example. But how wrong would it be to just blurt out to my wife: "Your sister sucks, and she's a whore, and I don't want her in this house?"

I'm off on a tangent again, aren't' I? It's hard for me when I get talking about Janine. I'm very frustrated.

Things are happening in my life. I feel like I need some support, someone to turn to, someone to understand. I just can't keep up this game we've had going on for so long. How do I tell her, "time-out"?

Well, it gets complicated when my wife does the right thing. Janine loved my Grandmother too.

That means a lot to me. She doesn't just tolerate Grandmother because she's married to me. She genuinely loves my grandmother. I've found Janine in tears quite frequently recently after she's been on the phone with Grandmother.

Janine is a good person, and I admit that. She makes sure that we remember Grandmother on her birthday, and it's always Janine who mentions that we need to go out to Grandmother's and work on her yard. They would talk for hours on the phone.

I'm talking about my grandmother as if she's still here. I'm having a hard time facing this. I don't have many friends, and losing Grandmother makes me feel even more alone. I'm realizing that it was good to have her in my corner.

The last couple of days every so often one of us will suddenly say, "Remember when Grandmother…" and then we'll just talk about something she said or did, and we'll chuckle together, and then it will get really quiet. Seems like at a moment like that we should start to share our feelings with one another, but we both end up looking at the floor.

I have to admit that the feelings Janine seems to have for my family are not the same as the feelings I have for her family.

So I'm burdened with the temptation to say what I think about Janine's sister, and at the same time I can't imagine Janine ever insulting my grandmother. Does that make me a hypocrite? I'd like to make a joke and say yes, but my grandmother has never tortured or insulted Janine.

Entry # 50

I'VE GOT TO SAY, I'VE BEEN TO TOO MANY FUNERALS LATELY.

Today was a hard day for me. It was like a continuation of the funeral. Remember how everyone ransacked Grandmother's house? Even though I got shafted by my cousins, uncles and aunts, and even by my brother and sisters, I still have to manage all grandmother's affairs. It sounds like I'm just as bad as my cousins, but I'll admit that I was hoping that some bank official would have something for me. I hoped that grandmother had remembered me somehow in her personal financial affairs.

She didn't.

There was no will. Grandmother didn't have much of a bank account. She had chosen me to put her affairs in order after her death. There weren't any debts. No accounts that had to be settled. And there was no savings account to speak of, and no investments.

One of my cousins called me as soon as I got home from the bank. She wanted twenty thousand dollars. She started going on about how she needed it to have some work done to her house and that she had talked about it with Grandmother before she died. When I told her that grandmother didn't leave any money, she got really mad. She demanded that I sell the house immediately and give her the money she needs. Funny how she took what she wanted from the house without checking with me to see what I thought, and now she wants more.

Well, my cousin got seriously angry when I told her that grandmother had made arrangements to have her house sold and then set the money aside in a trust that can only be used for life threatening illnesses or injuries that might occur in the family. My cousin started insulting our grandmother and claiming that she was a selfish old bitch who had never done anything for her family. She insisted that I get a lawyer and change the arrangements for the sale of the house. I told her that if she wanted to do that, she needed to do it all herself. I have no problem with grandmother's plans.

So my cousin called me a few vulgar names and hung up.

She won't be the last.

So that's what grandmother meant to the family she loved so much. Potential pay day. They just want money. Grandmother was not about money at all. She was about legacy. Nobody sees that. They never deserved to have her in their lives. I hate them all.

ENTRY # 51

SHE'S SUSPICIOUS.

Yesterday, when I was in here writing, she knocked on the door. "What are you doing in there?"

I told her I would be out in a minute, and I could tell that she was listening at the door. She must have heard the pages in the notebook rustling.

And today, I could tell that she had been looking for something in here. Everything was moved. She was looking for something.

She didn't find my notebook, or at least if she did, it didn't seem like something she should be concerned about.

I know what she was looking for. She was looking for porn. She's been talking at me a lot lately. She's been talking about the dangers of porn, and how it breaks up families.

She thinks I'm in here, in my bathroom, looking at porn. So probably when she saw my notebook she just moved it aside. She wasn't looking for words on a page, she was looking for evidence of pictures of naked women.

Follow up.

So, here's what I did.

I asked our IT guy at work for the cover to a Penthouse magazine. Not the actual magazine, just the cover. The IT guy is a real pervert and I knew he'd have some porn around. I took the cover he gave me and put it around a Time Magazine. Then I left the magazine there in my bathroom.

About an hour ago, I heard Janine scream my name. I ran upstairs like a frightened child. I didn't quite get the laugh I was hoping for.

I'm kind of confused, because she didn't believe for a second that I would really have an actual girlie magazine in the house, even though she was suspicious that something had been going on in the bathroom. She was angry about a girlie magazine cover over a normal magazine. She knew what it was right away, and she wanted to know why I would do something like that. I was trying to make a point. I was using humor to send a message. She didn't think it was funny. I've never seen her that furious. It was kind of scary. I only laughed a little bit, much less than I thought I would laugh.

I explained that I did it because I was offended that she would think that I was looking at porn. Of course that made no sense to her.

She screamed her point of view. The mere fact that I would play a prank like that proves that I don't see pornography in a healthy way. What's a healthy way to view pornography? I don't view pornography at all. Basically her point was that anyone who would find that prank funny at all has to be truly sick.

But holy cow, she was really mad.

ENTRY # 52

I WAS RIGHT.

By brother called me tonight.

He's suspicious that I'm not being forthcoming in everything that was discussed at the bank. Others in the family have approached him and asked him to double check what I have done about grandmother's supposed estate.

All the cousins, uncles and aunts, and my siblings have agreed to dissolve grandmother's trust, and sell the house, and split the money. They found a lawyer.

So I'm supposed to do a final cleaning of the house, and prepare it for the sale.

Yes, I've always felt that I was Grandmother's favorite, and yes, she did name me as the executor of her estate. I'm willing to do all of this.

But why is this my problem? Why do the rest of the children and grandchildren see me as some kind of foe that they will have to overcome to get what they want? Why do they want anything? Wasn't just having the woman as a mother or grandmother enough of a blessing?

The thing that's bothering me is how everything is playing out. First the house is looted. They leave it a mess. Then everybody's mad because there isn't a stash of millions of dollars to pass around, then everybody suspects me of hiding valuables from them, and now it's left to me to clean the house and sell it so that everybody can have a little piece of whatever is left of Grandmother.

I think I would die laughing if I knew what they all think the house is worth.

This whole thing has all ruined my comfortable bathroom writing.

ENTRY # 53

YOU'LL NEVER BELIEVE WHAT I FOUND.

I don't believe it myself. In my wildest dreams I could never have believed that something like this could happen to me.

This changes everything, and I'm the only one who knows about it. Like
I mentioned before, we had to go to Grandmother's house. We needed
to clean it out so that we could sell it. No one was willing to help, so it
was just our family. Daniel even came with us to help. We were going
through the house and we were discussing what to do with what is left
there. It's all garbage now. At least that's all that is left. I've been through
everything, and I'm sure. Funny thing, though, now that it's all con-
firmed to be garbage, it's all my problem. So everyone left me alone to
go through it. Janine took the kids out for dinner.

Anyway, as I was looking around the house, I kind of got lost in memories. I wondered what Grandmother would say about the garbage, and
what she would tell me to do about it. I think she would tell me to just
get a truck and haul it all off to the dump. She was never attached to
material things. Funny how she didn't feel that way when grandfather
died. I remembered one summer after Grandfather died when I was a
teenager and grandmother was wondering what to do with all Grandfather's things that were laying around the house. She wasn't ready to
throw it all out.

I suggested that we put it all in the attic, and she threw a fit. She didn't
want me going anywhere near the opening to the attic. She told me to
just forget it and drop the subject. So I did. We ended up stacking all of
Grandfather's things in the already cluttered basement.

I was remembering that day, and I went and found the attic entrance in
the ceiling. It's in the hallway by the bathroom. I was just standing there,
staring at it. I thought about getting a ladder and going up there to look.
It was strange. I started to feel so much fear. I imagined mummified
bodies and dead animals and other terrible things. It was like a horror

176

movie. I don't know why I was afraid. There was never anything sinister about my grandparents.

So I did get the ladder. The door had been painted over, so I had to get a knife to break the seal around the door. And then the dust and insulation that fell out when I moved the door was incredible.

I don't know what I really imagined I would see in the attic. Monsters? Aliens? Decaying bodies? It turns out that there was nothing in the attic. Nothing except about five or six boxes stacked and gathered around the hole there at the entrance. I looked into the closest one. It was full of money. Rolls and envelopes and bundles of bills that my grandmother had stashed away.

Sound incredible?

You didn't know my grandparents. They hated institutions of every kind. They hated the government. They were radicals in every sense of the word. They certainly didn't trust banks. So this isn't really a surprise. In fact, it is the very thing that my cousins were hoping to find. I'm sure that they found envelopes in drawers full of bills, and it might have even added up to be thousands of dollars. But it wasn't like this.

These were orange crates. I eased each one out of the attic, down to the floor, out the front door, and loaded it all out to the car very quickly. I didn't have even a second to think about it or act amazed or even say WOW! I also knew in an instant I could never tell anyone about what I had found in the attic. I knew it the first moment I saw it.

I have no idea why grandmother was keeping boxes of money in her attic. She never said anything to even hint about it, and I have no idea if she was planning to do something with or about the money. But the boxes are mine now. Loaded in my car and left to me to hide.

Not all the boxes were full of money. Some were stuffed with envelopes and papers. Behind the bigger boxes were six shoe boxes containing bags of coins. Grandma loved coins. She collected rare coins. Fifty or sixty years ago she used to make extra money by going through coins she would get from the bank, looking for valuable collectible coins. She used to buy large bags of different denominations from the bank, and then go through them, coin by coin, looking for collectible coins.

I thought I was going to have a heart attack getting it all in the car. I was sure that people were watching me. I thought I was going to die. I was panting like a dog and sweating like a pig. And I had to get those boxes somewhere safe before my family came looking for me!

I couldn't think of anyplace safe to take it all, so I took it to the office, of all the stupid places. I knew a utility closet that no one ever uses, and I put it all in some boxes of cleaning supplies. I know it's not safe there, but I was panicking. I was back at the house before Janine arrived. She complained that I was all sweaty. What did she expect? Cleaning out the house by myself is hard work! And cleaning all of Grandmother's money out of the attic was more exhausting than I can even describe.

Janine didn't notice that I had been gone, and she didn't notice that I was in an agitated state. This was one time when I was lucky that she doesn't pay much attention to my general state of wellbeing at all.

I was just in a daze after that. I could hardly find my way home. I was just staring at the walls the rest of the night. I was sure that someone was going to find those boxes before I could get back to them.

It was like being in a dream. I couldn't believe that I had stacks and stacks of money hidden away. I didn't even think about how I was going to spend it. It was just amazing that I had found it at all.

Where did all that money come from? It couldn't have been saved a little at a time, the way Grandmother saved money for projects and gifts. This was different. This money had to have been put together in large amounts. I've heard of things like this before. There was a famous case where a lady found out that her parents had stashed away large amounts of cash like this from money they had invested when their business was thriving. She had her son kill his grandparents so that they could get at the money. They succeeded in killing the grandfather and both the mother and the son wound up in prison. I think they made a movie about the whole thing.

So my first goal is to make sure that no one gets killed over this. Would someone want to kill me over this amount of money? Yes. This money could really complicate things. I'm going to have to be really careful with it.

I don't even know if this is all legal. Should I alert some authority about my find? I'm not going to do it. At least not yet.

ENTRY # 54

IT'S DIFFERENT NOW.

Something inside me has changed. Everything is different. Me, my house, my family, my marriage, everything.

I haven't written for a while, because I've been thinking more about all that money I've got hidden. I swear, it's the first think I think about when I wake up in the morning, and the last thing I think about when I go to sleep.

And who could blame me? This is a twist in the story of my life I could NEVER have anticipated.

In fact, it's amazing to me how much the discovery of all that cash in my grandmother's attic has changed my life. And I haven't even told anyone about it, or spent a dime of it.

It's hard to explain, and although everything changed when I found the money, I have to say that it feels like the change isn't really about the money. I see Janine in a new light. When she gets mad, I hear a whisper in my heart telling me that I don't need to listen to her, and my heartbeat stays steady, and I ignore her until she shuts up.

But she looks at me differently now, too. Maybe I'm causing that. I guess in a way I'm starting to stand up to her, and I don't think she ever thought I would do that.

Her new defense mechanism is the silent treatment. It made me nervous at first, but then I realized it was a gift. It's funny that she thinks that the worst thing she can do to me is to not speak to me. That's the time when it feels the best around here.

I find myself asking, when did things really start to change? Did it start when I started observing our relationship? I can tell you it didn't start with this notebook. But I don't remember noticing when things in my marriage started to change. One day I was just used to the fact that Janine bullies me and is always grumpy.

Attic money update:

I've had a chance now to go through the money.

At first I hid the boxes at work in a crawl space that no one uses. I swear, I couldn't sleep while I knew that the money was in there.

But now I've rented a small loft apartment above the retail shops downtown. It feels pretty safe there. It was definitely a strange feeling to carry box after box, back and forth from my car, as if it was the most normal thing in the world. I didn't dare to look around to see if anyone was watching me. I don't think anyone noticed me at all.

Now I can comfortably go through all the boxes. Can you imagine what would happen if Janine knew I had rented an apartment? Or that I had found all this money? Clearly she can never know about this. I've already decided. This has nothing to do with my wife. This is my own adventure. But it's scary, and it's going to be hard to keep it a secret. The stress of it all is already killing me. I don't know how long I can keep this up.

So here's what I'm looking at: Most of the money is in very good shape. The money in the envelopes had been protected, some of the bundles were a little ripped. A few rolls were very aged, and some had been eaten by insects and rats. But most of it is usable, normal looking money.

I counted about seven hundred thousand dollars in usable bills.

That's not even the interesting part.

The bags of coins were not quarters, dimes, and nickels. At least not mostly. There were a few bags of quarters, dimes and nickels, and many of them were older coins, certainly collectable. But most of the coins were double eagles, eagles, and half eagles. Gold coins. Very valuable gold coins. I don't have any idea exactly what they're worth, but I've done a little research. I'm guessing that the bags of coins are much, much more valuable than the bills.

There were also some papers about the silver mine they were involved with, and the bank that had help them manage their investments. I think they were stock certificates, or something along those lines. I'm pretty ignorant about such things, but I'm thinking they look pretty serious.

So that's it. I've got a lot of money now. My family doesn't, I do. Is that wrong? I don't know. Maybe things would be different if people were different. Maybe I'm a bad person for keeping this secret to myself, but that's exactly what I'm going to do. I'm never going to tell anyone about this.

One day I'll figure this out. I definitely want to help my children. But I'm not going to tell them about it. I'll have to find the right way to do this. I'm not sure that throwing money at my kids will help them. I don't want Janine to know about this, ever.

Sorry I haven't written in a week. It's doesn't mean I've been holding it. It just means that I haven't even thought about picking up this notebook and writing. There has just been too much going on in my life.

Entry # 55

You'll never believe this one.

It's crazy. This is taking a crazy situation and making it crazier.

We just got back from Las Vegas. Las freaking Vegas. Janine told me that she was noticing a lot of tension in my life, and she said that what we really needed was a getaway. She planned the whole thing. Wow! Something for me! From Janine! I guess it had something to do with my birthday, but Janine didn't say anything about that. The second day we were there was my birthday.

I couldn't believe how liberal she was with our trip budget. Our hotel was first class. We stayed at the Flamingo. The room was bigger than our first house. She had tickets to see Blue Man Group. Janine was relaxed and friendly. She casually suggested several expensive restaurants. We wandered in and out of gift shops, and Janine generously bought several items for family members, and for me, and for herself.

Janine held my hand several times as we were walking around on the strip. She seemed happy, but distant somehow.

I couldn't help watching other couples when we were wandering around the casinos and up and down the strip. I don't think I would have noticed before, but since I've been writing this, relationships just seem to jump out at me.

Girls and ladies that were with men, couples, I don't know if they were married couples, really stood out. I noticed that girls and ladies who were not with men were laughing and giggling and being really happy and excited. But those girls clearly with a guy, generally looked emotionless or even miserable. It was more than just a couple of girls that I saw, it was all of them. All the girls who were holding some guy's hand were grimacing and frowning. Is that what happens when men and women pair up? Someone becomes miserable? I just can't believe that's true.

So, there we were in Las Vegas. We had a pretty good time. Janine was actually pretty open to anything. The only weird thing I can report is that she seemed anxious to have a good time. She seemed to want to force it. She was exaggeratedly nice to me. She asked me over and over what I wanted to do. She was happy and willing to do anything I suggested.

We did have one funny experience. Janine had tickets to this old-time vaudeville show in a little casino way off the strip. Someone had told her we should go, so she got tickets online. So that was on the second day of our trip, my birthday.

The show was nice. It was okay. It wasn't the huge deal Janine was expecting, but we had fun. They did some little, ten-minute plays, and there were some singers and comedians. It was just a kind of variety show like you might have seen a hundred years ago.

At one point, they asked if there were any birthdays in the audience, and Janine started pointing to me. So all the actors jumped off the stage and pounced on me. They all started singing this funny birthday song. One of them was a voluptuous woman with lots of makeup. She sat on my lap and started running her fingers through my hair. She was acting like she was all turned on and aroused. She ran her hands all over my body and caressed around and around my head. Then she planted this big, very hard kiss on my check. It was a hard kiss so that she could be sure she left a lip stick mark on my cheek. The she blew lots of kisses to me as she went back to the stage and wiggled her behind at me. It was actually really funny.

I turned with a big smile to Janine, and Janine was absolutely steaming. People were razzing her, and yelling at her not to be jealous. It was all in good fun, and I think people thought that Janine was playing with me, but they don't know Janine. I tried to give Janine a kiss, but she pushed me away roughly. Everyone was really worked up by then, and I was started to feel embarrassed. The master of ceremonies came out to announce the next act, and everyone forgot about Janine and me. When the show was over, we went back to our hotel. Janine acted like nothing had happened.

Janine seemed so quiet and distant on the drive back to the hotel, I felt sorry for her. For a minute I saw the college girl I once dated. I gave her a surprise hug when we got to our room. She didn't respond. She was cold and stiff. I told her we could stop in a little town that we both like on the way home and stay in a bed and breakfast. She really brightened up at the idea. We talked about things we could do, and I suggested a hike through the forest on the mountain by the town. She loved that idea.

We got up early to hit the road, and we were both really cheerful as we drove the mountain roads to the little town of Garfield. We went for a walk to look around, and holding hands felt natural.

The bed and breakfast was really beautiful, and Janine was just glowing. Very feminine and flirtatious. That night in our room things got really heated up. Janine showered and came out nude to do her hair and brush her teeth. I was searching the channels on the tv, and I came across a whole section of channels that just played music. I was frantically looking for some romantic music, when I came across a channel of '80's pop hits. Lots of power ballads. Janine turned around with a big grin on her face.

"That one!"

Boy, it was incredible. You have to try to understand. This is the music we grew up on. We used to slow dance to these songs in high school. We dreamed of true love that would last a life time when we heard these songs. Now we were two adults making love furiously to these songs.

"Almost Paradise" from the movie Footloose

"Open Arms" by Journey

"Glory of Love" by Peter Cetera

"Never Say Goodbye" by Bon Jovi

"Waiting for a Girl Like You" by Foreigner

"Careless Whisper" by George Michael

"Saving all my love for you" by Whitney Houston

"I just called to say I love you" by Stevie Wonder

"Keep on Loving You" by REO Speedwagon

"In Your Eyes" by Peter Gabriel

We made love to songs like that for five hours. We just lasted and lasted and lasted. She was on top, and then I was on top, and then we were just all tangled up in passion. We were both just lost in ecstasy. I can't describe what an incredible thing it was. The music seemed to envelope us. I think people who grew up in the eighties always fantasized about something like that. It was like coming home. It was like someone had given me back my wife. I was almost crying. It was the safest, most comforting experience I've ever had.

When we finally turned off the tv and the lights, Janine snuggled up to me with her head on my chest. Although the room was quiet, the songs were ringing in our minds. I was openly crying by then. I kept whispering to her, "Janine, Janine, Janine". She didn't say anything and we fell asleep.

The next morning, we dressing and got ready to leave. We didn't talk. I cheerfully said, "I'll take the bags to the car before we go down to breakfast."

Janine spun around at me and snarled, "Why?"

I was stunned. What was wrong?

"Is that a problem?" I asked.

"Can't you wait till after breakfast?" she growled.

I was stuttering and stammering. I didn't want things to go back to the way they were.

"I just thought it would give you more time to get ready."

Janine seemed embarrassed and turned back to the mirror.

"I don't care."

We ate breakfast with very little conversation. We agreed that the food was good. I mentioned that I was looking forward to the hike. Janine looked confused and frustrated. She had forgotten. I told her we didn't have to go if she didn't want to, but she waved me off.

When we got in the car I told her I needed to stop at Walmart. She tensed up. "Why?" she asked.

I told her I needed some snacks, and I could see her resisting the urge to object. We got to the store and were walking in when I told her that I wanted to buy a new backpack, because the one I have is twenty years old.

She went nuts.

"What? You don't need a backpack! Why didn't you bring your backpack from home? Why do you always do things like this? Why can't you be responsible?"

I reminded her that we hadn't planned on a hike when we planned the Las Vegas trip. But she was already wound up.

"You don't need a freaking backpack! You drive me crazy with these stupid stunts! I can't believe you."

I was heartbroken. My beautiful love-making partner from the night before was gone. She was only visiting. I turned to face Janine.

"Why are you making a big deal about this? I just want a simple, inexpensive backpack. I've been meaning to buy one, and today I actually have a use for one. Why do you get so upset over nothing? You make all this up in your head, and then you get yourself boiling until the argument just seems crazy. Why do you do this?"

Janine stopped and looked stunned. Just absolutely stunned. She looked like she couldn't move. I tried to be compassionate.

"Let's just go home."

Her face contorted as if she was trying to shake herself out of a stupor.

"No. Let's go on a hike. I'll go pick out some snacks and drinks, you go get your stupid backpack."

Nice.

The hike was beautiful, but we didn't talk much. We were like a couple who had just met and were trying to salvage a bad date. Janine took a few pictures, and she pointed out a squirrel she saw. We got back to the car right about the time the sun was setting. I bought gas and hit the highway for home. Janine slept the whole way. I found a radio station that was playing oldies.

It's kind of funny to say, but I didn't bring any of the money that I found with me on our Las Vegas trip. She doesn't know about it, and I'm not going to spend it just yet.

I did go to the bank the other day, however, and I showed some of the money to the bank manager. I was very honest about it and I told him that my grandmother left it to me. He looked it over very carefully and said that the bills that I showed him were very old, but also very much legal tender.

I had taken the oldest bills I from the boxes. I'm spending them first. I've bought gifts for friends, people who deserved to be recognized but never received even a thank you note from me. There was a kid at the office who got married, and we didn't even respond to his wedding invitation. I got him a really nice table service. Plates and bowls and cups and everything. I use the old bills to buy gas for the car. I use them to run errands that need to be done but have been put off because I was watching my budget.

And one fun thing I bought that really made me feel good. I bought a pair of boots. I've always loved boots. I wore cowboy boots the whole time I was growing up. A few years ago, I told Janine that. I told her how I loved cowboy boots, and how I always wore them when I was young. She asked me, "Why don't you have a pair? Of Boots?" But she told me she thought cowboy boots were ridiculous. So I couldn't buy any.

But now I have a beautiful pair of boots, and they're not ridiculous.

I just can't explain what it's like to buy whatever I want and then look in my wallet, only to see many more large bills in there just making my wallet fat.

Now, don't get ahead of me. I know I'm in dangerous territory. This is a tax-free wind fall. At least so far. I don't know what to do about that. I know that if I start spending this money foolishly, it will draw a lot of attention to me, and I'll get into all kinds of legal trouble. And what if my cousins and siblings find out? It could all get really ugly really quickly. Still, I have been doing interesting things with the money.

One of the first things I started to do with the money was to leave big tips. I love to see the look on servers' faces when I leave a couple of twenties as a tip. Why shouldn't I make someone happy with this money? I can see that it could certainly make me happy.

I'm paying cash when I make purchases any time I can. That way I leave our savings and checking accounts alone.

Big things? Yes, I'm looking. But I'm afraid to buy. Janine is obviously a problem. How would I explain big, expensive changes in my life?

And the law. Taxes. Changes in spending habits draw attention. Does this mean I'm going to have to learn to launder money? So many adventures lie ahead for me.

Entry # 56

Things are changing at home, too.

Daniel called last week and said he wanted to come home for the week-end. He wanted to talk to us. We told him we were thrilled that he wanted to visit. He got here just after lunch on Saturday. He seemed so stiff and formal. It was like having a salesman in the house. I was caught completely off guard. I had no idea what was going on.

Daniel told us he's gay.

I'm stunned.

They talk about the percentages of gay people in our society, and I just take their word for it. But I don't really know any gay people. I mean, I knew Leon, and I've heard that one of our neighbors has a son who was fooling around with his roommates in college. I just don't really know any regular homosexual people. Are there really as many of them as we're told there are? Yes, I realize that gay people aren't going to come up to me and shake my hand and say, "Hi! I'm homosexual! Let me tell you all about it!" So I have no idea about homosexuality, how many people are homosexuals, or what their lives are like. So for good or bad, they are out of my line of sight.

And it's funny. With so little knowledge about homosexuals, I still con-sider myself to be very open minded and accepting of alternative lifestyles.

But to talk to someone from your own family, your own son, and have him explain that he's a homosexual, and why he is, well, that's a totally new thing for me.

I'm not equipped for this. He was waiting for a response, and I didn't know what to say.

I've still been trying to think of other homosexual people I've met. There was a guy in our accounting department. He's very nice, and very helpful.

Everybody likes him. But I don't get into conversations about sexuality with him. This is just new, difficult terrain for me.

Once I had an experience in a gay store years and years ago. I guess that counts.

I was looking for some lingerie to buy for Janine for her birthday. Lingerie and assorted sexual items. Yes, we're into that. Moving on. So I looked in the phone book and found out there was this "adult" shop downtown. I went and explored.

It wasn't a very nice shop. But it was clean and quiet. I started looking around, but everything seemed out of place. The lingerie looked wrong. Then the guy at the cash register came over to me and asked if he could help.

"I'm looking for some lingerie for my wife's birthday."

He smiled and gestured for me to follow him. In the back of the store, on a small rack, there was a limited selection of some pretty nice items. The sales guy stood there watching me go through the stuff. I didn't like that. Shopping in an adult store is kind of a private thing. Then he took it a step farther and started to talk to me.

"Young married guy, huh?"

I nodded. The lingerie was very, very inexpensive, so I picked a couple of outfits, and then I went to look at the sex toys. Again, very, very cheap. I was satisfied. I headed for the cash register. The guy who was helping me walked behind me.

"It's a pleasure to do business with a nice customer. We've had some real problems lately. People have painted really offensive insults on our store, and vandalized things. They threw a rock through our window and hit our front door with a bar of some kind. Anyway, it's nice to have a real customer in here shopping."

I was baffled. That's how naïve and backwards I am. I wasn't catching on. I was wide eyed and opened mouthed.

"That's terrible! Why would people single you out like that?"

The guy was ringing up my items and shrugged his shoulders innocently.

"Well, anyway, we want our heterosexual customers like you to know that we love you too! We care just as much about your sexual wellbeing as we do about our own! Yes sir! You're making a good, healthy choice in your marriage by tending to your sexual needs. You and your young bride are going to be very happy! And we want you to know that we love our heterosexual customers just as much!"

Got it!

Suddenly I knew where I was. And I was okay with it. Hell, the prices alone made me very happy. And horny!

The guy gave me a very kind, genuine smile.

"Anything else I can do for you, my friend?"

"No, just put that stuff in a bag and let me get the fuck out of here."

See? I admit that I'm a person who is very awkward with all this. And I was awkward with Daniel. It's not because of the sexuality. It's because of the huge life changes. It's because of the sudden awareness that there is a distance between us. It's because there have been important things that have gone unspoken.

Can I be honest here? I will confess. I'll just say what I was thinking. I know it's not the way people today think I should have reacted, but I will tell you what I was thinking.

I was struck by a massive impulse to throw my arms around my son and say, "Oh no! No you're not! Son, you're not gay! You're just confused. We can help you. We'll get you help. But don't believe for a minute that you're gay!"

That's what I was thinking and feeling for just a few moments. Then I tried to quiet my mind and listen. Another voice was telling me that Daniel is okay, and that I needed to listen to him. But I still can't deny that I sat there wanting to cry. In the end I just wanted to understand. I wanted to know that my son was okay.

And what was Janine doing while this was happening? Whatever is was, she's still doing it.

Janine is swinging out of control on this one. While he was here, she was really tense. She didn't offer much more of a reaction than I did, but she was clearly unhappy. Since Daniel left, she's had a lot to say. She starts to rant about homosexuality and choice and perversion. Then she swings the other way and talks about how gay people deserve the same rights and considerations under the law as anyone else has.

She talks about her confused son. At least she's not in complete denial. But I'm not so sure she's right. I don't know why she thinks he's confused. He seemed very resolute to me. When I asked her if she still loves her son she was so stunned that she almost fell over trying to sit down. I thought she would explode at me, but she just sat there staring off into space.

I'm not judging Janine. I'm doing some soul searching of my own. Am I a horrible person if I admit that this is not what I imagined for my son? How do other families react when their children have news like this? I know some families are hateful and unaccepting, but do others cheer and blow on party noisemakers and put on party hats?

I just don't know what to say to Daniel.

He was clearly waiting to see whether we would approve or not. Would we say it was right, or wrong? Personally, I would never tell anyone that I thought it was wrong for them to be gay, and that includes my own son. That's not the way things are anymore, and I know that. There was a day, not so long ago, maybe even just a generation ago, when this would have been seen as a tragedy. It would have meant screaming and threatening and cursing and insulting. It would have meant hiding and concealing and punishment and consequences. But that's not what we do now, is it?

But I still didn't know what to say to someone who was telling me the simple fact that he was indeed gay. What did he want from me? It felt silly to tell him that I thought it was great. It wasn't like he was telling me that he just got his dream job, or got a good grade on an important assignment at school. It felt wrong to tell him that I always knew he was gay. It sounded like an insult, and it wasn't true.

I think he was really devastated when he left. We asked him to stay overnight, but he refused. My boy. My buddy. Little guy. We live in different universes. How did that happen?

Entry # 57

I'VE ALWAYS SUSPECTED THAT SHE ONCE HAD AN AFFAIR.

Now I just look petty. It figures that with everything going on with Daniel, I just happened to start thinking about this. But that's the way these things go. Something big is revealed, and suddenly other secrets work their way back into our consciousness.

We had a neighbor about ten years ago that was always poking around here and acting like he was just stopping by to say hello. But he never wanted to talk to me. He liked to talk to Janine. He had lots of compliments for her. He shared a lot of interests with her. He would always come around when I wasn't home.

Janine was really friendly with him. They used to talk on the phone. Janine would leave the room and go somewhere where she could be alone when he called. She said it was because the kids and I made too much noise. Funny how she never left the room when her sister or mother called. But phone calls from her special neighbor friend were different. She told me that they had a lot in common, and that made them good neighbors.

Anyway, he came around a lot when I wasn't home. They did little favors for each other. This guy would come over and fix something at our house, and then come see me to get a 'thank you' from me. Yea, thanks for screwing my wife! Janine also tried to make friends with this guy's wife. She would send her little gifts like preserves she made at church. 'Thanks for lending me your husband'. One afternoon Janine disappeared and didn't come back home till eleven thirty. She refused to give anyone an explanation. She got very defensive when I pressed her and wanted to know where she'd been. A day or too later I pressed her again, and she admitted that she'd gone somewhere with the neighbor, but told me to mind my own business, and accused me of being cruel and dirty minded for not trusting her to do the right thing. That's all she would say about it. I know that if the date with the neighbor had really been innocent, she would have told me all about it.

I don't know why this is important to talk about. I didn't really care at the time. That's not true. I was mad. It was the deceiving that bothered me. Such a hypocrite!

Two years after it happened, I confronted Janine about it one more time. I told her everything about that night felt wrong. She wouldn't confirm or deny that anything had happened. She cried. She screamed over and over again for me to drop it. She's refused to talk about the situation ever since. She just says that I need to trust her, and that she would never let anything bad happen in our marriage.

Define bad.

Later I did feel hurt, not because she had been with another man, but because it made it so clear to me that our feelings for one another were changing. She didn't owe me anything. She didn't feel like it was important to communicate with me.

ENTRY # 58

THE PAPERS.

I went to see an investment officer about the papers I found in Grand-mother's boxes. Apparently, the mine sold shares. They're still good. They're going to let me know exactly what they're worth.

This brought up another question. Taxes? Remember my worries about taxes? What do I do about taxes? If I just go around spending all this money, I'll surely get into a lot of trouble. And I know I can't cash in these investments without reporting and paying taxes. How secret can I keep all this? I don't want anyone to know about it.

But these stocks, I don't think I can hide them from my family. Maybe this is my way out of hiding the money.

So I'm going to have to visit a tax professional and find out what I should do. I don't think I know anyone like that, but I'm thinking that I could talk to someone in the neighborhood who's really wealthy and ask for a reference.

Update:

I used to play golf with a man we called Big John. John's an ex-marine. He worked for a pipeline as a welder. Anyway, I ran into Big John at the golf course two days ago, and found out that John is retired. He's not sixty yet. And he hasn't needed to be very frugal to get by in his retire-ment. He's been to Alaska three times with his wife. He just bought a big trailer house, and a road bike, and he's been living life large.

I asked John how he does it. He laughed and said that everybody asks him that. Then he said to me, "I've got a guy".

I asked if I could meet this guy. Big John set up the meeting.

The "guy" turned out to be a financial planner, investment broker, and tax professional. He seems honest. And he knows all about how to find out if my stock certificates are valuable. There are a million ways this guy can help me. He seems very discreet. I haven't told him about grand-mother's money yet, but I feel like this might be my answer.

ENTRY # 59

I'M BECOMING MORE ASSERTIVE.

So today I had an appointment to see an attorney about Grandmother's will. I had been with my sister earlier, to get some advice from her. I trust Kay, and she has a compassionate yet firm viewpoint on the whole inheritance thing. I didn't tell Janine I was leaving. When I got home, Janine started yelling at me for not being around the house, and not telling her where I was going.

Then the phone rang, and someone was asking Janine if we could come over and help them with something or talk to them, I didn't even listen to Janine when she was ranting about it. She was telling them that we would be over in a little while. I was getting ready for my appointment.

When she hung up the phone, she started staring at me with her mouth open. She was still angry about my absence earlier. But then she saw me gathering documents and changing my shirt and combing my hair.

"What are you doing?"

I wasn't sarcastic, or evasive, or defensive. I was just matter of fact.

"I have something to do at five."

Her nostrils flared and she leaned in menacingly.

"You're not watching Sons of Anarchy!"

I did a spit take at the sink where I was brushing my teeth. She was just shooting wildly in the dark now.

"What the hell are you talking about?"

She was sure she was right. She's always sure she's right. Why can't she see? Why would I be brushing my teeth to watch Sons of Anarchy?

"I don't want you to watch that show anymore!"

I just shook my head and sighed and turned my back on her.

"I have an appointment and I'm leaving now."

"Where are you going?"

For a moment I felt that I had suffered enough. It was a moment of insanity, but I let it fly.

"None of your damn business!"

Actually, it probably was Janine's business. I believe that husbands and wives should arrange these kinds of things together, but I just wanted Janine to leave me alone. I could hear her gasping as I walked to the door. I've never, not ever, talked to her like that before.

ENTRY # 60

THINGS ARE CHANGING.

It's fun to walk around with this money.

A little at a time, of course. I stuff a wad of twenties and tens and a few fifties in my wallet, and I feel like I'm king of the world. I can buy what I want. I feel like I could do anything I wanted.

I have a few things I want, kind of like a kid at Christmas time. I mentioned earlier about my boots. So there's that. Now I've got a couple different pairs of boots. I bought a jack knife. And of course I will be buying a new set of golf clubs. There's no doubt about the clubs.

Here's a strange one. I went to the eye doctor to try contact lenses. I've always worn eye glasses. But I've been looking at family pictures lately, and I've realized that I look old. Old and weak. Old and weak and wimpy. But I've never even thought of contact lenses before, because the idea of touching my eyes with my finger gives me the willies.

But now my life is changing, and I decided that it's time to give contacts a chance. My eye doctor tried to talk me out of it. I wear bifocals, and apparently there's not really a good choice with contacts for people who need help with things close up and far away. And he knows that I don't want to touch my eyes. But I'm sick of other people making decisions for me, and I've learned to be a little assertive. So we agreed to try.

The doctor had some samples, but they weren't my exact prescription. He said that he needed to teach me to use them, and I needed to practice. So he put me in a special chair next to a countertop made out of a mirror. The doctor tried to pry my eyes open, one at a time, and tried to touch the lenses to my eyes. It didn't work. I couldn't help blinking, so he had to force my eyes open harder. I hated the sensation of his finger touching my eye. The contacts never stayed in, and they just fell out onto the countertop.

I told the doctor that maybe I should try it myself. After an eternity of trying, I finally got the damn things in. I looked like I had lost a boxing match. My face was red, and my eyes were swollen. But now I've got two boxes of contact lenses to make me feel younger and more attractive.

I paid the eye doctor in cash. I've been paying for everything in cash. I go pay the utility in cash, the credit card, the insurance. You could say that in this way I'm actually helping my wife and family with the money because nothing comes out of our checking account.

It's going to be a little bit hard to cash in on the gold coins, though. How do I do it? It wouldn't be possible to walk into a coin shop and say I want a million dollars for a bunch of gold coins. I would wind up on the news. All my cousins would find out. Janine would find out. I've got to figure this out.

I have been taking the collectible coins to dealers around town, and that has been an amazing experience. They can't believe it. But I think they've started to recognize me and that I'm building a reputation as someone with amazing, rare coins. I don't want that. I need to spread the whole coin thing out a little and take it slowly.

I've been looking up coin dealers around the nation, and I've decided that I want to cash in the gold coins a little at a time for the rest of my life. And that's great, because I've always wanted to travel around the US. If other coin dealers are like the ones around here, they'll just give me cash for my valuable coins. I'll take a handful at a time with me and see how it goes.

I'll probably leave some of the gold coins to my family as inheritance.

ENTRY # 61

I'VE MADE A DECISION.

My appointment with Big John's guy, the tax professional, opened my eyes. I've been taking some really huge risks. He was really discreet, and I felt like I could trust him. Still, I didn't tell him about the money. At least not all of it. I said my grandmother left me little cash. He told me that if it was just a few hundred, I'm probably okay. But if it's thousands, I need to declare it and keep everything out in the open. I tried my best to keep a poker face. I'm still not going to tell anyone about the money, but I'm going to share the stocks.

It turns out that the stocks are worth about a hundred and fifty thousand dollars. I've decided to tell my family about it. Cousins, aunts and uncles, everybody. I'm going to let them fight over it all like a pack of ravenous wolves.

I'm hoping that the fight over these stocks will cover my tracks. I'm hoping that no one will ever suspect that I've found those boxes of money.

I was thinking about Grandfather and Grandmother and wondering just how they came into all this money. They must have been outlaws in their own way. That has to be it. This money must have come to them in a clandestine way.

Grandfather used to wear a ruby ring. I loved it. I would sit in his lap and just gaze at that beautiful red stone. It was the kind of ring an outlaw would wear. It occurred to me that if by some magic this money has fallen into my hands, then I'm in league with my outlaw grandparents. Screw the family. Screw the IRS. This is my money now. I want a ring like my grandfather wore.

I went to some jewelry stores in town to look at rings. Most were wimpy and anemic. Feminine rings, even though they were in the men's section. That's not me anymore. Finally, at the Gem Smith's, I found a fantastic, heavy gold ring, with a square ruby in it. The jeweler discouraged me from wanting that ring, telling me that it was very expensive. He just about pooped his pants when I paid cash for the ring.

Just one more piece of the puzzle. One more step to becoming who I was always meant to be. Beautiful ring, but not glaring or gaudy. You don't even notice it unless you're really looking at my hand. But it feels really good.

I'm an outlaw now. A true gangster. I've decided to just live with my decision.

Entry # 62

We had a little intervention today.

No one called it an intervention, but that's what it was.

Janine took us all over to her folk's house. Her slutty sister was there. I planned to do what I always do at their house and just blend into the furniture. But soon enough, I figured out that I was the subject of the conversation.

It started with Janine's mother asking strange questions:

"So, what's going on with you two? What have you been up to?"

That led to,

"Scott, what's going on with you?"

And from there it spiraled into very personal questions and assumptions.

Here's what pisses me off. An intervention is only important when an intervention is NEEDED. What did I do? What's wrong with me that needs to be fixed by my wife's family? No one could answer that question. It seems that I needed an intervention because in their opinion, I just generally suck.

Danny really went off on me.

"I don't know why Janine has put up with you for all these years!"

I kept asking, "What have I done?"

No one would answer with specifics, and it seemed to make everyone more angry.

Worse than that is how Janine just sat there and let everyone rip on me.

Sammy got really flustered. She made some really mature observations. She started saying how I've always worked hard to provide for my family, and that I've never caused problems for the family. She pointed out a number of men that she knows about who have put their families through torture. I think she surprised everyone by defending me and she was shut down quickly. She got disapproving looks and several shhs and tongue clucks. Her grandmother shook her head and told Sammy that she didn't understand the situation.

"You're attacking my dad. I understand that."

The whole room erupted in objections.

"Nobody's attacking anybody! We're all just trying to help Janine work things out in her marriage. We want what's best for the whole family! This isn't about attacking anyone. It's about healing our family."

But everyone was starting to aim their increased anger at me, calling me names and shouting accusations. Accusing me of ruining my wife's life and destroying my children, as evidenced by Sammy's disrespectful behavior.

What did I do? The question kept coming back to me. I didn't deserve it. Typical of how I've always handled these things, I didn't say anything.

The night wound down in a very awkward way. They didn't have the courage to throw me out of the house, so everyone just kind of yelled themselves out, and then we just sat there staring at one another. Janine's mom had bought a cake for the evening, so plates were passed around. That's the kind of insanity that describes my life. That's the kind of insanity I can no longer bear.

One moment I'm the devil, I'm the reason for all the pain in the family, I'm responsible for all the problems in everyone's lives. The next moment I'm politely eating cake, and Janine's mom is asking me if I like the ice cream.

It's all insanity.

When we got home, Janine and I weren't speaking to each other. When we were ready to turn the lights off in our room and get into the bed, she finally asked me why I didn't say anything at her parent's house.

"It was your intervention. I thought that's why we were there. I thought it was important that you and your family had the chance to say all the things you wanted to say. It wasn't the time or place for me to have my say. That's what I thought."

Janine had a look on her face that told me she was having an entire argument with me in her head. She punched her pillow and twitched and rolled her shoulders and rolled her eyes.

"You just don't care, do you?"

Then she turned off the lights, and I tried to go to sleep.

ENTRY # 63

OKAY, I'M READY TO COME CLEAN.

I've been thinking a lot about this notebook. I said at the beginning that when I found it, all these feelings just started to flow out of me. I've said that there really is no good reason for keeping this bathroom journal. I don't think that's true anymore.

I think the thing that started everything, that is, me writing all this stuff down in this notebook, and me starting to chaff against my wife's iron fist, is the fact that my career is changing, or evolving, you might say.

Careers are monotonous, and repetitive. They go on year after year without anything ever changing. That's the way my job was. I was a guy in a rut, and it spilled over to my family. I think it even affected Janine. She counted on things always being the same. She wanted me to always be the same, and to always do exactly what she thought I should do.

A couple of years ago, I had the opportunity to change the way I'm paid at work. The company was growing by leaps and bounds and I was a big part of that. I've become one of the principles of the company. Kind of like an owner. Instead of a calculated paycheck, I am being paid a percentage of what the company earns on investments. That was a big deal when they offered it to me. I never told Janine about it. It seemed like a good idea at the time. Our company was thriving, and my paychecks were huge.

But our company investments have been losing for two years. That means that the money deposited in our checking account has come from a debit account that is racking up an amount that I owe. The work has slacked off, and staff has taken on a lot of the work I used to do. That means I'm not needed in the office as much as I used to be, and no one notices or cares when I don't come in. Sometimes I don't go into the office for as much as a week at a time.

Janine doesn't know anything about all this. I've talked to her about the importance of watching what we spend, and then I get a lecture about how she's the one who has managed our finances successful for all these years. I just can't bring myself to tell her that our monthly budget is a debit, and not a positive.

Because I haven't told Janine about my pay situation, she isn't trying to conserve our money at all.

Of course, if she knew, she'd absolutely die. But that no longer matters because of Grandmother's money. At least it doesn't matter to me.

The end of my employment story will probably be me losing my job because the company went out of business. That will have some obvious consequences. How will I explain it to my wife? What will I do with myself then?

Oh wait, at least I won't be poor. Right?

Entry # 64

Janine the Man

Well, here I am swinging to the other extreme, and that makes me look bipolar, or manic depressive. But I had to make this observation.

We've talked already about how Janine can be "man-ish". I've laughed and poked fun at this problem up till now, but tonight I want to talk about how this is a problem for both of us.

People have been telling me for a long time that Janine wears the pants in the family, and it shows. Here's where it gets bad for Janine.

I've told you that Janine is a beautiful woman, and it's true. She's beautiful and sexy. But the more she pushes me around and the more she makes the point that she runs things around here, the more man-ish she seems. She puffs her chest out and swings her shoulders when she walks, just like a man. I know it sounds sexist, but it's in everything she does. The way she talks, the way she interacts with people, and her overall attitude.

If she knew that she was slaughtering her feminine side, I think it would shake her. Maybe she'd wake up and see what's happening.

That's not to say I'm a chauvinist at all, but don't you think that there's something important about femininity? Yes, women should be sure and assertive. They should be successful and have equal opportunities. But don't you think that being feminine is important?

Janine's a beautiful woman, but she's not AS beautiful when she's being a bully or a jerk.

I've always tried to sweeten the image. My nickname for my wife is 'Mr. Janine'. I use it sweetly, lovingly, and almost like baby talk. I obviously came up with that nickname for my wife because of her personality and behavior, but she doesn't seem to get that. She's never reacted negatively to this pet name, or asked me what inspired it.

Does that make me 'Mrs. Janine?'

I'm not trying to say that I want Janine to be softer. Janine is who she is. I've become very familiar with Janine's tough side. It might be a surprise to hear that I don't want to change that part of her personality.

I think the problem with the feminine side of Janine is the fact that she's way too defensive. She has a protective wall built up against the whole world. She's not listening. It's not possible to communicate with her. She's never vulnerable. And all this makes her seem less feminine.

She could be so very beautiful if she would just stop.

Entry # 65

A bunch of idiots

That's my extended family. I was going to call them a pack of retarded monkeys, but I didn't want to insult monkeys.

I had my lawyer contact them all today with the news about how I found the stocks in grandmother's house. You'd think that this would all come as great news!

They weren't happy.

They wanted to understand the timeline. They wanted to know why I hadn't called the very instant I found the stocks.

They want a formal investigation. They want to accuse me of something.

Everybody is threatening to get a lawyer. Everyone has a reason why they deserve most, if not all of the stocks.

No one has given any hint that they are suspicious that I found anything more than the stocks. I think that is because they think they found all the money already. Let them keep their stocks. I hope they choke on them.

Entry # 66

I WENT GOLFING WITH DANIEL TODAY.

He called me to say that he wanted to spend some time alone with me. We talked about possible activities, and he said he's been playing a lot of golf. So I told him I thought that golf would be great, and suggested a couple of great local courses.

We met last Saturday morning at Wingepoint golf course at nine o'clock, and hardly said anything to each other. We had forty-five minutes to warm up before our tee time, so we hit balls on the range.

It seemed to me that Daniel wanted to pick a fight. He kept asking me stupid questions about golfing with a homosexual.

Would I be embarrassed?

I told him I didn't know how I felt about golfing with a homosexual, but I did know how I felt about golfing with my son.

We played the first two holes in silence. But then on the third hole, Daniel hit a really great drive. Suddenly he was beaming, and we had something to talk about. I raved so much about that great drive, I might have taken it too far. But Daniel only laughed at my enthusiasm. We talked for a few holes about great golf shots, and we avoided talking about relationships, family and sex.

I told him that I loved him, and that was an awkward thing to say on the golf course. He stopped for a moment and looked at me, but he didn't say anything at first. Then he told me that he loved me too.

After our round, Daniel asked me if I would ever be willing to meet his friend. Of course I would! Daniel's friend is important to him. Meeting Daniel's friend is the next step in understanding all this. Daniel said that he wanted to talk to his mom about a visit, and I said that we could plan it just as soon as possible.

We stopped at McDonald's on our way home. We started talking about times when he was growing up and we would stop at McDonald's. Those are the things that stay with me. Those are the things that I can lean on to remind me how I really feel about my family.

Entry # 67

I BOUGHT A MOTORCYCLE TODAY.

How do you like that?

It's a Harley Davidson Low Rider. It's from their Dyna line.

I've been stopping at the Harley Davidson store about every other day for a month now. I walk slowly around the motorcycles and look them over the way sixteen-year-old boys look at girls in bikinis. The ladies who work there as salespeople all look like Gemma from Sons of Anarchy. They all call me "babe" and "Hon" and "Sweetie".

Then a while back the sales lady suggested that I sit on one of the bikes I was looking at, so I did. No one suggested that I take a ride, but there I sat. I probably sat there longer than I should have. The sales lady motioned for me to get off. But she was very nice, and she encouraged me to keep looking until I was sure that I had found the bike I wanted. So I kept going back. I never said a word about this to anyone. And by anyone I mean Janine.

The sales staff at the Harley Davidson store started recognizing me. They covered their mouths when they laughed, and when I asked to sit on a bike, someone would start to hum the theme music from Sons of Anarchy until lots of them would laugh openly. But it didn't offend me. I'm way past that. Besides, I knew I had the money to buy any bike in there whenever I wanted. When I finally told the saleslady I was definitely going to buy that bike right then and there, everybody's attitude towards me changed.

You should see this bike. It's dark and wide and low and beautiful. I picked a black one, and it just looks classic. The lady told me to sit on the low rider. She thought that was the best one for me. I was like a kid at Christmas. It was seriously the best feeling I had ever had. I started to hum the theme music from Sons of Anarchy through my teeth.

So that was it! I pulled the trigger! I signed on the dotted line and all those other clichés. I bought a god damned Harley Davidson motorcycle.

I'm keeping it in a garage downtown where I'm renting some space. It's low and powerful and dark. Almost as fun as buying the bike was getting all the appropriate clothing. Leather boots, a leather jacket, and the coolest helmet you ever saw!

I thought I knew how to ride a motorcycle. That's what I told the sales guy. I had a dirtbike when I was growing up. But it's not the same. I needed to take a couple of lessons. The dealership offers a riding course, and I signed up. When I finish, I'll get my motorcycle license and everything. And I'm taking it easy until I really get used to it.

I know that life is not about material possessions. But I have to say, when I'm sitting on that bike, I feel like a part of me has been missing for a long time.

ENTRY # 68

INSIDE JOKES

I ran into Darin and his wife today. I was with Janine at the city summerfest picnic. Janine helped sponsor the local elementary school hamburger booth. Anyway, we were walking to the parking lot, and suddenly we crossed paths with Darin and his wife.

They were holding hands. Darin's wife grinned at me and asked me if I knew their secret. I started to stammer and told them I didn't know. They laughed at me and Darin said that he had told his wife that I knew all about it.

I couldn't believe that Darin actually told his wife that he had told me the whole masturbation story! But there she was, laughing at me and holding his hand. She said that everything between them had changed.

It was the communication that made all the difference. Janine perked up and was listening to us. Darin's wife was saying that a healthy sex life is very important to a happy marriage, but it's also important to one's own mental health. She pointed out that she had lived a very sheltered life, and that opening up about her sexual feelings with her husband had made her very happy.

Janine's eyes were very wide, and she was looking back and forth between, Darin, his wife, and me.

What should I have said?

Maybe I should have smiled knowingly and nodded at Janine and said: "Darin here hunts ducks while his wife stays home and masturbates. Yep, you could say that they both like to bang one off.".

Don't know how she would have reacted to that. But I do know how she reacted to what she did hear. When we got home, Janine grilled me about the conversation. She was sure that there was more to it. It was almost as if it was my fault that Darin and his wife had been so open about their private life. What kind of people do I associate with? What kinds of sick and twisted things do I talk about with other people?

Usually when we run into people, Janine is the center of the conversation, and I just lurk on the perimeter until Janine tells me to contribute something. Today it was the other way around.

I guess all this will only amp things up. Things are changing, and I know that Janine can feel it.

Entry # 69

It's shopping time.

It finally happened. I looked in my closet and said, out loud, "What the fuck is wrong with me?"

I took out everything I hate and put it all in a pile. Then I took that pile and put it in a garbage bag. Actually it took three garbage bags. Then I took the whole mess to goodwill.

Then I went to the outlet store and went shopping.

As I wandered through the shops looking at the clothes, I kept reminding myself that I'm a biker dude now. I looked at a lot of denim. I haven't had denim clothes since I was in college.

And flannel. I found out that I look great in flannel.

What's wrong with having a few different pairs of sunglasses? I bought ten. And I found out something amazing. I can get prescription sunglasses.

I bought some casual boots. Or maybe they're shoes that just look like boots. Either way, they're different from anything I've worn for decades. Okay, they're shit stomping boots. They're ass kicking boots.

Do I feel more manly in boots like this? I feel more like myself. Everything that is happening to me lately is making me feel more like myself.

So now I wear clothes that I want to wear, I drive the vehicle I want to drive, and I enjoy the pastimes I want to enjoy. And still a little part of me is uncomfortable. A little voice inside me says that things aren't right.

How does any of this make me the bad guy?

Shouldn't I have been living like this my whole life?

And guess what else I'm doing? I'm growing a goatee. A chin beard. A Van Dyke. Whatever you want to call it, it's starting to appear on my face.

I know, it's trite. It's a cliché. Everybody's doing it. But I want to know what it feels like to have a beard. It's my face, they're my whiskers. They make me feel mysterious and mean. They go with a motorcycle.

Maybe they'll get me laid.

ENTRY # 70

I'M GOING ON A LITTLE PLANE TRIP.

I've got a plan for selling a few of the gold coins. I've asked around about selling gold coins and how much privacy is involved. I've learned about several dealers throughout the US that deal in large amounts of gold coins. The next two days are going to be a whirlwind trip to Seattle, Denver, Atlanta, and then home again.

I told Janine that I needed to go out of town for work, and she barely even acknowledged me.

I can't help but thinking that what I'm doing is very illegal. I don't have any plans yet to declare any money I make from this trip. It's mine. It's all mine. I'm not sharing with my family (at least not directly) and I'm certainly not giving any of the money to the damn government.

I've got to say that I feel like Walter Freaking White. I'm one bad ass middle aged white guy.

It feels really good. Sometimes I don't care that I may never spend all this money. Just having it has changed my life. I've said before that I feel invisible. That's not Janine's fault. I felt that way long before I met Janine. I've always been a nobody, an 'also-ran'. I now feel like I've always got a continental smirk on my face. I give people knowing smiles.

And you know what? People seem to notice me. Cashiers in stores chat me up.

I really love being on an airplane. I love exploring new cities. In the last month I've wandered around Denver, and I've wandered around Seattle. And of course, wandering around a new city is even better with a huge wad of bills in my pocket. All the best restaurants, shopping in high end stores, all of it makes me feel like I'm on top of the world.

Then I come home and everything starts up again. There is no peace for me, ever.

Entry # 71

Janine has a secret, too.

It's funny how this stuff all piles up at the same time. I guess I'm just more sensitive to it. But I've been looking more closely at our family finances. Things don't add up. Our family spends more than it takes in. So I confronted Janine about it. I thought she would blow up, but she didn't. She seemed nervous and evasive. She kept telling me not to worry about it, and that she would handle it.

Handle what? She became more and more uncomfortable. I kept pushing. That's not like me, and I think I caught her off guard. She became defensive, but not aggressive. She finally told me that probably the discrepancy I was seeing was because of some money she has of her own.

Money she has of her own? Yes. It turns out that Uncle Leon left her some money.

This all explains her attitude in Las Vegas.

I don't know how much Leon left Janine, and I don't care.

I don't feel as guilty anymore about not sharing my money with my wife and kids. They're going to be rolling in money.

You'd probably tell me that rolling in money isn't important. I guess being obsessed with wealth and money is unhealthy. But the thought of failure eats us alive. The possibility of being poor and suffering hangs over all of us.

You know what? I'm glad. I don't want anyone to suffer. But I'm seeing how all this money is going to send each one of us on a different path.

ENTRY # 72

I MET SOMEONE TODAY.

Does that make me a horrible person? I don't think so. I'm not having an affair by any stretch of the imagination.

Her name is Cheryl, and she likes my bike. And she likes my tee shirt. Don't get me wrong. Nothing is going on. It's just that something in me has changed. I've met beautiful women before, but before I would have probably just politely said hello, and then I just continued on, minding my own business. That's what a good married man should do.

Why am even bringing this up? It wasn't anything. She just stopped me and told me she liked my tee shirt when I was at Wendy's for a burger today. I had this tee shirt on that had a cartoon panel on it. Mickey Mouse is telling us how to get a date. In one panel he shows Minnie that he has lots of money. Minnie is impressed. In the next panel he gives her lots of compliments. Minnie likes that. In the final panel he tells her he's in a band. He's playing a guitar and Minnie is going crazy for him.

We were just standing in line there talking about my tee shirt and my motorcycle. And it wasn't just her. After she said she liked my tee shirt, the girl at the cash register said she liked it too. So it wasn't me, it was the tee shirt. About the time we started talking Cheryl asked about my motorcycle gloves, and so I pointed out the window at my bike, and that sort of started a conversation.

"Is that your motorcycle?"

Boy, I really felt cool in that moment. I tried to nod casually, but I saw Cheryl's eyes sparkle as she looked at the bike and then looked at me and then back to the bike. She started telling me how much she liked motorcycles. How do guys feel about girls who like motorcycles? Why do you think guys buy motorcycles?

So that was it. I stood in line behind a beautiful woman and she started a conversation with me. What's the big deal? She liked my tee shirt and she thought my bike was cool. For the first time in my life I was sitting and talking with a woman who wanted to talk about me.

Okay, okay. You're all a bunch of gutter-minded busy bodies. I'll tell you what she looks like. She's about seven years younger than I am. She is fairly tall and slender. And I guess I'll add this: She's chesty. Beautiful melons. There, I said it. I like her boobs. And she's very very pretty. The kind of pretty that makes you take a second look because you just saw a woman that is so pretty. That's Cheryl.

Cheryl had a million questions about my bike, but I could tell she was going to take her food and go. So I gently hinted that I eat there almost every day. I don't eat there, but I wanted Cheryl to have a reason to come back to have lunch with me.

She smiles so warmly. It made me feel like I was fourteen again. It was the greatest smile you ever saw. She said, "I'll probably see you here sometime then!"

Entry # 73

It's tomorrow.

I went back to Wendy's and Cheryl went back too. She smiled and waved when she saw me. I can't even describe how that felt. That means that she was thinking about meeting me there just the same way I was thinking about meeting her.

Today I stood there and chatted for the longest time. Cheryl chatted back, and I've never felt like that before.

Am I a complete idiot? I never meant for things to go this far. Do I feel guilty? That's the funny part. I can't tell you how good it felt to sit and talk with a pretty lady. I mean just having a pleasant chit chat while smiling at each other. I don't remember the last time I had a talk with someone like that. And it doesn't matter that we were only talking about how cool my new bike is and how I've got wonderful taste in tee shirts. It's like I've been born again. It's like I've started a new life. I'm walking around everywhere with a smile on my face. I'm not trying to have an affair. I don't want revenge of any kind. That's not why any of this started. I just needed to vent a little bit. Maybe I knew I needed to stand up for myself a little bit. But I never wanted to hurt anyone. And right now, because all this feels so damn good, I can't imagine how any of it could hurt anyone.

What's wrong with this story? Nothing. Just me chatting with a woman about my tee shirt and my motorcycle. Well, there is one thing questionable about this story. We exchanged phone numbers and we plan to meet up again. It just came up that we are both planning to attend the school district art show. She mentioned that she has a son. He's a student at another high school exhibiting his drawings. Sammy is exhibiting her pottery at the very same show.

That made me feel a little twinge of guilt. Sammy is going to exhibit some of the pottery she made this year in her art class. I used that as a subject for planning to meet up with a woman who is going to see some art her son made. Janine isn't going because she went over to the community center when Sammy's pottery was shown over there. She's already seen it. She's done her parental duty. She doesn't want to drive all the way to Springville with me, so I'm going to go alone, and see Sammy's pottery and meet up with a woman I just met.

Icky? We'll see.

Okay, yes. I told Cheryl that I was married. I told her that Janine and I were separating. Was that a lie? I felt so dizzy when I said it that I almost passed out. Cheryl said that she was very sorry. I looked into her eyes to see if this meant that she wouldn't see me again, but it seemed really clear that our new friendship was going to continue on.

Cheryl's been married before. She told me about her first marriage. She has been divorced for eight years. She has one son. Her husband became frustrated with his life. Or he got bored. But he made some mistakes and the married ended. I guess everybody has a story.

Cheryl asked if she could have a ride on my Harley. My first passenger. What an experience. And dangerous! What if somebody saw us? I acted all casual. Sure! That would be nice! We could go up the canyon and stop somewhere for lunch.

It sounded so natural. Nothing unusual about going for a ride on a Harley. I made a mental note to go for a couple long practice rides.

What's happening to me? What am I getting myself into?

ENTRY # 74

JANINE IS GETTING SUSPICIOUS.

It's not about Cheryl. She has no idea about that. I don't think she has any idea that I could enjoy the company of another woman.

The problem is that I've been staying away from home more and more lately. I just don't want to come home. I'm not just out wandering the streets, either. I've been doing things that I love to do. I've been visiting antique stores. I've been going to museums. Not very macho, I know.

She asked me where I've been spending so much time. I told her I've been playing golf. It's not a lie. I have been out golfing a few times. But I've also met Cheryl a couple of times for lunch.

Janine screamed at me. She told me that she hates golf and that I'm never to play golf again.

So what am I going to do? I'm going to buy some great new golf clubs tomorrow. I've been shopping these clubs out for years. I've seen the model go through many design changes. I'm not waiting for anything anymore. I'm buying those damn clubs. I'm going to have some really great times on the golf course with the clubs I've always wanted. I'm going to play a lot of golf.

For years now, I've been very innocent. Janine has ignored me, and she's had no reason to be suspicious of anything. Now she has a million reasons to be suspicious, and her spider-sense is starting to kick in.

It's funny how the human mind works, isn't it?

Entry # 75

The Big Ride.

I'm back now. Nothing happened. But I can't believe the day I just had. I just can't believe it. And as I always do, I end up safe and sound back on this toilet. I contacted Cheryl. It didn't feel wrong, because I was honoring a promise I made to take her for a ride. I told her I had all day Saturday, and we could make a day of it. I suggested we get an early start.

Cheryl didn't say anything for a long time, and I wondered if she was having second thoughts. But then she asked me what time I could be there to pick her up, and what would she need to wear. I told her I could be there by seven thirty, and that she should wear heavy jeans and a tee shirt and a heavy shirt of some kind, and boots if she had them, or heavy shoes. She told me she would see me Saturday morning.

I left without saying a word to Janine about where I was going or when I would be back. I haven't felt my heart beat like that for a long time. I was smiling so wide I felt like my face was going to explode.

I admit that when I got to Cheryl's apartment, I felt like I was committing a crime. I had a new helmet, some leather gloves, a leather jacket, and some Harley Davidson boots that I had bought for Cheryl. That kind of started us off on the wrong foot. She didn't like that I had spent money buying things for her. She told me she wouldn't keep them. That made me panic a little bit as I wondered how I would explain the stuff to Janine if she ever found them.

We got past all that quickly.

Then Cheryl was on the back of my Harley and I was roaring down the highway. I felt like I had been released from prison. I felt born again.

Everything we saw seemed so beautiful. Cheryl noticed it all. She kept pointing and tapping me on the back and I was nodding at everything. We wound up the canyon, headed for the state line. There was a little river at the side of the road, and beautiful trees and wildlife, something amazing to see at every turn. The breeze got cooler as we went higher up the mountain. We stopped for a minute at a rest stop to get the jackets out. Cheryl was grinning like crazy when we got off the bike.

There was a little pond and a stream by the rest stop, and people were fishing there. Cheryl wandered over to watch, and I kind of just followed her. A guy commented on the Harley, and said it looked like we were having a lot of fun. Cheryl laughed out loud and said it was a great day.

Cheryl asked me if I liked to fish. I shrugged. Our family has never been the fishing type. She said we should come back soon and bring fishing poles. Then she headed back to the bike and I followed her. Cheryl walked all around the bike and brushed the tank and handlebars with her fingertips.

"I just love this Harley! I've always wanted to go for a ride on one. I'm having such a good time! Aren't you?"

I thought I was going to cry, or laugh, or explode. Cheryl had no idea. I had dreamed of a day like that for twenty years. She was extra snuggly when we got back on the bike. The roar from the engine seemed even more exciting, and I really gunned it as we headed back out on the highway.

We had been going for two hours when I finally stopped for gas. There was a wonderful looking barbeque place a block away from the gas station. We rode the Harley slowly past while we decided if we should eat there.

"Can we get our food to go and eat it in the park?"

I told her that it would be wonderful to eat barbeque in the park. We sat on an old bench under a big tree and just let ourselves relax.

"Have you taken other people out riding like this?"

Awkward question. I'm a novice, but I didn't want her to know that.

"I've always been kind of a loner. You're actually the first person I've ever taken on one of these long rides."

"You've never taken your wife?"

I looked away and tried to sound casual.

226

"My wife never liked things like this. She likes things like, shopping at the mall. That's more her style."

I couldn't believe it. I was talking about Janine in past tense, and I was making her sound shallow. It felt so good! But I could see it was making Cheryl uncomfortable.

"So, you're a lone wolf? Do you mind having me along this time?"

I tried to look at Cheryl right in her eyes. I smiled as warmly as I knew how.

"You're a great passenger. You seem to know just how to lean and balance. I hardly notice you're there."

Stupid stupid stupid. What was I thinking? What was I expecting? What if Cheryl wanted this right to turn romantic? Was I ready for something like that? I was already making it clear that I wasn't used to taking girls on rides, and that I was out of practice where it came to dating. Cheryl was studying me as if I were a bug in a mason jar.

"Well, I'm done. Should we keep going?"

I wasn't as enthusiastic that time when we got back on the bike, but Cheryl hugged me really hard that time, with her head resting on my back. The thrill was back, baby! Cheryl leaned her head over my shoulder when we got to the stop light and motioned that she wanted to say something. I turned to face her.

"I'm having a wonderful time. I think you're really great! I hope this won't be our last ride."

"It won't!" I yelled. I thought about that. This wasn't just a one-time fling on a bike with a pretty girl. I wanted rides like this to be a permanent part of my life. This ride was taking me some place, and it still is. I need to find the courage to hold on and see where this all ends.

So we roared out onto the highway again. Cheryl was a seasoned rider by then. She wrapped her arms around my waist much tighter than she had before. She leaned with me into the turns. I could feel her scooting her bottom to find a comfortable position. Then I felt her lean her helmet against my back.

The sun was setting when I got Cheryl back to her apartment. She laughed as she tried to straighten her hair. Neither of us knew what to say. She touched my hand.

"Call me?"

I just nodded. Then I took the Harley back to the storage unit, and I went home, where no one even noticed I had been gone all day.

ENTRY # 76

IT WAS JUST A JOKE.

I don't know what possessed me. I guess I finally snapped. Nothing like this has ever happened before in my life, not even in my wildest dreams.

But earlier today I had just finished my shower, and there was no clean underwear in my drawer. So I wrapped my towel around me, and went downstairs. I retrieved clean underwear from the dryer. Somehow I figured that the dryer would be full of clean whites. It was. Anyway.

I saw Janine in the kitchen, and I started to sing. I was singing and watching over my shoulder to see if she saw me. She seemed engrossed in something. I assumed it was the television. I sang a little louder. I was just singing along to a silly commercial that I heard playing on the tv one time. Then I started to dance. I danced my way into the kitchen, and she looked up impatiently at me. What was I expecting? Did I even think for a moment that she would smile and laugh? No. She was glaring at me. I swear she looked like Dr. Frankenstein in one of those old horror movies. So I threw my towel at her.

I threw my towel at her. I ripped it off and threw it as hard as I could in her direction. And I started to dance more vigorously. In the nude. I thought it was funny. I guess you kind of had to be there. But it didn't take long to see that there was a problem. I expected that. There's always a problem. This time it was different.

She wasn't alone. There were ladies waiting for her in the family room. Something about volunteering at the local elementary school for their carnival. Janine was yelling with her angry voice when she told me about the ladies, and I made a naked dash for the bathroom. I don't know how much they saw, if anything. I imagine they heard something though.

After she cooled down, Janine asked me what I thought her friends would say about my antics. She asked me with that tone that a person would use with a naughty six-year-old.

So I answered. They'd say: "Scott's hung like a horse."

Didn't she want the truth?

Entry # 77

It just gets better and better.

I actually think Janine finds my little prank humorous. I would have never believed it. I fully expected to be thrown out of the house. But she wouldn't speak to me for about a day. Then, when we would pass, she would mumble, "You're such an idiot", but it seemed like she was suppressing a smile.

Is that a good sign? I don't know. It doesn't matter. There's so much stress in our family right now.

I mentioned to Janine that we should call Daniel and talk to him again. Such a simple suggestion. How could she take offense to that? But she did.

"You're judging me!"

I told her that I didn't think that anyone was being judged at all and that we should really just focus on reaching out to our son.

Then she gasped.

I waited for her to say something for a long time, but she just stood there looking afraid.

Then she said it.

"You know, I understand Daniel better than you think. When I was in college, I did a lot of, well, experimenting. I got to the point where I was overwhelmed with confusion. I had all these crazy feelings exploding in me about same sex attraction. I was trying to sort out what was just college girl partying, and what were my real feelings. It was a crazy, difficult time for me."

She seemed so far away. She looked lost. It was like she had forgotten that I was even in the room. I was stunned. Janine the Lesbian. I couldn't wrap my brain around it. I wasn't even close to judging her. I swear it. I couldn't even begin to think of a joke or a snarky comment. Ten or fifteen years ago the revelation would have given me a boner. But at that moment, I was just frozen and wordless. Then she looked as if a thought had startled her and she continued.

"But none of that matters now. Look at where I am today. Look at my life! Look at my family!"

I didn't say anything. What was I going I say? I was flabbergasted. She was trying to make eye contact with me, and I was avoiding it. Then she gave me the coldest, ugliest, meanest glare she has ever concocted.

"You're judging me! It's none of your business!"

I didn't know what to make of the whole thing. It was the crazy cherry on top of the craziest decade I could ever imagine. Finally I just gently whispered to her.

"I just think we should call Daniel and invite him over."

She screamed at me.

"You're not going to say anything? You don't want to talk about this at all? It doesn't bother you to find out that your wife has struggled with this kind of thing before? Do you understand what I've been through? Do you understand how hard this is for me to figure out?"

"Don't tell me. Tell Daniel."

Then something happened that never happens in our marriage. We stood there staring at each other in silence. I felt very calm. I wasn't angry with Janine like I usually am. I wasn't frustrated. I was just staring at her eyes, looking for an answer. That's what it should always boil down to. We have a marriage. We formed a family. It's up to us to find an answer. It's up to us to decide what to do. I was searching her face, she was searching my face. After a minute or two, she shuddered, she hugged herself, and she stumbled out of the kitchen.

ENTRY # 78

I'M AN INVESTOR!

I've been looking for a bike shop to do maintenance on my new bike. Stuff like oil changes. Some guys who own bikes do all that themselves, but I'm the first to admit that it's just not my thing. And I want it done right. Maybe one day I'll learn to do the maintenance on my bike, but not now. I know, I should go through the dealer. But I'm a little, well, frugal. I thought I should look around and make sure I'm getting the best deal.

So I found this fantastic bike shop. It's run by a couple of young guys who are brothers. They've got a clean, large shop. They fix and service bikes, and they have a few used bikes for sale.

But they don't have a lot of business, and it occurred to me that my experience in the business world might help them a little bit.

And I've got a big pile of money to invest.

They liked the idea.

So we're going to fix the place up, give it a motorcycle club atmosphere, and start selling quality used road bikes.

I think we'll have a little café there too. A place where people can get a soda and a burger.

I walked through the property with the guys tonight. It felt a little bit like being on the set of Sons of Anarchy.

I gave them two hundred and fifty thousand dollars. We sat down with lawyers and figured the whole thing out. These young guys are great mechanics, but they have no idea about how much more business they could be doing with the right accessories, services, and other things like getting better used bikes from auctions and from other nearby states. So, I'm really going to build a new business.

This will solve my tax problem. Yea, money laundering.

I've got big ideas about this place. We could sell used bikes, carry a line of bike accessories, helmets, jackets, gloves, and all that stuff. We could even get a food license and have a café. I want it to be a real biker hangout. The kids who started it all are very excited about my ideas.

I was out at the property today, just looking around again. When I was done, I stopped downtown at this cafeteria I like for lunch. It's kind of an Italian place. They have good lasagna. One of the ladies who was at my house that day of the towel incident came in to order a container of soup to go. I knew she noticed me when she walked in, but she pretended not to. Ordinarily something like that would make me feel awkward and frustrated. But somehow I was enjoying myself at this lady's expense. I stepped close to her as I left the cafeteria.

"I guess Janine didn't marry me for my money, did she?"

The lady froze like a statue, but she didn't say anything. I thought it was a really fun moment.

Entry # 79

She said she hates me.

I'm stunned.

She's never said those words to me, at least not seriously or in anger. I was putting away clean clothes earlier. I was just standing there by the bed, folding things and putting things on hangers. I had a pair of pants in my hands, trying to get them on to a pants hanger.

Janine stormed through the bedroom. I don't even know why she was there. But when she passed me, she stopped and stared at me impatiently. Suddenly she snatched the pants from me, and they came unfolded. I told her that I could do it. I suppose I said it in a voice that was kind of whiney.

I had to snatch the pants back, and kind of pull them from her. For a moment we were having a pathetic tug of war. When she let go, I could feel her annoyance growing. Then, for no reason, and accidentally, I dropped the pants. It was a non-incident. I bent over quickly and picked them up. But Janine heaved a sigh and said: "I hate you!" And she stormed out of the bedroom.

Why?

What the hell happened? She said it with so much feeling and anger. It sounded like something that has been building up in her for a long time.

I hate you. We've all said it. Hell, some people would say it's the theme of this notebook. But if they did say it, I would argue. I don't really hate my wife. Sometimes people just say emotional things.

That's not what it was like when Janine told me she hated me. It felt real. It felt true.

ENTRY # 80

IT'S WORKING.

People are flocking to our garage. The advertising, the designing, the decorating, and all the hard work is paying off. The grill is always crowded. We can't keep our jackets and gloves and helmets in stock.

I've had the guys watching auto auctions and want ads within a thousand-mile radius. And I've run ads looking for bikes. I've bought thirty-six motorcycles in the last week alone.

I've encouraged the guys to really put some work into the bikes and make them as great as they can be. It's working. Every bike that ends up on our floor is incredible.

Our bikes sell in less than a week, usually. We're having to really work to find new bikes to sell. We're learning about auctions and we're getting the word out to people who want to sell their own bikes.

We hired two new, top-notch mechanics. One of the mechanics has ideas about building custom bikes from older models. I like that. He had some pictures of bikes he's worked on, and they are really amazing. People are finding out about our shop and bringing their bikes for service. This garage is really becoming a center of biker activity here in the city.

I did some research and we're picking up other things to sell. Things like bandanas and patches. So if you want to look like you're in a biker gang, we can make that happen. If you're the adventure type, and you're looking for gor-tex and reflective stripes, we've got you covered.

The money is rolling in. I've noticed biker clubs hanging out in our grill at lunch time. I was standing around talking about bikes with some guys from a club, when they asked me to take a ride with them. Wow. I hadn't even thought about something like that happening.

I suddenly found myself on my new Harley, heading west toward the desert, in a group of about fifteen riders. We went west and then south around the Stansbury Mountains. We went through a couple of the quaint towns out there. It was fun to see the looks people were giving us. Then we rounded the mountain and followed the lake back to the valley.

We stopped at a gas station before we hit the freeway. We talked about our bikes, and one of the riders offered to switch with me for the ride back to the garage. He was on a Victory bike. It was pretty cool. Other riders were switching bikes too. We stopped again at the south end of the valley where some of the riders left us. There were hugs and good-byes. These guys really feel a sense of comradery. Everybody started switching bikes again. I ended up riding a Fat Bob with a fairing. It was pretty cool.

When we got back to the garage, I felt like a real biker, and I felt like a new man. This garage is the best thing that has ever happened to me. This is something I did. No one told me to do it. And it's working.

ENTRY # 81

SHE HIT ME TODAY.

I can't believe it. I feel like such a wimp. I'm just staring into the bathroom mirror right now. My eye and cheek are starting to swell. I heard her walk into the bedroom a couple of times. Would you hate me right now if I told you I was a little afraid? Maybe I've been afraid for longer than I care to remember.

What the hell happened? Let me see if I can piece this thing together.

She asked me again what I've been doing when I'm not home, and I told her it was none of her business. I watched her go from annoyed to a full boil in just a few seconds.

I would have never believed that Janine could hit that hard. I'm almost laughing about it. Son of a bitch. If she's going to get violent, that puts a whole new spin on things. I'm not saying I'm going to get violent in return. That would be wrong and I know it. But it sure changes how I feel about things. For years I've tried to be long suffering because in some strange way, I was worried about Janine's feelings. I wanted to be supportive of Janine and hope that one day she would see the error of her ways.

Today she lost my support.

Now as I'm feeling angrier about this than ever before, and now that I'm in physical pain, a thought has occurred to me. I've talked about this before in these pages, but today I see that maybe it matters a little bit. What is Janine's side of this story? If Janine were keeping a secret notebook about her feelings regarding our marriage, what would it say?

There must be things in her story that I'm blind to. I don't know. I think of myself as invisible and harmless. I don't do anything to provoke anyone. I just do what I'm told. But somewhere in all of that, I'm starting to believe that there are things about me that really set Janine off.

I don't know Janine's side of this situation. I don't know if I'll ask her about it either. If I don't, I'll always carry part of the blame. But certainly something is rattling around in that brain of hers. She wouldn't turn into this person she's become just for no reason. I'm sure she could talk for hours about the changes that have happened in her life. I know I can. I guess the problem is that we can't talk about this stuff together.

Right now I don't care.

My new golf clubs are beautiful. At least I can look at them through my good eye.

ENTRY # 82

PEOPLE ARE FINDING OUT.

I guess Janine has told some people, some family members and some friends, about what she did. Her mom called to ask me if I needed to talk to someone. That was a first. I don't think it's ever been suggested before that we talk one on one about anything. She sounded concerned but I don't think she was on my side. I'd just about bet that most of Janine's family and friends would say that if Janine felt like hitting me, it must have been because I had done something pretty bad. I told her mother that it was a private matter, and not as big a deal as she might think.

Jose called me to talk. He wanted to see if he could help. I was surprised he seemed to know about what was going on. I told him there was nothing to talk about, so he came over. There were already people here who wanted to talk about all this. I didn't know why at first, but having Jose come over to talk to me about my marital problems felt like a bomb going off inside of me. So he got here and immediately started acting all wise and sympathetic.

Take responsibility for your part in this.

Try to understand her side.

Don't be difficult.

Why does Jose know so much about Janine's side of this? Why does he seem to understand so much about what Janine is feeling? Why does it always seem like Jose knows so much about Janine?

Well, I couldn't take it anymore. Not with what I've learned the last few weeks. I've been learning to face the truth. And suddenly, the truth came pouring out of me. I screamed at Jose. I don't know who else knows this, but I know that his wife left him because he was fooling around. He was cheating. His wife wasn't being cruel to him at all. Like the few other people who knew this, I pretended it wasn't true because no one was talking about it. I was trying to be polite. But I've come to realize that I was kidding myself. I always knew what kind of person Jose is.

Jose has always been a terrible flirt, and I have always known that he spends a lot of time with guys he works with at social events. I'm sure that when he's out with the guys, they're looking for girls.

It shouldn't have been so hard to see what was really going on. He cheated on his wife. I've always known it in my heart. So I asked around a little bit, I contacted some of his friends that he works with, guys I know, and they all said the same thing. I was right. It's true. He was going on little business trips and hooking up with girlfriends. His wife found out and left him. It wasn't any more complicated than that. How could I have been so blind?

You can't just say that everyone has their own point of view, or that there are two sides to every story. The truth is the truth. Jose is a lying bastard, and his wife did the right thing by leaving him. When everyone tried to look shocked, I yelled at them, too. Even if they didn't know the exact details, certainly they must have suspected. They just felt uncomfortable about admitting the obvious truth.

I guess I got so worked up about Jose because I've been feeling cornered lately. I don't think people face the truth until something corners them and forces them to do it.

My cousins and my siblings are getting suspicious. Somehow they've noticed, or someone's told them, that I'm not going to work as regularly as I used to. And my lifestyle has changed. I'm playing golf, and I have a motorcycle, and my taste in clothing has changed.

People think that grandmother left me some money, and I haven't been truthful about it. That's true, isn't it? Remember the will that doesn't exist? Well, it's also true that my situation at work was unusual, isn't it? I hate myself. I hate finding myself in a situation where I need to come up with a story to cover my tracks. And I don't want to pretend that things aren't changing for me. And I don't want to get into trouble with the law.

More than anything, I don't want to pretend. But my situation kind of requires some pretending right now.

That's what I've learned. Everybody pretends. Everybody pretends that everything is okay. Everybody pretends that they don't see the problem. And when a problem arises, everybody looks the situation over, chooses the side they think they should be on, and then pretends that their side is the victim side. That's not the same as two sides to every story. That's just hiding from the truth.

Entry # 83

Am I a biker dude, or an abuse victim?

We've done it. We've got all the licensing that we needed to make everything legal, and work on the place is continuing. Food handling permits and everything. We're expanding the variety of bike we showcase and we're going to be advertising nationwide. We're bringing in high quality used road bikes. We just got a huge neon sign, and lots of smaller artwork that identifies our shop. We've got custom work shirts and uniforms and shirts and hats and vests, all with our beautiful new logo. We've even got a great selection of quality tee shirts with clever biker slogans on them.

The grill is getting an upgrade and remodel. It was functional before, but it's going to be spectacular when we're finished. The property is improving. It's becoming an amazing place. I hang out there all the time. I park my bike in front and I wander around greeting people. Everybody's always happy and there are stories flying around about this ride and that ride and everybody is comparing and showing off their bikes.

And the can! The toilet is a thing of beauty. I made sure that our mensroom is top notch. Clean, large, simple, and private. It's down a hallway where people aren't watching where you're going. We've hired a company that sends in a crew to clean up every evening.

Sometimes when I'm sitting in one of our cool new garage chairs with my feet up on the table, I think about Janine hitting me, and I'm filled with a sensation I can't begin to describe. The guy hanging out in the garage is not the kind of guy who gets beat up by a girl.

Things are happening. I'm changing. It's time for the whole world to see what's happening in my life. When I say it's time, I'm not sure if I mean right now, or in a week or two, but bottom line is that the time has come.

Entry # 84

Dinner with Janine's folks.

At least that's what I thought it was going to be.

Turns out it was another intervention. I went to the dinner knowing that there were questions and feelings and lots of unresolved issues to work out, but this intervention was really interesting.

Supposedly for both of us this time. I guess they know about Janine's right hook. But just as I would have guessed, the conversation focused mostly on me. My behavior recently is causing damage to my family. I'm provoking people and upsetting everybody.

There were suggestions that Janine bears some of the blame in what's happening in our marriage, but I could tell they were rehearsed suggestions to try to make the intervention seem fair.

I already told you, Janine has lost my support. I don't care what her family thinks or wants. I just tuned out and stared out the window.

This whole story has gone beyond the point of figuring out a solution and then following steps to fix things. That's how other people see things. They see someone else struggling in their life, and they think they see a solution, and they want you to follow their instructions so that everything will be fixed. Other people need to shove their suggestions up their asses.

ENTRY # 85

I TALKED TO SOMEONE TODAY.

Obviously it was Cheryl. I've never talked openly with someone about everything I feel about my marriage with Janine. I really needed Cheryl today.

At first she was shocked, because she was under the impression that Janine and I were separated. But then she seemed to listen with a lot of compassion as I told her about the things I talk about in this notebook. I didn't actually say that I write in a notebook while I'm on the toilet, but I told her how I have documented the problems for quite a while. I thought that anyone who might ever know about this notebook would think that I was the most pathetic idiot who ever lived, but Cheryl seemed to understand.

Then I got to the point in my story where Janine hit me. I don't think I could ever have talked about it out loud with anyone else. I was surprised at Cheryl's reaction and comments.

Cheryl was very concerned and sympathetic. She said that while she felt that our story was really sad, she didn't think it was as unusual as I did. She did say that she absolutely felt that we needed professional help.

I asked her again if she was angry about finding out that I'm married. She was quiet for a long time.

When she finally spoke, she said that she had figured that my story was more complicated than I was letting on.

So I asked her the big question. Could we still be friends?

I don't know why, but that question made her laugh.

"I'm not your wife, Scott." That's what she said.

Then Cheryl did something unbelievable. She leaned over and kissed me right on the lips. She squeezed the back of my head with her hand, and she smiled at me.

ENTRY # 86

SHE WENT NUTS TODAY.

This time it was crazy. I don't even know what set her off. She was screaming at me as soon as I stepped in the door. She screamed about how I embarrassed her in front of Taz, and she screamed about how I embarrass her in front of her family, and she screamed about that thing with the email and my niece. I think something had happened before I got home, but I don't know what. I suspect she had been talking on the phone with someone.

Then she hit me on the head with a pan, and I really saw stars. I almost fell over. People joke about women hitting men with pans, but it's not funny. It really hurt. Then she hit me with a chair from the dining room table. It hit me in the head, the arm, the ribs and the hip. That really surprised me. I didn't even have time to defend myself from that one. I was surprised that she could pick up a chair and swing it like that. People get hit with chairs all the time in the movies. Believe me, it's not something you can just shrug off. I couldn't get to my feet. I was shaking. I felt like a three-year-old being attacked by a monster. I tried to push her away as she came at me again. Then she bit me, on the arm, really hard. My arm is bleeding. I screamed at her to stop. She was hyperventilating. She stared at me for a minute with her mouth open. Then she ran out the door. When I can get myself together enough, I'm going to go to the emergency room.

I wanted to document all this before I go. I took some pictures. I tried to bandage my arm. The pain in my head and ribs is severe. I can tell something is very wrong. I'm not going to call anyone. I don't want this insanity to spiral out of control. I probably shouldn't drive myself, but I'm going to.

I'm back from the emergency room. They called the police. I calmed everyone down. I kept Janine out of trouble. I lied a lot. They cleaned up the bite wounds. I asked them if I was going to get rabies. Everyone was whispering about Janine, and I felt the strong urge to defend her. How do you explain that? Finally, the whole world could see what has been going on in our marriage, and all I can think of is protecting my wife. At the same time, I laid there in my emergency room bed, going over every detail of the evening, trying to understand.

I never could make sense of what she was really saying, it was a lot more than the stupid things I do. She was ranting about humiliation and wasted life and other scary things. So I can't explain why she went nuts. She was saying something, her voice was shaking and she sounded out of breath. I wondered if she had found my notebook, but it looks undisturbed.

This isn't funny anymore. It isn't pathetic anymore. It's got to stop.

I can understand that she might be frustrated with me, or frustrated with her life. I can understand that she might be behaving this way because she doesn't love me anymore. But nothing in the world justifies this violence.

It was strange though. This time and the first time she hit me. She didn't say much. At least she didn't say much that made sense. She didn't seem to want to argue with me or make a point or accuse me or give any reason for her violence. It's like a goddam puzzle that I've got to solve. But I think I've got some clues.

It turns out that lots of people have seen me around town, living exactly as I please. That's what Sammy says. And that's what Darin Anderson commented to me. People come up to me with those large, nervous smiles and ask me what's new. Since I've lived for so many years doing exactly what I'm told, being seen doing what I want makes me appear to have left Janine. I haven't left her. I've defied her. There's a difference. People must ask her, "What's up with Scott?"

So she's been trying to explain something to people that she doesn't understand herself. I guess it's really frustrating for her. Apparently it all just became too much for her.

I wonder if someone said something about Cheryl. It had to be something that bad.

Entry # 87

We sat down and talked today.

I felt like wearing protective gear. I felt like bringing bodyguards. But she sounded very grown up when she agreed that we should talk.

For the first time in many years, I felt superior in our conversation. I told her that there was no way I would ever retaliate and get violent in return. She bristled a little bit at that, and asked if I thought she would do it again. I told her that I never expected her to be violent the first two times. I told her that I knew something was terribly wrong, because the women I fell in love with and married would never have been violent with anyone. She seemed very subdued at that, and she started to cry a little. I knew she wasn't ready to say that she was sorry for what she had done.

But she asked me if I felt that I was in any way to blame for what happened. I was quiet for a moment. I told her that I couldn't think of anything I had done or said that could have been the trigger for violent outbursts like that. I told her that if I had anything to do with her violent anger, then it was time for me to go.

I could tell by her flaring nostrils that my answer had pissed her off. I felt immediately ashamed after I told her that I didn't feel blame for what had happened. That's not true. I definitely have to carry some blame. Our poor marriage is a shared responsibility. I'm starting to see that now. Janine's annoying behavior and the crappy way she treats me are the results of things that both of us have done. Still, we were talking about the incident where Janine hit me, and I don't think I did anything to deserve violence. Janine flared her nostrils some more, and her breathing got more heavy and rapid, but she nodded quietly and said, "okay".

Everything had gone reasonably well up to that point, and she admitted that things had gotten out of hand. When I then pointed out that what she had done is illegal, and that I could press charges, she laughed a really evil laugh. She pointed out that if I complained to the authorities, then the world would see what a real loser I actually am.

It's time for me to go.

248

Entry # 88

She found my notebook today.

Somehow I always knew she would find it. I got it away from her before she could tear it too badly. I haven't seen her that defeated and frightened in years. She couldn't speak. She was crying so hard. I don't think she read much of it. But what exactly did she read? What if she knows about the money? This has really been freaking me out. I can't sleep, I can't eat, I can't function.

So what happened?

I walked into the bedroom, and she was standing in the bathroom with my notebook in her hand. She wiped her eyes and nose with the back of her hand and became like a piece of rock.

"What's this?"

I stood there shifting my weight from one foot to another like a guilty child.

"A notebook. It's a kind of journal I've been keeping."

"A diary?"

She rolled her eyes and threw the notebook on the bed.

"Figures."

She shouldered past me, and I lost my balance a little bit and had to step backwards to catch myself. I could hear her crying by the time she got to the top of the stairs. She slammed the door pretty hard. But I don't feel sorry for her. Whatever she read, it was the truth. Everything I've written here was summed up in that moment when she rolled her eyes and shouldered past me. I heard her run to the door and then I heard the car start up and the tires squeal as she drove away.

It was the last time she will ever shoulder past me. I swear to God. Janine will never, ever shoulder past me again in my lifetime. I'll go to jail first for head butting her. She will never shoulder past me again.

ENTRY # 89

I'M AN IDIOT.

I'm a child and I'm a hypocrite. I was so mad after Janine found my notebook that I just sat down on the bed and trembled. This notebook has changed my life. Everything that has happened this year, good and bad, took on a whole new meaning because I was writing about it. Yes, I had to hide it all from Janine. But is it so wrong to have something that is just for me?

But then I started reading the notebook. The months flew past me like people say their lives pass before them when they are about to die. I'm ashamed at what I saw. I looked at this notebook and realized that it's full of snotty, stupid, and childish complaints about my wife.

I'm just as much to blame for our trouble. I have been soft and weak and closed off. I needed to start communicating properly years ago. I needed to put my foot down and stop the bad patterns that were developing in my marriage.

I think that just about anyone in this world would say that I should have confronted her long ago. I should have talked to her. Even if I had to force her to listen. Even if the conversation would have turned into a screaming match, I should have talked to her. I should have told her what I was feeling. Any rational adult would have done that.

It's all become an exercise in searching through the past to find out what went wrong. Living in the past. That's all that's left for us. I don't recommend it to anyone. Don't let it happen to you. Life could be so much different right now, if I wouldn't have pouted, and if I would have confronted Janine and found the way to make her listen. Maybe I should have done some listening of my own.

That really sucks, doesn't it? We make terrible mistakes in life, and those mistakes make us feel all philosophical and self-righteous. But somehow our beautiful, developing understanding of what went wrong can't seem to help us figure out what to do from this moment forward. I'm just left the way I am, an idiot.

250

Entry # 90

Somewhere I lost ten years.

I was downtown earlier today, looking in the windows of the shops. The ski and snowboard people are getting their products ready for the season. I remember when I used to plan to take my family skiing. I didn't plan to take them just once. I used to imagine how we were going to buy ski equipment, and ski clothes, and then we'd get season ski passes and go skiing all winter long. It was going to be our big family hobby. We'd all be laughing and happy and we'd all get along. Janine would be there too. She'd be holding my hand and snuggling in the lodge with me by the fireplace. Skiing was going to be great. And it wasn't just in my imagination. I was really going to do it.

But when there was money, there wasn't enough time, and when we had time, we couldn't afford a ski trip. Each year passed that way. Waiting for time to be available, or waiting for money. So we never went skiing. I just spent ten years thinking about it. Or did I?

What the hell happened to the ten years I've lost? Where did my wife go?

You know, I'm not exactly a young man anymore. I'm not looking for an adventure, or a new start. I admit I spend a lot of time thinking about the past. But that doesn't make me a bad person. Maybe I'm a little hard to understand.

I was remembering a teacher I had in high school. He told us about this kid from the neighborhood where he grew up. When they were in cub scouts together, they had some kind of Scout Olympics activity. This friend he told about had won a medallion that meant a lot to him. Remember, we're talking about eight-year-old kids.

So my teacher told us that during high school, his friend had a rough time. He made some bad choices. After school he completely lost touch with his friend. But at their ten-year high school reunion, they ran into each other again. The friend had long, straggly hair. He had lots of tattoos. But the thing my teacher really noticed, was that the friend was wearing the medallion around his neck, the medallion that he had won at the Scout Olympics when he was eight.

The point my teacher was making with his story, was that his friend was pathetic. He told us that if we cling to accomplishments of our past, we're losers. We need to keep moving forward, and not get mired in the past.

I'm not sure I agree with that. Life is much more complicated than a simple example like my teacher gave us. Who knows why that guy wore a medallion he received as a child? Who really knows why anybody does anything?

Everything that's happened this past year has been baffling to me. It's made me doubt that I really understand anything that's happened since the day I met Janine.

I'm not writing in the bathroom tonight. I think it's important to mention that.

In fact, I didn't go home tonight at all. I've rented an apartment. I got rid of the studio downtown where I originally hid the money and found a nice place in a very lovely community. I called her, though. I wanted to let her know what I've decided to do. She screamed at me. She cried. She threatened. She said that I had ruined her life. All the things she's dreamed of, none of it ever came true, and it's all my fault.

What was she dreaming about? What didn't come true for Janine? She never let me close enough to her life to understand. That kind of marital support is a two-way street. You can't control and bully and belittle someone and then expect them to be at your side, willingly helping you achieve your dreams. Or even give a shit about them.

Whatever. I've got damage control to consider. Worrying about this crap is making my chest feel like it's in a vise. The past is behind me, and it has almost killed me. Forward is the only direction left to me.

I'm sure now that Janine doesn't know about the money. I don't think she saw very much at all about what was in the notebook.

I went over this morning and took a lot of my personal things from the house. Janine wasn't there. I knew she would want to be with her sister and her mother.

I thought I would feel sad as I carted off the things in our house that are important to me. But I wasn't. It felt natural in a very creepy way. It was if I had over stayed my welcome long ago.

Entry # 91

I GOT CAUGHT.

Daniel saw me with Cheryl today. We were downtown, just about to enter a restaurant for lunch. I think Daniel had been following us, spying on us. He loudly called me out and people turned to see what was going on. He was really upset. He called me a hypocrite. He screamed some insults at me and called Cheryl some names. Then he stormed off before I could say anything. I was really embarrassed, but Cheryl told me not to be.

While he was yelling, I tried to calm him down. I tried to introduce Cheryl to my son, I tried to explain what was happening, but Daniel wasn't having any of it. I didn't want Cheryl to be hurt or insulted, and Daniel was being hurtful and insulting. I tried as hard as I could to take control of the situation down.

I thought about explaining that nothing is going on between Cheryl and me, but what does that really mean? We don't do sexual things together, but we spend time together, and we've become good friends. Should that make my son angry?

In the end Daniel stormed off grumbling insults over his shoulder. I'm guessing that he isn't the only one trying to find out what's going on in my life. This won't be the last confrontation.

I've always said that what other people think doesn't matter. But that's crap. People see things. Our families see things. They form opinions based on what they see, and not what we try to explain. We do care what they think. We want them to think the best of us, or at least some version that we've invented.

So what does it mean to be caught? Who is Daniel going to tell? How is this going to change my life? I don't want to live my life in hiding. I don't want to hurt anyone. But I don't know how to make the big leaps that will be needed to live the way I want to live.

It doesn't matter what I want. Those big leaps are coming whether I want them to or not.

ENTRY # 92

JANINE'S ARMY

I think my questions are being answered.

I was walking into our Target store today, and Janine's sister Danny was suddenly walking right at me.

"You're dead."

That was what she said to me as I passed.

Okay. Whatever.

I finished my shopping and I was leaving the store with my small bag of socks and shampoo. I walked toward my car in the parking lot, when I noticed two skinny guys approaching me. They weren't walking, but they weren't exactly running. They looked silly. I could tell they were coming for me.

I recognized one of them as a friend of Danny's. He was the brother of the guy she's dating. I couldn't believe it. Danny was having some guys beat me up.

I could feel myself smiling. I'm not Janine's victim anymore. I haven't got her leash around my neck anymore. I'm a biker dude now.

The first guy grabbed me by the arm, and the second guy took a swing at me. I easily ducked his punch. I head-butted the guy who had grabbed me and he went down like a house of cards. It was painful for me too, but I was too angry to notice. I grabbed the second guy by the front of his shirt and swung him around and threw him against my car. I don't remember what I was saying, but I was grumbling "fuck" a lot.

The first guy was now curled up in fetal position, holding his bleeding nose, and the second guy was on all fours trying to breathe. I had knocked the wind out of him. I clenched my teeth and tried to sound like Clint Eastwood.

"Get out of here before I call the cops, or kill you. And tell that creepy family to leave me alone, or things are going to get out of hand. And that's a promise."

Corny.

But the guys stumbled to their feet and ran to where their car was parked on the other side of the store.

Janine's family wants me beat up? What's next? This is turning out to be the greatest adventure of my life!

Entry # 93

Sammy came to see me today.

Apparently she had talked to her brother. I guess he had figured out exactly where my apartment is. It was really a weird experience to hear a knock at the door, and then to see my daughter timidly peering around to see me. It felt really strange to invite her in and ask her to sit down. She doesn't live in my condominium. That was my choice and not hers. Kids are supposed to move away from home, not dads.

At first, she just cried. I couldn't believe I was doing this to her. I can honestly say that I never, ever wanted anything bad like this to happen.

Then Sammy asked me what was going to happen next. It was the kind of question that sounded like pleading. It was a question that reminded me that I had the power to do great damage to our family. It was a question that showed me that I've always had the power to really hurt our family.

Sammy started to cry again.

"We're a family! I know what mom is like. But she's my mom. She's your wife. You need to fix this. I know what you're like, too."

How could I explain this to my daughter in a couple of sentences? I felt so helpless. I knew my answer would be unsatisfying.

"I don't know what to do anymore."

Sammy's voice was rising. It was almost a scream now. The veins on her neck and forehead were starting to show.

"You need to come home! You need to work this out. That's what people do! You need to talk to mom."

"I've tried talking to your mother."

"You need to try again! That's what people do! It takes hard work to make a family happy."

I had nothing else to tell her. I just sat there, blinking and hyperventilating. Sammy leaned in close to me as if trying to wake me from a dream. She sounded so desperate that my heart leapt to my throat.

"You're destroying everything. My family is falling apart, right in front of my eyes."

Sammy now looked bewildered by my silence. She sat on the edge of my new fancy couch. She looked around like she was Alice in Wonderland.

She tried again to reason with me. This was her second try, but it hurt as much as the first. She cried. She cried really hard. She left, and there was no resolution between us. I wished in that moment that it was that easy. I wished that I could make this all right just by wishing it to be so.

Then I remembered what my dad told me one time, I should have it carved on a sign and hanging over the door of this bathroom: "Wish in one hand and then crap in the other. See which hand gets filled first."

No. Wishing means me giving in and changing who I am. I am not all of the problem. I could change completely, but Janine would still be the same. No. We all have some changes to go through. But how do I explain that to Sammy without sounding like a stupid prick? Before she left, I hugged her and let her cry herself out. I whispered to her that it was all going to be okay. And I wasn't lying.

There was a voice in the back of my mind telling me that all this would one day be in the past. One day we will all be alright, living the lives we should be living, and only remembering these hard times like stories we once heard.

But this is it. This is the life we are living. Everything that happens leads us along. We can either embrace it, or go crazy pretending it isn't happening. I don't have any regrets. I feel a lot of weight, and I've felt a mountain of sadness. But I'm going to embrace this life I'm living, even if it makes everyone in my life hate me.

ENTRY # 94

WE VISITED A DIVORCE LAWYER TODAY.

This is all becoming more real all the time. I was really calm. Almost friendly. I held the door for Janine and she smiled at me. The lawyer was so upbeat as he greeted us that he almost gave me the giggles. How does a guy like that make divorce negotiations seem like planning the details of a trip to Hawaii? He started right off by talking about forms and time frames and legalities. Then he tented his fingers and got serious.

We talked about the violence. Janine said she hit me once. I told her it was many times. She objected and suddenly changed her mind and said it was twice. Then we argued about the difference between occasions, incidents, and actual blows.

Then we moved on to expectations. Janine doesn't want me to get my hands on her money. That's okay with me.

The lawyer slowed things down a little bit and then asked me the question that I've been asking myself. I knew he would ask me, but the question startled me. He asked if I thought that any of the problems in our marriage were my fault. I didn't even hesitate. I said yes. I know that our problems are at least half my fault.

Janine leaned forward in her chair with her elbows on her knees and stared at me. The lawyer didn't say anything for a while. Janine's voice sounded harsh, like a smoker's voice when she spoke.

"You think some of this is your fault? I thought you've been saying that I'm the evil bad guy in all this."

I didn't look her in the eyes.

"No. A lot of what has happened over the past fifteen years, has happened because I don't assert myself. I'm withdrawn. I don't communicate. I just roll with the flow. That's not a good thing. It leaves a vacuum. That's what I did to my marriage. I allowed a gaping, sucking, black hole to form in our life and it festered until it became a problem. Sometimes, and I'm saying that it was just sometimes, Janine was only trying to step up and fill that void. That's on me. That's what I did to hurt our marriage."

Janine's face twisted in bewilderment and a grimace of disgust started to form.

"Fifteen years? What are you talking about? The first time I hit you was just a couple months ago."

I blew out a sad breath.

"I'm talking about our marriage, Janine. Things have been bad for about fifteen years. That's the way I've figured it. I feel like you've been aggressive and controlling and demeaning toward me for about fifteen years. And I'm saying that I've dealt with it all in a very unhealthy way by just checking out. I've just shut myself down and I've just floated along like a coward, trying not to upset you. That's the damage I've caused to our marriage."

There was horror in Janine's eyes as she processed what I was saying to her. She straightened her back and stretched her shoulders. She twitched the muscles in her mouth and face and her eyes went back and forth in her head as she considered what I had said. She held her hands out and raised them as if she had finally understood. I wasn't surprised. I knew she would try to capture the situation, like a butterfly in a net, and take control of it. She offered her snap resolution proposal.

"Well, then. That's something, isn't it? That's communication. That's something we can work with, right?"

I looked into Janine's eyes for the first time.

"What do you mean?"

"What do I mean? I mean that I understand you. I understand what you did. It makes sense to me."

Janine leaned forward again and put her elbows on her knees again. She reached for my hand, but I leaned back in my chair and out of her reach. She pretended not to notice.

"And do you know what? Here's the most important thing. I forgive you."

Janine nodded her head ominously. She waited to see if I would look her in the eye again.

"I forgive you. What do you think about that? None of this is necessary. We can move past it all. Now. Can you say the same to me? Can you say that you forgive me for hitting you? There's no reason to tear our family apart. There's no reason for a divorce. We can forgive each other. All it takes is a little communication, like you just did a moment ago. Can't we just do that?"

Janine's voice was starting to falter, and she fell quiet. The lawyer didn't seem ready to speak. I looked up at Janine's face and was surprised at what I saw.

Confusion.

Fear.

Longing.

Weakness.

That was all. Janine was finished. The lawyer saw his moment and cleared his throat. He addressed me by my name. He asked me what I wanted. That was more startling to me than Janine's little speech. I felt my heartrate increase. This was not about 'forgive and forget'. Not anymore. What did I want? I had to think about that for a long time.

I want the abuse to end.

I don't want to ever have to see that sneer again, and I never want to see the eye roll. I don't want to be insulted. I don't want to be ordered around.

I want to be happy. I want to get up in the morning and stretch and yawn and smile.

Janine looked shocked. I was saying things that were beyond her comprehension. I was proving to her that I was just crazy. Or at the very least selfish.

What I've had in my life for the last few years is not what I've wanted. Does that sound selfish? I suppose it is. I'm not talking about having a family and a home. I'm talking about the way things are, day to day. And I think I've illustrated how bad things have become. I never wanted any of this. I know I share the blame for the ways things are, but there is no way I would have ever chosen any of this. What I want, or what I wanted, was very different from my current reality. I wanted a story book marriage. I wanted the white picket fence. I wanted my wife to be my friend. I wanted to grow old with my wife. When I was younger, I dreamed of what I wanted for my life. Things started out pretty good. The last ten years have not been what I dreamed of at all.

But once upon a time I had dreams of what I wanted for my life. Yes, just like the damn song. I dreamed of a happy family in a happy home. Then things started going sour, little by little, until the whole damn thing was misery.

Now it's all gone.

Really?

Maybe not gone. Maybe different. Maybe that's the key. Things changed. Our course was altered, and I didn't notice. I was caught not paying attention.

Everything is not gone.

My relationship with Sammy is better than I could have ever dreamed, but things with Daniel are more different than I could have ever imagined. But good. Daniel is my son. I feel the same way about Daniel now as I did the day he was born. The only difference is the way our relationship has grown. Were there mistakes? Were there times when I wasn't a very good dad? Absolutely. But my love was never different or less.

Here's what I've learned. I have to find new things to dream about. If I let myself give in to despair, I'll sink. Thoughts of failure, thoughts of hatred, thoughts of revenge, they are all poison. And yet there is very little else in my heart and mind sometimes.

I've determined that I'm going to empty the revenge and hatred and failure from my heart. I'm going to find love and hope and new things to hope for.

ENTRY # 95

I SAW HER TODAY.

It's been about a month since the visit with the lawyer, and the divorce is going forward. I've had no contact with Janine, until today.

I was downtown. I was on my bike. I had plans to meet Cheryl for lunch. Thankfully Cheryl was a little late. I saw her coming down the sidewalk. Janine was walking to her car. I was surprised I hadn't noticed the car parked almost right in front of me. It was surreal to see her. She didn't seem to react at all to my appearance or my bike. She looked at me over her shoulder as she walked. Her mouth was open a little. It almost seemed like she wanted to say something. But she didn't. She just looked sad, and she got in her car. Janine is not the same person anymore. She seemed disheveled. She seemed confused. She was in a daze.

I walked over quickly and stopped her. It felt like something I was supposed to do. She looked awkward and confused, but she rolled down her window. I asked if we could talk a minute. I moved to one side so she could open the door. She exited the car like someone being hassled by the police. We walked to the sidewalk and stood under an awning. I asked her if she was okay, and she didn't answer. I thought she was going to cry. She was humble. She was timid. She struggled to find the right words to say.

She didn't ask, but I told her I was doing okay. She kept looking around as if she was trying to spot somebody. Like she was worried that someone was watching us. She wouldn't make eye contact with me. Very abruptly she mentioned that she started talking to me the other day before she realized that I wasn't there. She said it just seemed like I should always be there. She laughed nervously as if it was a joke, and then she said she had something she had to do, and she shuffled off quickly.

Beaten. That's the only word I can think of to describe her. And it brought me no satisfaction at all. I never wanted to beat her. I just wanted her to change the way she treated me.

It may sound like a trite cliché, but I don't wish her any ill. I only hope for the best for Janine.

I'm not the same person anymore, either.

You probably think I'm going to say that I'm harder and tougher and more cynical. But the truth is that I'm softer and more introspective.

I hardly ever write in this notebook anymore.

I just don't feel the need to. I'm not hiding from anyone anymore.

Entry # 96

Writing from the hospital.

Where do I even begin?

My cell phone went off the other night, about ten thirty. It was Daniel. He was hysterical. He was saying over and over that he couldn't take it, and that it all had to end. I couldn't get him to calm down or to tell me what was going on or where he was. I knew something really bad had happened. I tried to keep Daniel on the phone, but the line went dead.

I called the police. I told them I thought my son might be suicidal, or hurt in an accident. I was surprised how fast the police got to my apartment. They demanded to see Daniel, and they weren't listening as I tried to explain what had happened. When they finally got the picture that Daniel had called in distress, and that I didn't know where he was, they asked me why I wasn't at my home in Layton. Layton? I've never lived in Layton.

We all started arguing about why I wasn't in Layton, and why Daniel wasn't with me, until everything seemed insane. While this was going on, another police officer had called his headquarters and the dispatcher had taken Daniel's phone number and had "pinged" his cell phone.

They found Daniel. He had tried to commit suicide. They had to take him into custody. He was all cut up, on his arms and on his neck. He was on his way to the hospital. That's all we could find out.

I called Janine and told her I would meet her in the emergency room.

No one would tell us what was going on. Daniel is an adult, and they couldn't share much information with us at all. Janine and I sat in the waiting room and stared out the window, waiting for a county health official to come out and talk to us.

It turns out that Daniel's friend, Stuart, has decided to return to his family and religion and submit to his family's wishes to make an effort to overcome his homosexuality.

Is this the reason behind this? I refuse to believe it. What else is going on his Daniel's life? Why would he do this? Was it just the breakup with Stuart? Are Janine and I aggravating his life with our problems? We don't know yet.

Update:

Two days have passed. The county health department lady gave us Daniel's things and told us that he had cut his wrists. He wasn't in serious condition, and he would be moved to the psychiatric ward in the morning. That was all she said. She wouldn't answer our questions. She pretended to not even hear our questions. She smiled as if everything was alright and just walked away.

The next day we went to the police department, and they wouldn't tell us anything at all about Daniel's situation. They did suggest that we try to go to the hospital at seven for visiting hours.

At seven we were at the front door of the psych ward, waiting for the guard to talk to the doctor, who was going to ask Daniel if he would accept a visit from us.

I cannot properly describe or explain what it was like to see Daniel in his hospital room. He looked so pale and skinny. There were bandages on his arms and neck. He let us hug him. I started to apologize for everything that has been going on the last few months, but he stopped me. He said that things had been going on in his life, too. He said he has been seeking psychological help for some time now. He said he's been struggling with his feelings, and that the incident with Stuart had been too much for him to deal with.

Daniel asked us not to try to get him to say too much about everything. He said that there would be time for questions and explanations later. Right now, he just wants help. He wants love and comfort. That's what we can do. We can help him. We can love our son. I can be there for my boy. I gathered Daniel up in my arms one more time before we left. I felt the swell of emotion as I fought the urge to cry. I whispered close to

Daniel's ear: "Little guy." When Daniel heard that, he grabbed me tighter, and I heard his breath break as his own sobs surfaced. We both were wiping our eyes with our hands as we pulled away.

"I love you dad."

They were magic words. I patted his shoulder and the doctor ushered us from the room and down the hall and through the security doors.

I know it sounds strange, but it felt like we were a family again. Janine and I weren't the center of the problem this time. We were the parents, and we were side by side. We asked Daniel if we could visit the next day, and he hugged us again. The doctor said he was being very cooperative, and that he had already made friends with the other patients there.

It may sound weird, but I was proud of Daniel. He was in the psych ward there, helping and encouraging the other patients. That's my son. That's the boy I've always known. He'll get through this. He's going to be okay.

I went with Janine to the house, and we talked with Sammy. I was surprised at how calmly she took the news. She wants to go with us tomorrow night when we visit Daniel. She wanted to know what the doctor had said.

The doctor said that Daniel has been battling depression for years, and that he will need counseling and medication. But he assured us that Daniel is not crazy, and that he will be back on his feet sooner that we think. He said that he was sure that we had every reason to be very hopeful for Daniel.

Talking with Sammy, we were all tempted to say that we had been selfish and uncaring. We all wanted to blame ourselves. But it was Sammy who pointed out that everyone has problems. We all do our best to love each other and reach out to each other when we need help.

Is that true? Why couldn't I see that my son needed help? Where was I a month ago? A year ago? How long has Daniel been struggling?

We don't blame his friend Stuart. We never even had the chance to meet him. We don't know what his reaction to all this has been.

I swear I'm not blaming myself, but I feel very small. I've been moaning and complaining for a long time, and I haven't been able to see the needs of my own family. I don't even know if there's anything I can do about it at this point.

ENTRY # 97

SOMETHING NEW

I'm going on a big trip. Daniel is out of the hospital, and he says he's doing much better. It's been almost four months since that horrible night in the hospital. We've all come a long way in four months. Daniel came to my apartment the week he got out of the hospital and we had a long talk about his life. He doesn't feel that everything that is happening with me and Janine has anything to do with his attempted suicide. But I'm sure it added to his stress.

I don't want to talk about all the details in this journal. I've been through the whole thing too many times already. Daniel's going to be okay. The medication is helping, and he says the therapist has helped more than he ever thought possible. I know that Janine is going to focus on him, and I will too. But for the next few days I'm going to be out of town.

Cheryl and I are taking a bike trip to Durango Colorado. It's going to be incredible. It will be the longest ride I have taken on the Harley yet. We got a blue tooth intercom system for our helmets so that we can talk and listen to music and even make phone calls on the cell phones.

And here we are. It's funny. Getting away felt wrong at first, with everything that's going on at home. But now that we're here, I see my situation in a new light.

First of all, I'm tough. A lot of these folks here in town trailered their bikes. I didn't. I don't even have a trailer for my bike. I drove on my Harley the whole way, with Cheryl on the back. We loved every mile of it. And when we got here, I realized that our leather jackets looked broken in and used, not all shiny and new.

I mentioned before that nothing is going on between Cheryl and me. By that I mean that we're not sexual. We really aren't. We just like spending time together.

There is a biker rally happening here in Durango, and I wanted to participate in this and represent our shop.

Wow. Did I just say that? Have I gone from being Janine's whipping boy to being a biker dude? A whipped husband to representing a cool biker garage?

Seems funny.

Want to know what I was feeling as I was wandering around, mingling with other guys, all of us wearing leather jackets and talking about bikes? I felt like myself. I've heard a lot of people making fun of biker types. You know what I mean. Accountants and doctors with bushy moustaches who dress up like guys in a gang wearing lots of leather. They get together on their Harleys and annoy people out on the highway. But let me tell you, they know who they are, and they know what they want. I'm starting to be accepted by them, and it feels really good.

I did an incredible thing when we got to our hotel. I showed Cheryl my notebook. We sat and looked through it together. She really laughed at parts. That surprised me. I didn't think I was writing anything funny in here.

I thought she was going to tell me that I was a horrible person, but she didn't. In fact, she didn't say anything at all for a very long time. Then she just told me that she understood. She said that everybody needs a way to express their feelings. I never thought it would be that simple. This whole thing isn't about a notebook. I'm learning that.

We were out walking in town when I got a call on my cell phone. It was Sammy. She asked to talk to Cheryl. I admit that it made my heart race. Actually it was like a bomb went off in my head. I felt like I had suddenly lost all control over the situation. But it turned out okay. From what I could see by watching Cheryl's side of the phone call, they laughed and talked about fun things. It all sounded really friendly. Then Cheryl passed the phone back to me.

I asked about Daniel, Sammy said she had taken him to lunch, and he seemed really happy. I asked about her mother. Sammy says she's working things out. So am I. But I reminded Sammy that her mother and I won't be working things out together.

When I hung up with Sammy I asked Cheryl if she had talked with Sammy before. She told me that yes, they had spoken a few times.

Apparently the first time was confrontational and Sammy tried to threaten and insult Cheryl, but the last couple of times were really friendly. When I asked Cheryl to tell me what happened when Sammy first confronted her, she was reluctant to talk about it. She said she was able to remain calm, and that she understood why Sammy was upset.

Cheryl and I sat and talked about the whole thing for quite a while she told me that she wanted to take things really slow between us, because she has a feeling that things aren't really over between Janine and me. That comment was like a shock in my brain. I can't explain it. Part of me wanted to run around the room screaming that it would never happen, and part of me suddenly remembered a moment in our marriage shortly after Daniel was born.

Janine and I took a little trip. Totally spur of the moment. We got to this beautiful little town just as the sun was setting. We found a really cheap motel. We hurried and got into our swimsuits and went and sat in the hot tub, which was tucked in corner by the little pool at the edge of the parking lot. We got there just in time to see the most beautiful sunset you've ever seen.

Have you ever seen images in clouds? Well, I saw images in that sunset. It was like I could see Janine in the sunset. She was holding Daniel on her hip. She was playing with the rays of the sunset like they were toys, maybe strings on a giant red harp. She was dancing and singing to Daniel and playing in that sunset the way you might play at the beach. She was hiding behind the mountain peaks and giggling and waving to me. At least, that's the vision I saw in that sunset while we sat in that hot tub at that little hotel in that little town.

I remember Janine laughing at me because I had kind of zoned out looking at the sunset, and she asked me what I was thinking. I remember that moment like it was yesterday. I remember hugging Janine and trying to tell her about what I was imagining in that sunset. I felt like the richest man in the world. I felt like life was ahead of me, and all my dreams were coming true.

BOB WHIRE

How do I get that feeling back again? I think about today, and it occurs to me that things are very beautiful today, and the sunset is shaping up to be incredible. Getting that feeling back doesn't necessarily mean reconciling with Janine. Obviously, my kids will never be babies again. I can't have that. What else is beyond my reach? And what is within my reach? Am I smart enough to hold onto it? Do I love people enough to tell them that they matter to me?

On the way back toward the hotel, Cheryl asked if I'd like to hold hands. She just gave me this flirty little smile and took my hand. I felt like I was sixteen years old again.

Walking back to the hotel that evening, enjoying the sunset, holding hands with the girl I'm dating, knowing that my family is okay, it was all I could have asked for in this world.

One final note, I don't write in this journal on the toilet anymore. I even bought a new journal. It's a real journal, with a leather cover. I sit on the couch and make daily entries right out there with anyone who might be present.

And I don't write about how other people hurt me or limit me. It's time to stop that. Now I'm writing about the people I love, about my hopes and dreams, my joys, my fears maybe, and I'm writing about myself.

272